M000297244

# The
# Woman
## in
# Carriage
# 3

## ALISON JAMES

*Bookouture*

Published by Bookouture in 2023

An imprint of Storyfire Ltd.
Carmelite House
50 Victoria Embankment
London EC4Y 0DZ

www.bookouture.com

Copyright © Alison James, 2023

Alison James has asserted her right to be identified as the author of this work.

All rights reserved. No part of this publication may be reproduced, stored in any retrieval system, or transmitted, in any form or by any means, electronic, mechanical, photocopying, recording or otherwise, without the prior written permission of the publishers.

ISBN: 978-1-83790-395-5
eBook ISBN: 978-1-83790-394-8

This book is a work of fiction. Names, characters, businesses, organizations, places and events other than those clearly in the public domain, are either the product of the author's imagination or are used fictitiously. Any resemblance to actual persons, living or dead, events or locales is entirely coincidental.

*To all the survivors out there,*
*and to those who helped them survive.*

# PROLOGUE

Hattie leaps back instinctively, staring in horror at the motionless body slumped near her feet. Her breath shortens and her vision begins to swim. Because this is not a stranger. She knows this person.

Stumbling backwards, she quickly grapples for the emergency button to summon the guard. What happens next is a blur. There is commotion in the corridor; feet running, shouting. Someone searching for a pulse, for a breath. The train grinds to a halt and sits immobile on its tracks, next to a large playing field. Her fellow passengers stand up to peer through the windows; their expressions confused or irritated. Hattie is ushered back to a seat, some distance from where she was originally sitting. The guard takes down her details, saying something about talking to the police, but she's barely able to take in what he's saying. She stares past him, her limbs shaking uncontrollably, as paramedics appear on the train, then, minutes later, leave again, taking their equipment with them.

After what feels like an eternity, the two carriage doors at the rear of the train are opened, and Hattie and her fellow passengers are evacuated through them. There's a general murmuring, and some throw curious glances back at the train. About a hundred of them are shepherded down a slight embankment, along a track and through a gate onto the main road, where marked patrol cars and an ambulance are stationed.

A police officer tells them they have to stay where they are, ignoring the mutters of dissent. After about half an hour, several men in hooded white Tyvek suits and blue disposable shoe covers walk carefully along the edge of the track until they reach the carriage where two uniformed policemen are standing guard. They have to duck under a blue tape to enter, and Hattie realises with a lurching sensation in her chest that the train is being treated like a crime scene. Other officers bark instructions into their airwave sets, trying to make themselves heard over the drone of the police helicopter circling overhead.

Two coaches arrive to bus the passengers away. The police officers confirm that they have her details in case they need to question her further, and let her go and join the others boarding the coaches. Climbing up the steps of the vehicle, Hattie sees a body bag stretchered off the train, carried by the men in the Tyvek suits to the awaiting ambulance. She turns away with a shudder as its doors are closed, but she can still hear one of the police officers speaking into his radio.

'Yep, one fatality... cause of death TBC, probably cardiac arrest, but we can't rule out foul play at this point... Yes, on the train... It's the 18.53 from Waterloo.'

# PART ONE

# ONE

## HATTIE

The lights in the tube carriage flickered on and off and, as it snaked round a bend, an empty McDonald's cup rolled across the floor and into the space between Hattie Sewell's feet, splashing the dregs of a strawberry milkshake onto her shoes.

The sweet, rancid smell made her feel queasy, as did the jerking movement of the train. She'd had precisely ninety minutes of sleep in the past thirty-six hours, and despite six paracetamol tablets and several strong black coffees, she was still riding the wave of a hangover. Plus, she was still dressed in the clothes she had put on yesterday morning, when she'd set off for work, and they were now creased and grimy. Mostly because she had slept in them.

The train stopped abruptly between Green Park and Westminster stations, and Hattie glanced anxiously at the time on her phone – 18.44. She really wanted to be on the 18.53 train from Waterloo. It was the fast service, and if she missed it there wouldn't be another train to Summerlands for forty minutes. Unless she caught the stopping train that took twice as long. And in her current state, she couldn't face that.

After a couple of minutes, the tube lurched forward again,

and five minutes later it pulled into the Jubilee line's Waterloo stop. Pushing her way through the crowds, she charged up both escalators, taking two steps at a time and tutting impatiently at anyone standing her path. The 18.53 always left from Platform 2, and as it had been part of her daily commute for the past eight months, Hattie's feet knew their way there by muscle memory alone. She darted across the concourse and reached into her bag for her rail pass. She couldn't find it. Surely she hadn't left it at Ethan's flat the night before? She didn't remember taking it out at any point, but the truth was that she had been so drunk that she couldn't remember very much of what happened. Some dancing and a silly game of spin the bottle. Then eventually passing out in Ethan's bed after everyone else had left. Had they had sex? She wasn't sure. It was possible. Ethan was someone she'd met online a few months ago. They weren't – and never had been – in a relationship, but they had slept together a couple of times after a night out that had turned a bit messy. Much like last night.

She rummaged again, deep in the recesses of her bag amongst the dirty tissues and sweet wrappers, and eventually found her rail pass in its plastic wallet. Slamming it on the sensor, she lurched through the barrier just as the guard blew his whistle and the train doors began to close. With an impatient shake of his head, the guard pressed the button to open them again. Hattie jumped in, the doors closing a second later as the train shuddered, then slid forward.

She had to walk through several carriages before she reached the forward section of the train, which she knew from experience was usually more sparsely populated. Sure enough, carriage 3 had a few free seats. She needed to sit down. It was only a thirty-nine-minute journey to Summerlands, the affluent suburb south of the Thames where she was headed, but her head was still thumping and she felt as though she might pass out if she was forced to stand. God knows how she had got through an entire day in the office feeling as she did, but somehow she had.

At the centre of the carriage there were two tables on either side of the aisle, with a pairs of seats facing in both directions. Table seats were always at a premium because they allowed for working or eating, or both. The window seat of the left forward-facing row was free, but Hattie was forced to hover, wandering how to climb across the lap of the person in the aisle seat. To her relief, the woman leaned forward and shuffled herself across into the window seat, leaving the aisle seat empty for Hattie. She sank into it gratefully, turning to give a smile of thanks to the woman who had vacated it. She had Mediterranean colouring, a pleasant, slightly careworn face and was probably in her forties.

Opposite them on the other side of the table was a distinguished-looking man, dressed in a camel overcoat, pinstripe suit and polished black brogues. His greying hair was swept back in waves from a high forehead, and he wore tortoiseshell glasses with square frames. The empty space next to him was taken up by a much younger man, who sat down just as the train started to pull out of the station. He threw an apologetic smile at the other people round the table.

Hattie found her gaze drawn in his direction, because he was handsome; distractingly so, with dark blond hair and clear grey eyes. His looks reminded Hattie strongly of Jude Law in one of her favourite movies: *The Holiday*. She caught his gaze and looked down, embarrassed by her appearance. Nothing said 'walk of shame' like two-day-old make-up and dirty hair. He continued to look straight at her, and she reached her fingers to her undereye area and rubbed self-consciously at the mascara smudges, trying to minimise them. The faintest smile played around his lips as he turned his gaze away.

On the other side of the aisle was a man a little older than the Jude Law lookalike, but heavily muscled and fit-looking.

There was the edge of a tattoo showing above the neck of his T-shirt and one on the section of right wrist emerging from his leather jacket. His hair was shaved into a savage fade. Lowering herself into the seat opposite him was a woman around the same age as Hattie. Her straight hair was scraped back at the nape of her neck and she wore a matronly high-neck blouse and unflattering glasses. Which was a shame, thought Hattie, because she could be quite pretty if she made more of an effort. She caught Hattie scrutinising her and gave a tentative smile back before returning to her copy of the *Standard*.

It shocked Hattie a little to realise that she recognised some, if not all, of her fellow commuters by sight. Had she really been making this commute long enough to become a regular? It seemed she had. Summerlands was the first stop on the fast service to Portsmouth, and pretty much the same group of people caught this train after work every day, most of them also favouring the non-stop 7.48 from Summerlands to Waterloo in the morning, and the relative space in carriage 3. When she had first moved back to live at her parents' house, Hattie had assured them that it would only be for a few weeks, and yet here she was, eight months later. Eight months ago, she had a flat in London, a permanent job, and a boyfriend. Now she was living in her childhood home again, working for a temp agency and hooking up with a series of men she met on dating apps. No one, including Hattie herself, would have said that getting drunk every night and sleeping around was a good strategy for dealing with her changed life circumstances. After all, she was twenty-nine, not nineteen. But that was exactly what she was doing.

Her nausea intensified as the train picked up speed, hurtling over the Thames and through the inner suburbs of Putney and Barnes. She tried to distract herself by observing her fellow travellers. The younger woman to her right was still flicking through the *Evening Standard*, the man in the pinstripe suit had put his laptop on the table and was tapping away on it, the others were all studying their phone screens. No one was speaking, or even acknowledging the people sitting mere inches away. So far, so normal.

And then, with a shudder, the train ground to a halt.

It had been travelling for about twenty minutes, and had just passed the outer edges of Kingston when it stopped. Assuming they had just been held up by a signal, Hattie pulled out her own phone and opened one of her dating apps, swiping through profile pictures while she waited for the train to start moving again. It did not.

After a few minutes, people started to move restlessly, looking up from their phones or newspapers and directing their gaze through the internal carriage doors or out of the window in an attempt to work out a cause for the delay. The two men opposite Hattie exchanged glances and shrugged, with the older man sighing heavily and giving an irritated shake of the head.

With the whole journey usually taking under forty minutes, five minutes without moving felt like an age. The heating system was belting out hot air at full force and Hattie was starting to sweat inside her winter coat.

Eventually, a disembodied voice came over the PA system.

*'Ladies and gentlemen, apologies for the delay... this is due to a passenger incident... Please bear with us and hopefully we'll be on the move again shortly.'*

The woman next to Hattie tutted under her breath.

'Passenger incident?' snorted the man in the pinstripe suit. 'What in the name of God is that supposed to mean?' He rummaged in his overcoat pocket and pulled out a vape pen, holding it up with a flourish. 'I know we're not supposed to use these things on board, but if we're going to be stuck here with no decent explanation, then I'm sorry, but I'm not following their stupid rules.' He hauled his not inconsiderable bulk into the aisle and strode to the toilet cubicle, pulling the door shut behind him with a decisive slam. The Jude Law lookalike raised his eyebrows in mock shock, and Hattie suppressed a giggle.

When the rebellious vaper emerged from the toilet cubicle, he didn't come back to his seat but strode off in the opposite direction. When he eventually returned a few minutes later, he was carrying a couple of the white paper carrier bags that were handed out in the buffet car. He dumped them triumphantly on the table.

'Thought we might as well have some refreshments, since it looks like we're going to be here for a while.' He pulled out cans of pre-mixed gin and tonic and lager and single serving bottles of white and red wine, a stack of paper cups and a few packets of crisps. 'Please: help yourselves.'

Hattie gratefully accepted a can of gin and tonic, feeling her headache recede and her nausea subside as she sipped on the cold liquid. Jude Law was helping himself to gin and tonic too, and the woman to her right accepted a bottle of white wine and poured it into one of the cups. The man with the tattoos took a can of lager, but the girl in the glasses shook her head meekly and whispered, 'I don't drink.'

Pinstripe Suit Man slapped his forehead with a theatrical gesture. 'Sorry! Should have got some soft drinks too. Didn't think.' He poured himself a red wine. 'I'm Julian, by the way. Julian Cobbold.'

And so they all introduced themselves. The Jude Law lookalike was called Casper Merriweather, a name which fitted his flamboyant good looks perfectly. The woman to Hattie's left was called Carmen Demirci, and she explained that although she had lived in London for fifteen years, she was originally from Turkey. Tattoo Man said gruffly, 'Lewis. Lewis Handley,' and the girl in the glasses, looking a little reluctant to join in, mumbled, 'I'm Bridget Dempsey.'

'And I'm Hattie.' She smiled, relaxing as the alcohol hit her bloodstream. 'Hattie Sewell.'

They exchanged small talk, starting with the question 'What do you do?', as though they were at a cocktail party. Julian, surely to the surprise of no one, was a barrister. Hattie told them she worked in digital marketing, omitting the bit about being reduced to temping because she had been fired. Casper worked in a fine art auction house, Carmen was a university administrator, with two young children who were cared for by her husband while she was at work. Lewis simply gave a sardonic laugh in answer to the question. Nobody asked the painfully shy Bridget for fear of making her even more uncomfortable.

About fifteen minutes after Julian had brought the drinks, their conversation was interrupted by a loud, insistent beating sound.

'Air Ambulance,' Lewis observed, pointing out of the window.

Sure enough, a red HEMS helicopter had landed in the field, and paramedics in orange high-vis suits hurried towards the train. They all craned their necks to watch as an elderly woman was carried out on a stretcher, which was then loaded onto the helicopter. As it began its ascent, the guard's voice came over the PA again.

*'Ladies and gentlemen, the medical emergency has now been dealt with, and we should be on the move again shortly. Once again, apologies for the delay to your journey.'*

'Thank God for that,' Julian said, draining his second paper cup of red wine. 'Looks like the old dear's still in one piece too. Thought for one awful moment we were dealing with a body.'

They all smiled and laughed with relief at this, none of them knowing that in a few months a dead body would be carried off the very same train, and that it would be one of them.

# TWO

## JULIAN

Twenty-five minutes later than scheduled, the train pulled into Summerlands. On the border of Greater London and Surrey, it had grown up with the rise of the suburban railway. Art Deco apartment blocks near the station gave way to solid, bourgeois streets with detached homes and well-kept gardens. There was a tennis club, a golf club and expansive parkland along the banks of the river.

As their little group shuffled through the ticket hall of the 1930s station and out into the car park, the man who had introduced himself as Casper announced: 'I think I'll pop into the Railway Arms for another drink: anyone care to join me?'

Only Lewis agreed to join him. The young woman called Hattie was tempted, Julian could tell. She chewed on her lower lip, her expression frozen with indecision for a few seconds.

'I'd better not,' she said eventually. 'I was out really late last night. I ought to get home.'

This, in Julian's opinion, was the right call. To borrow one of his late mother's favourite expressions, the girl looked like she'd been dragged through a hedge backwards. Clearly she could use a hot bath and a long sleep. Cleaned up and rested, she'd be very good-looking though. She had a lot of golden-brown hair that would look magnificent if it was clean, and large green eyes fringed with dark lashes.

Julian pulled his car keys from the pocket of his suit trousers and waggled them at the assembled group. 'Can I offer anyone a lift?'

Lewis shook his head and Carmen refused too, saying she was only two stops away on the bus.

'Which way are you going?' Hattie asked.

'I live the other end of Northborough Road.'

She gave him a grateful smile. 'I'm on your way, then. It would be great if you could drop me.'

Once she was in the front seat of the Jag, the young woman turned to him as she clipped her seat belt into place.

'I usually walk back,' she confided, 'But I'm so knackered I really can't face it.'

Julian lifted an eyebrow as he eased the car into gear and slid out of the station car park. 'Tough night, was it?'

Hattie flushed slightly. 'Let's just say I didn't go home.'

'Ah,' Julian nodded sagely. 'One of *those* nights. I just about remember them. And it's hardly ideal to have your train journey delayed when you need nothing more than a soak in the bath and to sleep in your own bed.'

She glanced at him sharply, as though he was implying she was dirty. Which he wasn't, although the truth was, she did smell less than fresh. Stale cigarette smoke, rancid coffee, London grime.

'Still, it was quite jolly in the end, once we'd had a few drinks to break the ice. Nice bunch of people, I thought.'

She nodded, then pointed out of the windscreen as they turned into a wide tree-lined street. 'I'm just down here, on the left.'

She indicated that he should stop outside a substantial 1930s detached house, with two newish cars on the driveway.

'Your parents place?' he asked, because although she was old enough to be married, that didn't really seem to fit with such an established home.

'That's right,' she said, with a rueful little twist of her mouth. 'Long story.'

'You can tell us about it on the train tomorrow,' he told her with a smile as she climbed out of the car.

She hesitated next to the open door, as if she wanted to tell him something. According to Julian's friends he had a kind face, so maybe she was about to share a confidence.

'Off you go then,' he said briskly, impatient to get home after what had been a much longer commute than usual.

Hattie slammed the car door, raised her hand in a brief salute and trudged wearily up the drive.

Julian pulled out into the road again and within a couple of minutes was pulling up outside his own house, a double-fronted Arts and Crafts mini-mansion with seven bedrooms and a large, landscaped garden.

'Anybody home?' he called as he walked through the front door. The question was redundant given his wife Ginny always was at home when he got back from work, but it was a little ritual he always acted out. He dropped his keys, overcoat and briefcase on the circular walnut table at the centre of the entrance hall and strode into the kitchen. 'Sorry I'm late darling, train got held up for ages. Some sort of medical emergency on board.'

Ginny, stirring something in a pan on the hob, nodded coolly, but didn't say anything. That was his wife: always reserved, cold even. The daughter of a distinguished former high court judge, in her late forties she was still pretty, with expensively curated creamy highlights hiding the silver in her hair, and smooth skin that owed a lot to expensive facials and a discreet use of Botox.

'I'll pour us a drink, shall I?' Julian took out two tumblers from a kitchen cabinet. 'Better make mine a small one, given I've already had wine on the train.'

He poured two gin and tonics, clinked his glass against his wife's and clicked his heels together in a formal little salute. This too, was all part of the evening ritual. *Stick to the familiar routine, and it will provide a handrail to prevent you falling into the gaping, aching hole at the centre of your lives.*

'Is there time for me to get changed?' Julian was tugging at the stiff detachable collar of his shirt, and the tie which during court sessions was replaced by starched white bands. 'You know how I hate eating in fancy dress.'

Ginny took a mouthful of her drink before turning back to the stove. 'This will be ready in five minutes,' was all she said.

Julian drained his glass and leaned in to give her a swift kiss on her cool, powdery cheek. She ignored it. 'Five minutes, darling.'

He bounded up the stairs to the first-floor landing, turning right in the direction of the large principal bedroom suite. Then he stopped, hesitated. On either side of the corridor were two closed doors, each with a child's wooden nameplate screwed to it. On the right, the sign was embellished with pink fairies and read 'Louisa'. The sign on the left had red and blue trains. 'Edward', it stated.

Julian took in a long breath, and opened the door.


The sports trophies were lined up in a neat row on the shelf to the left of the window – 100-metre sprint, hurdling, hockey, swimming. Two wooden alphabet letters were perched on the fireplace; an 'E' and a 'D'. The 'WARD' had been banished to some charity toy donation many years ago. It was always Ed or

Eddie outside of the family, never Edward. A guitar case rested against the wall in the corner of the room and posters of Ariana Grande, Mabel and Jorja Smith were attached to the walls with Blu-Tack, now curling slightly at the corners. A montage of photos was stuck up over the bed; crazy, happy teenagers wielding bottles of Smirnoff Ice and sticking out their tongues. The bed was still neatly made with fresh blue and white striped linen, but it hadn't been slept in. Not since that night a year and a half ago when Julian's eighteen-year-old son had been killed by a drunk driver after celebrating his A level results.

Julian sank down onto the edge of it now, and bowed his head. The tears came, as they still did so frequently. But only when he was alone. He had returned to work two weeks after Edward's death and never once cried in front of his colleagues. He didn't cry in front of his daughter either, or in front of Ginny. His tears distressed his daughter and irritated his wife.

Unwilling to bring Ginny upstairs in search of him and for her to find him like this, he quickly collected himself. This evening he had a specific reason for coming in here. Prompted by something that had been nagging away at him ever since the conversation with his fellow travellers on the train.

He bent down by the bookcase next to the bed and started to thumb through the shelves. Lots of the Alex Rider spy novels, Philip Pullman, his own childhood Adrian Mole collection and of course Harry Potter. All the Potter books. A Petit Robert French dictionary and a maths A level text. The Official DVLA Driving Test Theory. This last one made the lump return to Julian's throat.

Eventually, he found what he was looking for: a large hard-back on the bottom shelf. Sitting back on the edge of the bed, he started thumbing through the Contents page. And there it was. He'd found it. He jabbed at the page triumphantly as though he was making a point in court. All part and parcel of being a successful barrister: having the courage of one's convictions.

'Julian!' Ginny's voice floated up from the foot of the stairs. 'Supper's ready!'

Julian darted into the main bedroom and tugged off his work shirt, reaching for the informal flannel one on the back of the chair. 'Coming!' he shouted back.

As he headed downstairs, he was unable to suppress a smile of satisfaction. That nagging voice in his brain had been right.

# THREE

## HATTIE

Much as she was grateful for the lift from Julian Cobbold, Hattie felt awkward as soon as she was in his car.

It wasn't just the sumptuous leather seats, the walnut dashboard and professionally valeted interior which made her feel even more stale, even more grimy. It was Julian himself, with his expensive cashmere overcoat, starched collar and bespoke tailored suit. He smelled of clean laundry, sandalwood soap and aftershave with exotic, spicy notes. She looked at his hands on the steering wheel, complete with gold pinkie ring and flashy Piaget watch. They were so clean, the fingernails so immaculate. And she, in contrast, was unwashed and unkempt. As he handled the car with a smooth mastery, Hattie decided that this was a man who was always in control. A man for whom everything worked out just as he wanted it to. Who never knew any uncertainty, any unhappiness.

She had been tempted to go for a drink with Casper and whoever else had accepted his invitation. Casper had intrigued her, even sparked a little frisson of desire. But she recognised that on this occasion discretion was the better part of valour.

She was dog-tired and, after the gin and tonics on the train, a little light-headed.

'Good God, Harriet,' her mother said disapprovingly when she stumbled in through the front door. 'Where on earth have you been? And look at the state of you.'

'The train was held up by an emergency,' Hattie mumbled, heading for the stairs.

'We've already eaten, I'm afraid.' Susannah Sewell kept her tone neutral, but that look was there in her eyes. The look that said her daughter had been a disappointment yet again. A waste of university tuition fees. 'But there's some casserole you can heat up if you're hungry.'

Hattie hadn't had a meal all day but had gone past the point of hunger. 'I just need a bath,' she said weakly, adding, 'I might make myself a sandwich in a bit.'

She knew her mother wanted to ask where she'd been the night before, and pick a fight about it, just as she would have done when Hattie was in her teens. But since her daughter was almost thirty years old, she simply gave a disapproving little shake of her head and retreated to the kitchen.

Hattie went upstairs to the attic-floor bedroom where she was currently living. Her old childhood bedroom was on the first floor, next to that of her younger sister Beth. This room, converted from the loft a decade ago and with the addition of an en suite bathroom, used to be the guest room. But when circumstances had forced Hattie's return to the family home, it was decided that it would be better if she was on the top floor. There, she had a bit more privacy and the illusion of independence. And it was just an illusion. She was contributing money from her earnings to the household bills, but Susannah and Alan Sewell couldn't give up the role of fretful parents, and they monitored her comings and goings, her progress – or lack of it – in finding another permanent job. Hattie was the older of their two daughters, but Beth had always been the more sensible one, the steadier one. At twenty-seven, she was a qualified optometrist, and owned a flat in Ealing with her solicitor boyfriend.

Hattie removed her make-up while the bath was running, then sank back into the steaming water. After a couple of minutes, she submerged her head completely and, as she sat up again, reached for a bottle of shampoo and massaged it into her dirty hair. Already she felt better, just knowing that she was clean.

Her mind strayed back to the unconventional little drinks party on the train, and Casper Merriweather's eyes studying her face. There was no denying that he was very good-looking. Sexy too. When she'd turned down his offer of a drink, she was pretty sure that he'd looked a little disappointed. But after less than two hours' sleep in the past forty-eight, she couldn't be certain that she hadn't just imagined that.

Wrapped in her dressing gown, and with a towel twisted round her wet hair, she sat down on the edge of her bed. It was neatly made, which meant her mother must have been up here. With a mental eye roll, Hattie reached into a wicker basket under her bed. Her mother insisted she use it to store her shoes, and it was full of them, even though there were still plenty of stray shoes littered round the room. Hattie fumbled underneath the layers of assorted trainers and ballet flats and pulled out a screw-top bottle of Pinot Grigio. She couldn't always be bothered to go down to the kitchen in search of a drink, and besides, her parents monitored her alcohol consumption, on top of everything else. Pouring a generous serving into her tooth mug, she leaned back on the pillows and pulled out her phone.

Her first, reflexive instinct was to google Casper Merriweather. Sure enough, with the very first hit, there he was at Van Asbeck's auction house in Mayfair. He was listed as 'Consignments Manager' in the Japanese Art department, and there was a photo of him in a navy suit and gold tie, his hair swept back rakishly from his forehead. She found an Instagram account for him too, although there wasn't a lot on it; some close-up shots of paintings, some travel to European cities, a few grinning selfies. No photos with a girlfriend or wife, she noted, and no mention of a significant other in his bio.

Her curiosity piqued, Hattie opened one of her dating apps, set the geographic search area to within two miles of her current location and swiped through the results. If Casper was single, then surely he would be using apps, she reasoned. Everyone their age did. But he did not appear. Perhaps he lived more than two miles away, although if he got on and off the train at Summerlands that wouldn't make much sense. Perhaps he preferred men. It was possible, although her instinct told her otherwise.

Out of habit more than desire, she swiped right on a couple of the profiles that attracted her. She matched with someone called Antonio, who messaged her immediately.

*How's your day been gorgeous?* He'd added a winky face emoji.

Hattie sighed, and topped up her beaker with wine. So far, so unoriginal. She looked at Antonio's profile again. He had a beard, black curly hair and a wide, engaging grin that revealed a gap between his two incisors. There were the obligatory workout shots for good measure, showing off his chiselled abs and substantial biceps.

*Let's just say I'm glad it's over*, she messaged back, with a sweating face emoji.

Antonio sent a laughing face emoji.

Sighing again, Hattie knocked back half of her wine before typing a longer reply.

*Cards on the table, I'm not a big fan of endless online chat-*

*ting. If you want to meet up in person for a drink or whatever,
then great. If not, no hard feelings but I'm out.*

Her phone pinged five minutes later. *What's 'whatever'?*
With the predictable addition of the aubergine emoji and a
tongue out emoji.

Hattie switched off her phone in disgust and tossed it onto
the duvet. What she needed was to sleep, but first she needed
some food. She shuffled down to the kitchen in bathrobe and
socks and found a half-eaten stick of garlic bread on the counter.
Suddenly ravenous, she tore off a chunk and pushed it into her
mouth, while simultaneously grabbing an apple and a banana
from the fruit bowl and shoving them into the pockets of her
robe.

Alan Sewell came into the kitchen; a solidly built man with
a tonsure of grey hair and a florid face. 'Hullo, sweetheart!' he
exclaimed when he saw his daughter.

'Hi, Dad,' she said thickly round the mouthful of garlic
bread.

He leaned in to plant a kiss on Hattie's cheek, but she
flinched and ducked away, not wanting him to smell the alcohol
on her breath.

The feeling that accompanied her as she made her way back
to her room was all too familiar. A deep, burning shame. She had
felt it so many times in the past year. First when her boyfriend,
Leo, had moved out of their shared flat after she got drunk at an
office party and ended up sleeping with one of her colleagues. It
hadn't been intentional. With Hattie, it never was. There was a
guy called Hamish in the IT department who everyone referred
to as 'Hot Hamish', and although she was perfectly happy with
Leo, Hattie used to flirt with him in that innocuous, collegiate
way people did at work. Just a way of making the day go a bit
faster. She'd even joked about it with Leo, and he'd laughed, just
as they always laughed about the absurdities of office life.

But then, at the work Christmas party, she'd had several tequila shots too many and snogged Hamish in the office kitchen. And then somehow – and even now she wasn't quite sure of the sequence of events – they'd had sex in the stationery cupboard. Her memory was so hazy she couldn't be sure if he'd used a condom. So the next day she'd been to the chemist for the morning-after pill and, like something out of a bad sitcom, Leo had found the packaging in the bathroom bin. He had been shocked, and very, very hurt. There had been no blazing rows, just an extended and painful period of not speaking. Then, after three years as a couple and a year of living together, Leo abruptly announced that he was moving out. He still loved her, but he could no longer trust her. According to him, Hattie became a wholly different person when she drank. Someone he didn't recognise. She'd pleaded and bargained, but he wouldn't change his mind.

A few months later, she was let go from her job after turning up late and hungover for a critical client meeting. It had been a good job too: content strategist for a prestigious digital marketing agency. But Hattie's way of coping with Leo's departure had been either to go to a bar or pub and get blackout drunk, or stay at home and get blackout drunk.

And then the shame had hit again when, with no work for several weeks and no second income to cover the bills, she had been forced to give up the lovely one-bedroom garden flat in Stoke Newington that she and Leo had moved into together. That feeling had returned frequently since then, when she had stayed out late and hooked up with some stranger she had met online. There had been so many of them that they all blurred into one. Rarely did they ask her on a second date, but that didn't matter, since there was an endless supply of young, single men looking for casual sex. Some of them probably not even single.

Hattie ate the fruit and fell asleep with the banana skin and apple core still on her duvet. She woke at four and switched her phone on again. She logged onto the dating app and found the chat thread with Antonio.

*How about a drink tonight, or tomorrow night. Somewhere in central London. Let me know if you're interested x*

Then she groped under the bed for the bottle of wine, took a couple of large mouthfuls and went back to sleep.

# FOUR

## HATTIE

Having turned in for the night before ten o'clock, Hattie woke unusually early the following morning.

After showering, she sat at her dressing table and contemplated her reflection. Her hair, now clean, was shiny and luxuriant. The bruise-like circles under her eyes had faded and the greyish pallor was gone. In short, she looked a lot better. She reached for the overflowing make-up bag in front of the mirror and set to work applying foundation, bronzer, blusher and mascara.

'Do you not want any breakfast, Hat?' her mother called as she ran down the stairs and into the hall.

'No thanks,' she shouted back, wrenching open the front door. 'I'm going for the fast train.'

It was one of those mild February days that carried the faint promise of spring, with sun breaking through gauzy white clouds. Hattie walked the mile to Summerlands station at a brisk pace, and arrived feeling too warm under her red wool coat. Since she had over ten minutes to spare before the 7.48 arrived, she decided she would go to the station's small coffee concession. At this time of day, it did a brisk trade in hot drinks.

'A large cappuccino please,' she told the barista, reaching for an anaemic doughnut in a cellophane wrapper. This was her breakfast after all, she reasoned.

'Hi!' a voice said behind her. 'It's Hattie, isn't it?'

She turned round to see Bridget, the girl from the train the night before, standing behind her. Her mousy brown hair was pulled back into a ponytail: not a high, flirty ponytail on the top of the head as Hattie sometimes wore it on a night out, but low at the nape of the neck. Behind her round glasses, her eyes were a pretty shade of hazel. She had beautiful skin too, which was quite devoid of make-up.

'Hi,' Hattie returned, holding up the doughnut. 'Just grabbing some refreshment.'

'Are you catching the 7.48?'

'Yep. That's the plan.'

'I am too,' said Bridget, flushing slightly. There was something curiously old-fashioned about her, with her calf-length skirt, frumpy court shoes and blouse buttoned to the neck. 'Perhaps we can sit together?'

'Sure,' said Hattie easily, taking her coffee and doughnut and heading to the platform, although she had planned to spend the commute to her current temp job messaging Antonio about their meetup.

As the train slid into view, she noticed Julian Cobbold waiting, copy of *The Times* tucked under one arm. He gave a little salute when he saw her, but the carriage was so crowded that he ended up sitting some distance away from Bridget and Hattie, who managed to secure the only pair of forward-facing seats in carriage 3 that were free.

'So, what do you do for a living?' she asked Bridget, remembering that she had been the only one not asked this the previous night.

'I'm a civil servant.' Bridget flushed again. 'In the Office of National Statistics. Pretty boring, I'm afraid.'

'I'm sure it's not,' Hattie lied.

'And you said yesterday that you worked in marketing, is that right?'

Hattie nodded, as she bit into her doughnut. 'Just temping at the moment, though.'

The hazel eyes, behind the glasses, scrutinised her with a sudden intensity. 'Really? Why's that?'

'Oh...' Hattie waved a hand airily, as if the recent collapse of her life's structure was no big deal. 'All sorts of reasons. You don't want to hear about that.'

'Yes, I do,' Bridget said earnestly.

'Another time, maybe. Over a drink would be best.' As she said this, Hattie remembered that Bridget had said she didn't drink. 'Or whatever,' she added.

The conversation ran dry at this point, and after fifteen minutes or so of silence, Hattie pulled her phone out of her pocket and discreetly opened her dating app, scrolling mindlessly through profiles. Man after man. So many men.

Antonio had replied with a tongue out emoji and *When/where?*

Hattie sent a location pin for the bar she favoured for such assignations, then finished her doughnut, discreetly wiping her sugary fingers on the scratchy velour of the seat. When she looked up to see Bridget studying her, it was her own turn to colour slightly.

'Oh look, we're here!' she said jauntily, standing up, as the train pulled into Waterloo. 'Have a good day at work.'

'Will you be on the 6.53?'

Hattie shook her head. 'I'm going out this evening.'

As she walked up the platform to the barriers, she scanned the moving tide of commuters and spotted Lewis Handley, loping along in a denim jacket and Converse high tops. But it wasn't Lewis she had been hoping to spot. She'd wanted to see Casper.

. . .

'Harriet... it is Harriet, isn't it?'

'Hattie,' she replied flatly, not looking up from her computer screen.

'May I have a word?' Sonia Nixon, the office manager at her current place of work, was standing next to Hattie's desk. She was a squat, rather untidy-looking woman, with hair dyed an unflattering shade of aubergine.

For the past ten days, Hattie had been employed to create online content for the digital newsletter of a construction supplies business. The offices were in a drab building on the wrong side of St John's Wood, the permanent staff members acted as though she was invisible and the work was dull and beneath Hattie's skill level. As a result, she hadn't been trying very hard, and hadn't done a very good job. She was aware of this.

Sonia Nixon must have shared this view, because she told Hattie that at the end of the following week they would be letting her go; her services no longer required.

'Obviously we've been more than happy with your input,' the older woman said disingenuously, 'but now you've got the newsletter up and running, and with your agency's rates being sky high...' She gave a helpless shrug to indicate that this decision was beyond her control.

'It's fine,' said Hattie, forcing a smile. It wasn't fine, not really. Not because she wanted to continue working in this uninspiring place, but because it meant that she would have to go cap in hand to the temp agency again and ask them to find her something else.

What she really needed was to find a permanent position, something she could really get her teeth into, and with a salary that would allow her to move out of her parents' house. As soon as Sonia had disappeared, she opened LinkedIn on her web browser and started to search content strategy roles in central London. Immediately, she saw a listing that caught her eye, posted by rising fashion brand Saints & Sinners.

> *You'll be able to offer our brand culturally relevant data and insights, and head a team turning these insights into meaningful solutions for us, helping us plan our content strategy in the fast-paced and constantly evolving world of high fashion. You will understand the passions of our online tribe, and be able to use sophisticated AI to aggregate digital content to understand their engagement and grow our audience...*

There were several more paragraphs of this marketing speak, which Hattie scanned through, looking for the critical pieces of information. Ah, there it was. *'Lovely, state-of-the-art offices in Hoxton'* and *'£80,000 plus generous benefits'*.

The salary was at the upper end of what someone with Hattie's experience could be expected to earn. The money, in conjunction with the brand's cool credentials, would mean a bumper crop of applications. Did she have the faintest hope of even scoring an interview? Given that she had left her previous permanent job under a cloud, it seemed unlikely. Nevertheless, she downloaded the job details and spent much of the morning updating and reframing her CV before submitting an application via LinkedIn. At four o'clock, she surreptitiously logged off and spent nearly an hour in the ladies' cloakroom, putting waves in her hair with her cordless styling wand and perfecting her make-up, before setting off on her date.

Hattie had asked Antonio to meet her at the Authentic Grape, a bar near Holborn that she had been to many times. It was an unpretentious place, with an accessible wine list and friendly sommeliers who would not look askance at her meeting up with a different man every time she visited. There was also a clean but cheap chain hotel a block away, that she had made use of on a few occasions.

Hattie pushed open the door of the place at exactly five forty-five, and was greeted with a discreet nod by one of the servers, who must have recognised her. The walls of the interior were covered in deep blue tiles, and there was a curved, copper-topped bar ringed with tall wooden stools, behind which were floor-to-ceiling wine racks. She ordered a glass of Bourgogne Aligoté and took it to one of the small tables tucked away under the window. Their agreed meeting time was six, but Hattie wanted time to get in the mood, which for her involved getting a little tipsy. As the chilled, minerally liquid slipped down her neck, her body responded with a warm glow. She could feel the blood rising in her cheeks, which she knew would give them an attractive flush. Seconds later, she was holding up the empty glass and tilting it in the sommelier's direction to indicate that she needed a refill.

Antonio arrived at ten past six. He had said in his profile that he was 6 feet tall, but Hattie immediately noted that he was no more than 5'10". No matter; she was only 5' 6" herself. It was a commonplace lie in online dating, and he was otherwise attractive, dressed in black jeans and a tan suede jacket over a colourful Hawaiian shirt. Hattie had the advantage of a few seconds to scrutinise him because he had walked right past the corner table and stood in the centre of the room, slowly scanning it for a lone woman. She took pity on him, standing up and tapping him on the shoulder.

'Hi... Antonio? I'm Hattie.'

His surprise gave way to relief, and he reached in to kiss her on both cheeks, European style.

Once he'd sat down and ordered a glass of what she was

drinking and she had corrected him and asked for a bottle instead, her blind-date mode was fully activated. It was like putting on a performance, she decided, acting the part of the woman these strangers wanted her to be. This uninhibited, giggly and confident character was not the real Hattie, she was just that: a character. Although, these days, she could barely recall who the real Hattie was anyway. Maybe this was her. Maybe she had become this person. Once they'd started on the second bottle of wine, she hardly cared.

As for Antonio, he seemed nice enough. They talked about generic stuff: work, family travel. He told her that he had been born in Barcelona, but moved to London nine years previously and worked in a tech start-up. Once or twice, she thought she saw him flinching at the volume of her shrieked laughter, and the way she stumbled through the door of the Authentic Grape and on to Gray's Inn Road. But then again, he seemed happy enough when she leaned back against the wall of the bar's frontage and pulled him in for a passionate kiss. Swaying slightly, she reached for his crotch and started sliding down his fly.

'Not here, okay?' he murmured, glancing over his shoulder at the mid-evening commuters striding past them towards the tube station. 'Can we go to your place? My flatmate will be home this evening.'

Hattie thought about the ludicrousness of dragging him back to Summerlands on the train. Antonio aside, she had drunk too much to want to embark on a journey to suburban Surrey. He seemed nice enough. Why not, she thought. She was free and single: if she wanted to sleep with him, there was nothing stopping her.

'There's a place we can go round the corner,' she slurred in his ear.

And so they ended up in the lobby of the chain hotel having an awkward discussion about who was going to hand over their credit card to the clerk on reception. In the end, it was Hattie, desperate to take their encounter to the next level, who handed over hers. Minutes later, they were on the bed in the small, cramped room, tugging frantically at one another's clothes. The sex was over so quickly that when Hattie woke a few hours later, dry-mouthed and disorientated, she could have convinced herself it hadn't happened at all, if it weren't for the condom wrapper on the carpet next to the bed. Antonio and his clothes were gone.

There was a message from him on her phone, which she ignored. There were also several missed calls and an angry text from her mother, demanding to know where she was.

Hattie sighed heavily, climbing up from the bed and setting the doll-sized plastic kettle to boil. Once she had poured the water into a chipped mug, she composed a reply.

*Sorry, Mum, didn't want to wake you by texting. It got late so I stayed over with w/a friend xx*

This was true to an extent, she reflected as she washed down paracetamol with the tasteless tea.


Having taken a shower in the cramped bathroom and re-applied her make-up, Hattie set off for work via the shops in the Strand, buying herself a cheap white shirt in River Island so that she wouldn't have to wear yesterday's crumpled and stained one.

Hattie may have looked fresh enough, but she felt jaded and spaced out, and the day was not a productive one. Several times, she felt her eyelids closing as she stared at her computer monitor. Eventually, six o'clock rolled round, and she dragged herself through teeming drizzle to the tube station, arriving at Waterloo in time to catch the 18.53.

She headed instinctively for carriage 3, choosing a window

seat so that she could lean against it and doze for the thirty-nine minutes of the journey. She had just wriggled out of her coat and tucked it round herself as a blanket when an amused voice said, 'Well, well, well... we meet again, Ms Sewell.'

She opened her eyes again and found herself looking straight into the face of Casper Merriweather.

# FIVE

## HATTIE

Without asking her permission, Casper moved her bag off the empty seat next to her and sat down.

He was wearing a well-cut blazer and a blue button-down shirt under a classic trench coat of the type worn by spies in film noir. It was damp from the rain and he stood up again to remove it, folding it carefully before putting it on the overhead shelf. The label said 'Burberry', Hattie noted.

'Rough day?' he asked, staring directly at her face. For a second time, she found herself in awe of his looks; that combination of a strong, square jaw and a full, almost feminine mouth.

'Bit of a late night,' she mumbled, grateful at least that this time her hair was relatively clean and she didn't have mascara smears on her cheeks.

'I'm sensing a theme here,' he said with a grin. 'Didn't you cry off the pub a couple of nights ago because you were hungover?'

Hattie was pretty sure she had told him no such thing. That had been his inference, even if a correct one. Before she could defend herself, he went on.

'Still – work hard, party hard, eh? Why not, if you're young, beautiful and single.'

She felt colour rising in her cheeks at his substitution of the more usual 'free'.

'You are single?' he asked.

She nodded, glancing down automatically at his own ring-less left hand.

'Dating anyone?' he persisted.

'No one in particular.'

'Dating around, then.' His eyes fixed on her directly as he said this, steel grey with thick black lashes, and she felt a little shiver travel the length of her spine.

'I suppose so. How about you?'

But before he could answer, the tall figure of Julian Cobbold loomed in the aisle. 'Oh look, my compatriots are here! Hello again.'

He sat down on the other side of the aisle and was soon joined by both the older woman, Carmen, and Bridget, who smiled shyly at Hattie and gave her a little wave. Carmen also smiled, but to Hattie she seemed distracted, tense even.

'I fancy a sharpener... anyone else?' boomed Julian, and a few minutes later he was back from the buffet car with a selection of cans and mini wine bottles.

As Hattie sipped pre-mixed gin and tonic from a plastic cup, she was sure she could feel the length of Casper's leg pressing up against hers. She wasn't just imagining it, was she? That the pressure was more than just normal train-seat proximity. When he twisted to his left to speak to Carmen on the other side of the aisle, his right arm trailed behind him over the seat divider and his fingers rested, ever so lightly, on the top of Hattie's thigh. So lightly, it almost might not have been deliberate.

And yet she knew it was deliberate. Her body was telling her so. Every single cell fizzed with an electrical current she had never felt before. Joyous, but also scary. There was a magnetic pull towards this man that went way past superficial attraction, or even plain lust. *I want him*, her brain said. *I want all of him, mind as well as body.*

Casper was talking to Julian about a series of high-profile auctions that were coming up which meant a lot of promotional and media events to attend, but now Hattie was barely listening, staring instead at the dark gold curls at the back of his neck. She wanted to reach out and touch them. But despite that curious magnetic pulling sensation, she managed to refrain from doing so.

There were no delays to the journey this time, so the informal drinks party was over swiftly, with Julian once again taking time out to shut himself in the train toilet to smoke his vape. As their little group emerged onto the forecourt of Summerlands station, he pointed out his wife's car waiting outside and asked if she'd like a lift. Hattie turned down the offer, even though it was still raining, hoping that another trip to the pub might be suggested. But none was forthcoming. She thought fleetingly about making the suggestion herself but, given her lack of sleep and two-day-old clothes, decided that discretion was the better part of valour.

Bridget scuttled off down the main road in the opposite direction to the way Hattie would go, and Carmen followed her, walking as far as the bus stop. After giving Hattie a barely perceptible wink, Casper turned up the collar of his trench coat and trudged off in the same direction as the other two women.

Checking her inbox as she left work the following day, Hattie was pleasantly surprised to see an email from Saints & Sinners, inviting her to attend an interview in two weeks' time.

Her mood buoyant, she caught the 18.53 train, hoping to see her new drinking buddies and share her news with them.

But as she walked through the train to carriage 3, the only person she recognised was Lewis Handley. As she sank into the free seat opposite him, he clearly noticed her glancing around for the others, and said with a rueful shrug, 'Just me today, I'm afraid.'

'That's okay,' she smiled back, quelling her disappointment.

'Carmen doesn't work on Fridays,' he reminded her. 'And didn't Rumpole of the Bailey say he was doing a case at Reading Crown Court today?'

Hattie laughed at this nickname for Julian. 'I think he did say something about that, yes.'

*But what about Casper?*

She waited for Lewis to mention him, desperate just to hear the sound of his name like some infatuated schoolgirl, but he didn't. He was probably at one of the art world events he had spoken about the evening before.

Lewis was drinking straight from a can of lager. 'Can I get you a drink?' he asked politely.

'No, I'm fine thanks,' Hattie replied, although she was longing for one.

'Share mine, at least,' Lewis insisted, pouring some of the lager into the unused plastic cup provided by the buffet car, and she sipped on it gratefully. 'How's your day been?' he enquired genially, and she found herself telling him about the upcoming job interview.

'Wow, that's fantastic news; well done!' Lewis seemed genuinely pleased for her, and she noticed how his warm brown eyes crinkled attractively at the corners when he smiled.

They talked about the highs and lows of the digital marketing world for a while, before Hattie asked, 'And what's your job?... Sorry, if you told us and I've forgotten already.'

'I didn't,' said Lewis with a slight shrug.

'So what do you do?' Hattie persisted.

'I work in security.'

He did not elaborate.

'Security? You mean like being a bouncer?' Given his muscular build, it wouldn't have surprised her.

'More along the lines of cyber security,' Lewis said, but again did not elaborate.

They lapsed into talking about sport and fitness. Lewis confessed to a serious gym habit, as though his biceps were not evidence enough.

'I keep meaning to get back into working out,' Hattie said with a sigh, remembering the gym she used to belong to in Stoke Newington. 'I'm horribly out of shape.'

She noticed that he did not correct her. 'The Helix Fitness place on Kingston Road is very good, if you're looking for somewhere local. I know a couple of the trainers there. I could put in a word if you like.'

'Thanks.' Hattie drained the remaining half inch of her lager. 'I might look into it.'

As they were disembarking at Summerlands, she caught sight of a familiar figure on the platform, scurrying, head down, as though determined not to be noticed.

'Bridget!' Hattie called, raising a hand in farewell to Lewis, then running after her. 'Hi!'

Reluctantly, Bridget slowed and turned round. She was wearing a dowdy calf-length skirt and a blouse with a row of pearls, and carrying a navy raincoat in a style that even Hattie's mother would have disdained as old-fashioned.

'I didn't see you on the train,' Hattie was puffing breathlessly. God, she really was out of shape. 'If I had, I would have sat with you.'

'It's okay.' Bridget kept her eyes downcast.

'I sat with Lewis in the end.'

Bridget pulled a face, implying this was a piece of bad luck on Hattie's part.

'What?' Hattie demanded. 'It was fine. He's actually quite

sweet.' She fell into step next to Bridget. 'He recommended a gym to me, and I was thinking I might sign up this weekend. I don't suppose you fancy coming along.'

'I can't, I'm sorry. I can't go to the gym.'

'Why not?'

'I have this condition.' Bridget's face turned pink. 'I suffer from chronic fatigue, and fibromyalgia. I'm not really able to do any sort of exercise.'

'Oh God, poor you.' Hattie meant it. 'That must be really tough: I'm sorry. But you're able to work okay?'

'Sometimes I have a relapse, and I have to take time off. Mostly I'm okay. But I have to make sure I rest at weekends.'

'Of course,' Hattie said, giving the other woman's shoulder an encouraging squeeze. They had reached the main road now, where they took different directions. 'See you on Monday, I expect.'

She was already wondering how she was going to fill the next two days herself. That was one of the worst things about living at her parents': the yawning chasm of the weekend. Perhaps she would go to the gym anyway. But as she trudged towards Northborough Road, the rain on the pavement splashing her ankles, the only thing on her mind was the bottle of wine stashed under her bed.

Hattie had definitely intended to go and sign up at the gym. But after waking late on Saturday morning and having a prolonged argument with her mother that ended in her agreeing to sort out her dirty laundry, it was already midday. And then she was texted by her friend Avril, who lived a few miles away in Twickenham, asking if she fancied a trip to the pub.

'You can borrow the car if you like,' her father suggested when she announced that she was going out.

But Hattie declined, catching a bus instead. If she drove,

she wouldn't be able to drink. And if she couldn't drink, what was the point in going to the pub?

She met Avril at a pub on the riverside, a place whose redeeming feature was a large terraced beer garden stretching along the water's edge. The damp, dreary February afternoon forced them into the rather characterless interior instead, but Hattie didn't mind. It was warm and dry, and there was an unlimited supply of alcohol. There was a noisy hen party in one corner, complete with veils and 'Team bride' T-shirts, but otherwise the only customers were the sort of gnarled, solitary men you found nursing a drink in every British pub.

'So, what's the latest with your love life?' Avril demanded, as she carried a tray with a bottle of wine and two glasses back to their table. She was tall and buxom, with a mass of brassy blonde curls and an unremarkable face brightened up with a slash of scarlet lipstick. She and Hattie had met at university and, while not exactly close, still saw each other a few times a year. 'Seeing anyone?'

Hattie shrugged, reaching for the wine. 'Just doing the dreaded apps, you know?' she said, eliciting a comedic shudder from her friend. For some reason, the image of Casper Merriweather came into her mind, but she decided against mentioning him. Crushing on a man she commuted to and from work with would sound pretty teenage if she said it out loud.

Avril was also single, having recently broken up with her boyfriend of five years, and so the two of them spent a happy couple of hours comparing notes about the pitfalls of the London dating scene while sharing a bowl of chips and downing two full bottles of Pinot Grigio. Hattie insisted they had some tequila shots before they staggered out into the drizzle, giggling loudly.

Her parents had gone out by the time she got home, so she carried on her impromptu party for one, raiding the drinks cabinet in the dining room and playing Beyoncé so loudly that the husband of the family next door – who had small children – came round to complain.

There was no visit to the gym on Sunday either, because, obviously, she was nursing a hangover. Lying in bed with a mug of coffee, Hattie picked up her phone and found the message Antonio had sent in the early hours of Thursday morning.

*Was great to meet you xx*

Hattie hesitated for a moment then, because she was bored, typed back.

*Only just seen this... sorry. Was good to meet you too. How about a drink tomorrow?*

*Really? Only if you're sure you want to!*

Hattie frowned. Was he implying that she was a flake, because she hadn't bothered to answer the message straight away?

*Definitely*, she typed. *Same place as last time. 6.30 x*

# SIX

## HATTIE

On Monday morning, her head having finally cleared, Hattie took special care over her appearance. She dressed in high-heeled boots, a flattering, figure-hugging teal blue dress and clipped her hair up with a sparkly slide.

This was because she was going on a date with Antonio, she told herself. Nothing at all to do with the fact that she might see Casper on the train.

Bridget had saved her a seat on the 7.48, but, frustratingly, although Carmen and Julian were sitting at a table together at the far end of carriage 3, there was so sign of Casper.

Never mind, she thought, taking the cappuccino that Bridget had bought for her, if she had missed the opportunity to talk *to* Casper Merriweather, then at least she could now talk *about* him. The shy smiles, her remembering Hattie's coffee order – this all indicated Bridget had a bit of a girl crush on her. So surely she would be only too happy to discuss Casper, if that was what Hattie wanted.

'What do you think of Casper?' she asked, raising her take-away cup to her lips.

'What do *I* think?' Bridget stammered, tightening her grip on her own coffee. She seemed flustered by the question. 'I don't know... I haven't really thought about it.'

'He's incredibly good-looking, isn't he?'

'Is he? I suppose so.'

'Oh, come *on*,' Hattie scoffed. 'Don't pretend you haven't noticed. Anyone with a pulse would notice him.'

Bridget gave an awkward little giggle at this. 'Yes, he is. I think so too.'

She seemed pleased to be party to a girlie conspiracy, so Hattie then told her how Casper had surreptitiously pressed himself against her when they had last been on the train together. 'I really don't think I was imagining it,' she finished.

'I'm sure you weren't,' Bridget said, with a firmness that surprised Hattie. 'I can tell that he likes you.'

'How?'

'Oh...' Bridget smiled shyly. 'I've caught him looking at you a couple of times when he thinks no one can see him.'

Slightly surprised, Hattie nonetheless filed away this piece of information to consider later. 'I enjoyed sitting next to Lewis on Friday,' she continued. 'We had a nice chat actually. I quite like him.'

But Bridget was frowning at this. 'I'm not sure about him at all,' she said, turning down the corners of her mouth.

'What d'you mean?'

'I don't know... there's just something about him that makes me uncomfortable. Creeps me out.' She gave a little shudder to reinforce her point.

When the train pulled into Waterloo, Harriet made a point of walking past the table where Carmen and Julian had just been sitting.

'Hattie!' boomed Julian from the other end of the aisle. 'Glad I've seen you! We were planning on going for a drink at the Railway Arms this evening, if you'd care to join? Casper and Lewis too, of course, if they're on the 18.53.'

'Of course,' she smiled. 'That would be lovely.'

As she walked up to the ticket barriers, she had already pulled out her phone and composed a message to Antonio.

*Sorry, can't make tonight. Something's come up* ☹

The Railway Arms was a few hundred yards from Summerlands station; a plain but solid brick building with mullioned windows and slightly bedraggled hanging baskets.

Hattie arrived with Carmen, who she had sat with on the train from Waterloo. The older woman was friendly enough, but there was something about her that Hattie couldn't quite put her finger on – an energy – that made Hattie uncomfortable. She was fervently hoping that they would find the others already at the pub.

To her relief, Lewis and Julian were seated at a large table with a bench on either side, and already had drinks.

'Ah, ladies! Come and join us!' Julian called, motioning them over.

The pub was already busy with the after-work drinkers, and Hattie and Carmen had to squeeze their way through the crowd to sit down. Hattie accepted Lewis's offer of a drink, requesting a tequila and soda, and positioned herself facing the door. She wanted to be able to see who was coming through it. Bridget did so a couple of minutes later, wearing her frumpy navy raincoat and apologising for being late.

No sign of Casper. Perhaps he wasn't coming, Hattie thought, now regretting having cancelled her meetup with Antonio.

But fifteen minutes later, there he was, dashing in a dark suit, white shirt and subdued red tie, his hair damp from the rain.

'Don't you look nice?' he said to Hattie, his eyes took in the clinging blue dress and diamanté hair clip as he pulled out a chair opposite her. 'Going on somewhere later?'

'I might do, yes,' Hattie answered. She didn't want Casper to think that she had dressed seductively just for his benefit, even if this was partly true.

Julian was quizzing Bridget about her work in the civil service, while Carmen and Lewis were discussing a Swedish crime drama they both watched, so Casper and Hattie fell into what felt like their first proper conversation. He told her about his job at Van Asbeck's, which involved liaising with clients about where they wanted their purchases shipped to and organising all the security and red tape involved in moving priceless pieces of art around the globe. He was clearly very knowledgeable but wore it lightly, with a quick, teasing wit and a degree of self-deprecation.

But what Hattie really wanted to know about most was his private life. Why was he living in Summerlands? she asked. Surely someone at the heart of the glamorous world of international art dealing would have a pied-à-terre in Mayfair or Chelsea, or Knightsbridge. What on earth was he doing in dull old suburbia?

'It's complicated,' he said evasively. 'All to do with being between properties, moving assets around.' Hattie waited for him to elaborate, but he just said, 'I'm only here temporarily. Bit like you really.'

'And are you living with a partner, or...?'

Casper just smiled and said, 'You know what, I'm much more interested in finding out about you.'

And he did seem genuinely interested in Hattie. He asked lots of questions about her family and her upbringing, and when it came to the subject of her living at home again after losing her prized independence, he was surprisingly sweet and sensitive.

'It'll all come good again, you'll see,' he told her warmly. 'A smart, attractive girl like you. All it needs is for one thing to change.' He fixed his light grey eyes on her face, bringing his gaze to rest on her mouth, as people were supposed to do when they were experiencing desire. 'Just one thing.'

After a while, he turned to talk to Carmen, and Hattie made small talk with Julian about the golf club he and her father both belonged to. Another round of drinks was bought, and then another, until Carmen said she needed to get back to her children and Bridget hurriedly got to her feet, seeming grateful for the chance to flee.

'Well, this has been jolly,' observed Julian, repeating his sentiments about the night they'd all first met. 'How about we start a WhatsApp group for the six of us, then we can share travel tips, save seats, et cetera.'

The others agreed, and numbers were exchanged. Sure enough, soon after she had been driven home in Julian's Jag, Hattie received the invitation to join the group entitled: 'The 18.53 Crew'. Carmen, Julian, Casper, Lewis and Bridget had all joined, and Hattie couldn't quite suppress the thrill of pleasure that she now had Casper's phone number, and he had hers.

Sure enough, as she was turning off her bedside light just before midnight, a new WhatsApp message arrived, below a profile picture of Casper looking just like Jude Law.

*Goodnight, gorgeous xx*

# SEVEN

## HATTIE

Over the next few days, Hattie and Casper continued to send messages in their private chat thread.

They exchanged the usual banalities about their activities during the working day, and they flirted: hard. Inevitably – as was now the norm with digital communication – they started exchanging photos. Nothing explicit, just content that teased, hinted at more intimacy to come. Hattie would have been happy to talk all day long and send thirty or forty messages in a twenty-four-hour period. Maybe more. But Casper rationed his, sending them every couple of hours or so. This only served to heighten Hattie's dependence on the line of communication, constantly checking her phone to see if he had been in touch.

Antonio sent a message asking if she wanted to rearrange their liaison. She ignored it.

The following week, a message from Carmen appeared on the 18.53 Crew group chat.

*Hi guys... I wondered if you would all like to come over to mine after work one evening for some supper. Won't be anything fancy! Could you let me know which days you're available? X*

Reading it, Hattie was mildly surprised. The last thing she had expected from the tense, rather wary Carmen was a dinner invitation.

She added her address, then a third message.

*Friday is best for me as I'm not in the office, but I realise it may not work for everyone.*

Bridget was the first to reply, saying that she would be free on Friday and asking what she could bring, prompting Hattie to write a similar message. Julian chimed in an hour later telling them that he was prosecuting a trial at Southampton that day but could probably be there by '8-ish'. Lewis simply said he would try to make it. Casper said nothing.

Hattie went to their private chat.

*You going to go to Carmen's thing? xxx*

He didn't reply for a while, eventually just sending an emoji of bared teeth.

*What's that supposed to mean?*

*It means that kind of get-together's not really my thing*

Hattie was in the office, and glancing around her, she saw Sonia Nixon staring at her. But since this was her last week, she didn't care. She flung Sonia an insolent stare as she typed her reply.

*Not mine either, but at least we'll see each other. We could go
on somewhere else after xxx*

She checked her phone every couple of minutes for the rest
of the afternoon, but this did not draw a response.

Eventually, as she was heading for Waterloo, she saw a
reply land as her phone picked up signal again.

*I'll go on one condition*

Racing up the escalator so that her phone signal was strong
enough to send a message, she typed a reply. *What's that?*

*That you wear the sexiest thing you own. And that you let me
see what's underneath it*

She read this last message over and over again. Once she
was at home, she went up to her room, stripped naked and took
a picture in front of the mirror, which she sent to Casper.

He did not respond.

There were very few seats on the 18.53 the following evening,
and Hattie was forced to sit next to someone she didn't know.
She did spot Bridget, however, as they were heading to the
ticket barriers at Summerlands, and waved to her.

'I was thinking about Friday...'

Bridget stared at her blankly.

'About the supper party at Carmen's.'

'Oh. Yes.' Bridget's voice did not hide her lack of
enthusiasm.

'Only why don't you come over to my house beforehand
and we can get ready together? It will be my last day in my
current job, so I'm planning on heading home early.'

'Get ready?' Bridget looked confused.

'You know,' Hattie urged, 'change into our going-out outfits. Do our hair and make-up. While having a drink, obviously.' As she was speaking, she remembered that Bridget didn't drink.

'Oh,' Bridget said again, her expression quite blank. 'I was just going to go in my work stuff.'

Nevertheless, she agreed to make a note of Hattie's address on her phone, and at six forty-five on Friday evening, she appeared on the doorstep of the Sewells' house.

'I caught an earlier train,' she explained, as Hattie led her up to the top-floor bedroom. 'Only Carmen said to be there for seven thirty, so the 18.53 would have got in a bit late.'

Hattie had already made a start on her make-up and had tonged her hair into waves. She waved a plastic beaker of rosé hopefully at Bridget's hand, but she shook her head firmly. Then, ignoring the other woman's horrified expression, she stripped down to her underwear and pulled off her bra, before climbing into a tight black chiffon dress with a short, flounced skirt and a plunging neckline that revealed most of her breasts.

'I bought another top,' Bridget said meekly, holding up a carrier bag. 'But I don't have anything like... like what you're wearing.'

'Don't worry,' Hattie said blithely, putting on some gold chandelier earrings. 'I can do your make-up for you, at least.'

She made Bridget sit down on the chair and remove her glasses, before getting to work with highlighter, bronzer and blusher.

'Oh my God!' Hattie said eventually, pushing Bridget round so that she could see her reflection in the dresser mirror. 'You look amazing.'

And it was true: she really did. She had a perfect complexion, almond-shaped hazel eyes and a straight little nose. Her teeth were perfect too, apart from large and unusually pointed canines.

'Why don't you leave your specs off tonight?'

Hattie went to pick them up, but before she could, Bridget had grabbed them and put them back on. 'No,' she said firmly. 'I need to wear them to see.'

'Okay, but you should seriously invest in some contact lenses,' Hattie persisted. 'Then everyone can see how pretty you are.'

In reply, Bridget merely shrugged on the ugly blue raincoat, obscuring the broderie anglaise top she had just put on. 'Come on, we really ought to get going. I'm sure Carmen has gone to a lot of effort, so we mustn't be late.'

Hattie took a bottle of red wine from her father's makeshift cellar in the utility room, and the two women walked back to the main road and caught a taxi to a large 1930s block of flats on the far side of the suburb.

Once they were inside, Hattie's high spirits gave way to discomfort. There were several reasons for this. Firstly, she realised she was stupidly overdressed, in her sexy dress and high heels. Carmen was wearing joggers and a T-shirt, and her husband Steve was in jeans and a sweatshirt. Secondly, Carmen's two young sons were still up, albeit in their pyjamas. They were racing around the cramped, untidy flat, roaring with excitement and jumping on the furniture. Hattie did not much care for children, and she was relieved when Steve rounded them up and put them to bed. Thirdly, Julian and Lewis arrived about thirty minutes after she and Bridget did, but there was no Casper. And now all that Hattie could think about was that she had sent him a nude. And that he had not contacted her since. Had she repulsed him? Put him off in some way?

It was still the only thing on her mind when the guests squeezed around the small dining table at one end of the living room. Carmen had made a delicious Turkish chicken dish, but Hattie barely touched it, instead helping herself to the wine on the table and, once that was empty, opening the bottle of red she had taken from her parents' house. She overheard Bridget and Carmen talking. Carmen was explaining that the flat was just rented, and that Steve was at home doing most of the childcare, because he had recently been made redundant. It was difficult managing on her part-time salary, she was saying, but they did their best to make it work.

Lewis, Julian and Steve were discussing the merits of various London football teams and Hattie was communing solely with the drink in her glass, half listening to the others. One thing she overheard that surprised her was Lewis referring to himself as a single father. It was the only personal thing he'd disclosed about himself, and not one she had expected. But he was old enough to be a father, so why not?

At nine o'clock, the intercom buzzed and Steve got up to answer the door. A minute later, Casper came into the flat, wearing an expensive-looking grey overcoat and carrying a bouquet of lilies, which he presented to a delighted Carmen, kissing her on both cheeks.

'So sorry I'm late, guys, got held up at work.' He slid into the empty chair between Carmen and Julian. As he took his seat, his eyes strayed fleetingly over Hattie's cleavage, but he made no eye contact. 'Big things happening at Van Asbeck's at the moment. Very big things.'

Steve extended a hand and introduced himself as Carmen's husband. 'Sounds interesting. Tell us more.'

'Sadly, this particular event is embargoed at the moment. But you'll read all about it in the press soon enough, trust me.' Casper gave the assembled group an enigmatic little smile, before accepting a reheated plate of chicken and a glass of wine.

Hattie tried and failed to catch his eye, and in desperation accepted a glass of port from Steve. She hated port: it was too sweet and gave her a headache. By the time the meal was finished, she was so drunk she could barely walk, mumbling her goodbyes and staggering out into the night. The recent spate of spring showers had filled the air with a fungal earthiness, and there was a chilly breeze. Hattie's teeth chattered, and she pulled her flimsy coat more tightly around her.

'Fancy a lift, Hattie?' Julian's Jag appeared out of the darkness, gliding to a stop at the kerb.

'No, s'okay, I'll walk,' she mumbled. She didn't trust herself not to pass out in the car's warm interior, or worse still, vomit. 'Thanks all the same.'

The alternative was covering around two miles on her four-inch stilettos, but in her inebriated state, she convinced herself this was perfectly doable.

'Hey!' As Julian's Jag roared off, a voice called behind her as she set off down the main road. 'Hattie?'

She lurched round to see Casper, his long overcoat billowing behind him as he approached. There was a street light behind him, and his golden hair was glowing as though there was a halo above it. When he caught up with her, he put a hand on her shoulder and let his gaze roam the length of her body, taking in the dress and the shoes.

'Can I just say,' he murmured, 'you didn't let me down with the outfit. You look sensational.'

Hattie merely stared at him, her eyes wide, her mouth slightly open.

'And as for that photo you sent, you naughty girl...' He was very close to her now, his groin pressed against hers. 'I can't wait to see the real thing for myself.'

He grasped the back of her neck, his fingers entwined in her hair, and all of a sudden they were kissing, deeply and passionately, Hattie arching against him.

'Let's go back to your place,' she whispered.

His expression darkened. 'We can't. It's not... convenient. We'll have to go to yours.'

'But my parents...'

'Surely it's not that big a deal? We can sneak in really quietly.'

Hattie glanced at her watch. It was almost midnight. When they were spending the evening at home, her parents usually went to bed after the ten o'clock news, turning out their light around eleven. They'd almost certainly be asleep by the time they reached the house.

'Okay, okay,' she was still slurring. 'But we'll have to be super quiet, okay?'

They flagged down a passing cab, and five minutes later, shoes in their hands, were creeping up the stairs to the top-floor guest room. Casper tossed his coat on the chair and went straight for the zip of Hattie's dress, toppling her onto the bed and easing himself into her with a suppressed groan of pleasure.

What followed was very intense, but almost silent sex. An hour and a half later, Casper disentangled his limbs and left her sprawled naked on the bed as he crept down the stairs again and out into the night.

The next morning, when she tried to remember the intimate choreography, it was all a bit of a blur, but Hattie was pretty sure it had been good. Then she received a WhatsApp from Casper.

*My God, you were amazing! xxx*

So it had been good. It had been very good.

# EIGHT

## JULIAN

'How was your little train thing?' Ginny Cobbold asked across the breakfast table.

Her husband was munching toast, his attention focused on Saturday's edition of *The Times*. Ginny reached over and refilled his cup with coffee from the French press.

'My what?' Julian asked distractedly, his lips spraying crumbs.

'Your get-together with your train chums. Isn't that where you were last night?' Her tone was wintry. 'I heard you coming in around midnight, I think.'

'Sorry,' Julian said, with a self-deprecating grin. 'I did try to be quiet.'

'I can't think why you'd want to spend your evening with a bunch of glassy-eyed commuters. Hardly your thing, surely?'

He shrugged. 'They're nice people. And it was fun. A lot of us squeezed into a small space, admittedly. Food was good. Couple of people drank rather a lot.'

He instantly had a mental image of Hattie Sewell on the pavement outside Carmen's flat, swaying like a tree in a gale. She seemed like a nice enough girl, but, my God, she was a bit of a lush. In his opinion, she needed to sort herself out. He'd overheard her talking about her upcoming thirtieth birthday. At her age, he and Ginny were married with a child and another on the way.

There was no sign of Hattie on the platform at Summerlands on Monday morning, but Julian did glimpse Lewis Handley, who he had enjoyed getting to know a little at Friday's supper. He was chatting to Carmen, and the two of them boarded the train together, but Julian pretended not to see them, choosing to sit alone in one of the rear carriages. He had a plea hearing at the Old Bailey that morning and needed to use the thirty-nine minutes on the train to go over the brief and work out what he was going to say.

'Don't forget you have a lunch at one thirty, Mr Cobbold,' Terry, his clerk, said as he intercepted Julian in the corridor of chambers as he was leaving for court, wig tin and gown tucked under his arm.

'I do?'

'Yes, sir. With Mr Laszlo.'

Julian slapped his forehead in exasperation. 'Bloody hell, Terry. Is that today?'

'It is. A table is reserved at Simpson's. Would you like me to rearrange it, sir? Only this morning's list should be finished by twelve, I would think.'

'No, it's all right. As you say, we should have wound up by then. I'll go straight from court and come back here after. If anyone particularly wants to know.'

Ernst Laszlo was a former client of Julian's, a wealthy Hungarian businessman who he had defended a few years earlier on charges of tax fraud. Having successfully kept Laszlo out of prison, he had earned the man's eternal gratitude and an expensive lunch every six months or so.

After he had finished with his cases, Julian decided to walk to the Strand to meet Laszlo. It was a clear, bright early spring day and he was grateful for the chance to stretch his legs before what was sure to be a heavy meal.

Ernst was waiting for him at the table in the opulently panelled Grand Divan dining room. White-coated waiters poured wine and silently wove their trolleys between the tables, delivering the trademark silver cloches. Not wanting to spend the afternoon fighting sleep, Julian requested a Dover sole and opted for sparkling water, despite his companion pressing a bottle of Puligny Montrachet on him. Ernst was keen to embrace the full carvery experience, ordering aged Scottish roast beef with several types of vegetables, traditional gravy and a bottle of Burgundy. He even lit a cigar at one point, only to have the maître d' scuttle over and request he put it out.

Julian was reluctant to divulge details of cases he was working on, so instead they made small talk about Ernst's business dealings. He was investing heavily in art, he informed Julian.

'After drugs and arms, it's the world's most lucrative commodity,' he said with a rasping laugh. He was a large, square man with thinning black hair and a slight underbite that made him look like a bulldog.

Only then did Julian spot something familiar in the pile of papers Ernst had next to him on the red leather banquette. A glossy magenta brochure with a distinctive gold logo. Van Asbeck's.

'You buying from those people?' he enquired, pointing to it and raising an eyebrow.

'Ah, now!' Ernst sounded exceedingly pleased with himself. 'This – this is something exciting.' He picked up the brochure. 'You know much about early nineteenth century Japanese art? From the Edo period?' He speared a roast potato with his fork and crammed it into his mouth.

'Very little, I'm afraid.'

'Even so, you've probably heard of Hokusai?' Ernst spoke around the mouthful of potato. 'He created the famous woodblock of The Great Wave. The most reproduced image in history.'

'Ah yes,' Julian nodded.

'Well, towards the end of his career, he also painted in oils. And someone in Japan has found a previously undiscovered painting he did of a courtesan in a red kimono.' He flipped through the pages of the brochure and showed it to Julian.

'Beautiful,' agreed Julian. And it was, the image of the opulent kimono being both delicate and full of subtle strength.

'Lot of buzz around the sale. Quite a bit of attention in the press. Oriental art is having a bit of a moment just now.'

And then Julian remembered that the auction house in question was where Casper Merriweather worked. Was this the reason for his late arrival the previous Friday, and his teasing comments about an exciting development that they would all hear about?

'Interesting,' he said, taking the brochure from Ernst and looking at it more closely. Some of the items had a starting bid listed, but underneath Hokusai's painting, it just said, 'Guide price on enquiry'. 'Is it expected to fetch much?' He handed the brochure back to Ernst and took a mouthful of his fish, washing it down with water and wishing he'd agreed to white wine instead.

'The record price for a Hokusai is about two million pounds, but I'd be very surprised if it didn't top that by quite some margin.' Ernst wiped his mouth with a thick white linen napkin and beckoned the waiter over to pour him more wine. 'The fact that it's just come to light after two hundred years adds to the excitement. And therefore to what it's worth.'

'Very interesting,' Julian repeated.

. . .

He thought about the painting as he walked back to chambers later, not quite able to get the hauntingly exquisite image from his mind. He made up his mind to ask Casper more about it when he caught the 18.53, but he wasn't in the usual carriage 3: just Lewis and Carmen again. Nor was there any sign of the mousy, silent Bridget, or Hattie. Julian thanked Carmen for the dinner she had hosted, and she responded with a nod, but seemed out of sorts. The woman always looked distinctly unhappy he thought. Haunted, almost.

Hattie, he now remembered, had recently finished a temporary contract and so for the time being would not be commuting regularly. Lord knew what the girl would find to do all day holed up at her parents' house with no gainful employment. Drink, presumably.


At home, after he and Ginny had eaten in near silence, Julian went upstairs to Edward's bedroom.

The pain of loss tore at his heart as it always did the second he opened that door, but this time he pushed it down firmly, marching straight to the bookcase and pulling out the same book he had picked up before. That same nagging feeling had been with him all day; the feeling that something was out of kilter.

He flicked through the pages. And there it was again. He hadn't been imagining it. There was a pack of bright orange Post-its on Edward's desk, next to the pot of pencils, an assortment of neon highlighters and a ruler. Julian peeled one off and stuck it in the book, on the relevant page, before using one of the pencils to firmly underline two words. Seconds later, he was downstairs in his study, pulling up his internet browser and searching Google.

Ginny appeared in the doorway, asking if he wanted a hot drink, or a whisky. 'Is that a case you're working on?' she demanded.

'Something like that,' Julian replied vaguely. He closed down the page and turned to look at her. 'I was thinking I ought to organise a drink with Nigel Hayes. Might ring him tomorrow.'

Nigel was a detective chief inspector at the Met who had been the lead officer on a big criminal case Julian had prosecuted for the CPS a few years ago. The two men had become friendly and stayed in touch, meeting up every so often to discuss the ills of the criminal justice system.

'Really? Why?' Ginny demanded, looking at him intently.

'No, no reason,' he told her with a smile. 'Just that it would be nice to catch up.'

'No reason, Julian? You suddenly need to see an acquaintance completely out of the blue, and he happens to be a police officer?'

'Exactly.'

She stared back at him, and he could tell from the set of her jaw that his wife did not believe him.

# NINE

## HATTIE

On Tuesday morning, Hattie phoned the agency who had been finding her temporary work, only to be told, 'We have nothing that fits your skill set at present.'

'Are you sure?' she pleaded, but they simply stated that there were other agencies she could try. Her desperation did not stem so much from a need to earn money or fill her time productively, more from an increasingly obsessive need to see Casper. Since his message on Saturday morning, she had heard nothing further. She'd sent a couple of light-hearted messages which had received no response. Not even two blue ticks to indicate they'd been read. And given that Hattie had no idea where he lived, the way she saw it, her only chance of seeing him was on the train between Summerlands and Waterloo. But no job meant no commuting.

Just before six o'clock that evening, she announced to her mother that she was going for a walk.

'But it's almost dark, darling!' Susannah Sewell protested.

'I need to pick up a couple of things from the chemist.'

As expected, this shut down the discussion, and Hattie walked in the dusk to the station. Casper would almost certainly be getting a train back from London; the problem was that she didn't know which one. She was in time to see the 17.53 from Waterloo arrive, but he was not among the passengers that emerged from that. Nor was he on the slower, stopping train that got in just after seven fifteen. He must, surely, be on the 18.53 then, that arrived at 19.32. She checked the WhatsApp group for any updates, but from what she could see, only Lewis had signalled any intention of being on the train that evening with his jaunty message:

*If any members of the crew get there before me, save me a forward-facing seat pls!*

It had just started to rain, and Hattie had no hat or umbrella. She bought a cup of tea from the kiosk, and sheltered under the eaves of the station building, positioned so that she was partly hidden, yet could see everyone who was leaving. She was still trying to work out what she would say to Casper as the 18.53 pulled in to Summerlands, just after half past seven.

Sure enough, seconds later, there was Lewis, striding out with a newspaper held up over his head to keep off the rain. Eventually, the crowd started to thin until people were coming out of the building in ones and twos. She spotted Bridget in her matronly navy coat, opening an umbrella, but she was almost the last passenger.

Hattie darted back into the station hall to check, but the train had pulled out en route to Portsmouth, and the platform was now empty.

She ran out onto the rain-slicked street and shouted out to Bridget. Hearing her name, Bridget turned round, a frown of irritation on her face. Was it Hattie's imagination, or was the smile that followed it slightly forced?

'Hello,' she said, sounding puzzled. 'Were you on the train? I didn't see you.'

'No; no I wasn't.' Hattie gave a rueful grin. 'I'm not temping at the moment. I just popped out to pick up a few things from the shops.'

Bridget nodded, even though Hattie wasn't carrying any shopping, or even a handbag.

'Was... Did you see Casper on the train?'

'No. He probably wasn't on the six fifty-three.'

'Only... the thing is, Bridget...' Hattie grabbed hold of the sleeve of Bridget's coat and pulled her to the edge of the pavement so that other people could get past her umbrella. 'You're the only one I can really tell this to. Something happened the other night. After the supper party?'

'What d'you mean, something happened?'

'We... Casper and I slept together. At my house.'

Bridget was staring at her now, and Hattie was shocked to see that her expression was not merely disapproving. Worse: she seemed almost repelled.

Feeling her cheeks colour, Hattie ploughed on, her need to confide in someone now overwhelming. 'And the thing is, well, he hasn't been in touch with me. And since I'm not going into town to work anymore... well, I wondered, if you see him could you just... without being obvious about it or anything... could you just try to suss out what's going on with him?' Hattie was babbling now, her anxiety getting the better of her. 'But please, please, you have to be subtle about it. I don't want him thinking I've put you up to it.'

'Me?' Bridget looked horrified. 'But I never speak to him. So surely it would look really odd if I did now.'

This was true, Hattie realised with a jolt. She had never, ever seen Bridget and Casper exchange a single word. But she was on a mission now, and not to be deflected. 'The thing is, he didn't want me to go back to his place, and since he hasn't been in touch, I'm even more convinced he might have a wife, or a partner.'

'And you think he's just going to tell me that?' Bridget's face was impassive, her expression hard to read.

'Well, no...' Hattie's shoulders slumped in defeat. Rain was soaking her hair and the back of her coat. 'I don't suppose he is. Look, I'll let you go. Sorry.'

Bridget adjusted her umbrella and walked off, picking her way through the puddles, with a slight shrug of her shoulders.

'See you,' Hattie called bleakly, but the other woman appeared not to hear.


Later that night, having drunk a bottle of her parents' wine that she'd smuggled upstairs, Hattie messaged Casper again, taking a more direct approach this time.

*Hi... everything okay? xx*

Forty minutes later, just as she was switching off her light, her phone bleeped. Her heart pounding with excitement, she grabbed her phone. *Message from Casper Merriweather*. Just a single thumbs up emoji.

Frustrated in the extreme, Hattie started typing furiously, composing an indignant response. But despite the wine she had consumed, she had the good sense to delete it. If she started coming off needy and demanding at this delicate, early stage of their relationship, no good would come of it. Her endless succession of dating-app flings had taught her this, if nothing else.


In the morning, she decided that if the mountain wouldn't come to Mohammed, then it would have to be the other way round. She posted a message on the train WhatsApp group.

*Guys... anyone travelling on the 18.53 tonight?*

Lewis responded with a thinking face emoji, Julian wrote *Not sure,* and Carmen said simply *Yes.* Nothing from Casper or Bridget.

After getting up late and trawling job websites for an hour or so, Hattie changed into jeans and a linen blazer and caught the train into London. She walked over Waterloo Bridge and amused herself trawling the shops in Covent Garden, buying a dress and some boots that she couldn't really afford. After sitting alone in a brasserie nursing first one, then a second large glass of wine, she headed back to Waterloo station in time to travel on the 18.53.

Carmen spotted her as they were walking onto the platform, and they found table seats together. Still feeling ill at ease with the older woman, Hattie was relieved when they were joined by an out-of-breath Julian just as the train pulled out. Yet again, Casper was conspicuous by his absence, but at least Hattie had the vicarious enjoyment of hearing him talked about. Julian told them about the art world being agog at the discovery of a very early nineteenth-century Japanese masterpiece, and that it was Casper's auction house, Van Asbeck's, that were holding the auction.

'There'll be bidders from all over the world, and apparently it's expected to fetch several million at least,' Julian reported with satisfaction. Then, ever the gentleman, he offered to buy drinks from the buffet car for Hattie and Carmen after he'd been into the toilet cubicle for his customary vape. He told them he was only going to have coffee himself since he had to work on a big case that evening.

'Nothing for me, thanks,' Carmen said with a smile, holding up her hand. 'I try to have a night off from the alcohol every once in a while.'

'How about you, Hattie?' Julian raised an eyebrow in her direction.

Hattie hesitated. She desperately wanted another drink, but the other two could probably smell the wine on her breath already. 'I'm fine,' she answered disingenuously.

'Been into town for a spot of shopping?'

'Actually, I had a meeting to talk about a potential project,' Hattie wheeled out her pre-prepared lie, hoping she didn't sound too defensive. 'And I've got an interview on Friday, for something that's looking pretty promising.'

This last part was true, at least. *Please God let Saints & Sinners offer me the job,* she thought fervently, as she accepted a lift from Summerlands station in Julian's car in order to avoid walking home in the rain. *And let Casper get in touch.* This pretending to have a satisfactory adult life was so draining.

On Thursday, she was woken by a WhatsApp message. Not from Casper, but from Bridget.

*Hi Hattie. I talked to Casper and I can tell he's definitely still keen. So no need to worry. I'm sure he'll be in touch.*

That was all. No information about when she had managed to speak to him. It definitely hadn't been on the train the previous evening, unless both of them happened to travel together on a later service. Perhaps they'd commuted into London at the same time on Wednesday morning.

A mere five minutes later, another message arrived, this time from Casper.

*Hi, gorgeous. How about we grab a drink tonight after work? xxx*

Hattie felt a warm surge of pleasure run through her veins, tingling at the memory of his touch the other night. She felt energised, lit up. He wanted to see her. But immediately her spirits sank again. Tonight was no good. Her interview with Saints & Sinners was at ten the following morning, and she had a firm plan to be in bed early, and sober. She needed to be firing on all cylinders because she badly wanted – and needed – this job. Bridget knew about the interview of course, since they'd talked about it on the train together, but there was no reason she would have mentioned it to Casper.

*Would love to, but not tonight. Could do tomorrow evening, or Saturday? xxx*

His reply came a couple of minutes later.

*Sorry I'm off on a business trip tomorrow. Tonight only night I'm free for a while xxx*

Hattie stared at her phone for several minutes. She didn't want to go out tonight, but nor did she want to leave it, and risk never seeing Casper again. He had not said how long he was away. And what if he stopped answering her messages again? Surely she could meet him for a quick drink, just to find out when he'd be back from his trip, and make an arrangement for after his return. She could be home early if she just stuck to one drink. It would be all right.

*Fine,* she typed. *Let's do it xxx*

# TEN

## HATTIE

In Hattie's mind, she was definitely only going to have one quick drink with Casper.

But without a job to go to, she had far too much time to think about and plan for their date, and therefore it took on a larger and larger significance as Thursday wore on.

She walked up to the local parade of shops and had her hair cut and blow-dried at the salon her mother favoured, before going into the beauty spa next door and pleading with them to fit her in for a leg and bikini line wax. Back at home, she tried on and rejected half a dozen outfits, leaving drifts of clothes across her bedroom floor and her bed.

When the time finally came to get ready, she was so nervous that her hand shook as she tried to apply her make-up. What was wrong with her? she wondered. Why did the thought of this particular man have her insides both fizzing and churning? She had never felt like this about anyone before, not even Leo. There was something both magnetic and mesmerising about Casper's presence, as though when she was near him she was being helplessly sucked into his orbit.

She thought about going down to the dining room and

helping herself to her father's Scotch, but tonight she had resolved not to mix wine and spirits, so instead she connected a dance playlist to her Bluetooth speaker and allowed the music to distract her as she painted on winged eyeliner and a dark cherry red lipstick.

Susannah Sewell observed Hattie from the kitchen as she picked up her bag and hurried to the front door. 'You look very... alluring,' she said, taking in the buttock-skimming skirt and heels. 'Where are you going?'

'Just meeting a friend.'

'He must be a pretty special friend,' her father cut in, peering over her mother's shoulder.

'It's just a quick drink, okay?' Hattie wrenched the front door open. 'I've got to be up early for that interview, remember?' She did not linger to explain further, since she was already running late.

Casper had suggested they meet at a tapas bar near the station at eight. The place had faded saffron yellow awnings, and a lot of dusty artificial greenery and was virtually empty. Hattie wondered if that was why he'd chosen it. It was already after eight fifteen when she walked through the door, but there was no sign of her date. So she did the only thing she could do: bought herself a drink. On a normal night out, she would have ordered a bottle of wine, but tonight she stuck to a medium-sized glass of red and waited, glancing nervously at her phone every few seconds. By the time he appeared, looking tanned and glamorous in a white shirt and dark jacket, it was almost nine o'clock and she had consumed most of what was in her glass.

'No, no, it's okay,' she protested as he flagged down a passing server and requested a bottle of the same red Hattie was drinking. 'I'd better not have any more. Got to get up early.'

But Casper did not retract his order and the bottle arrived a few seconds later. Hattie tried ineffectually to cover the top of her glass, but he distracted her by grabbing her hand with his left and kissing the tips of her fingers while pouring more wine into her glass with his right. 'Just have the one glass,' he coaxed, letting go of her and handing the drink to her. 'I'll get through the rest, if you're so determined to be virtuous.'

'All right,' she agreed, forcing herself to take just a couple of small sips.

'I'm so bloody happy to see you,' he murmured, pouring a glass for himself. 'I know I've been a bit evasive but...' He was looking her directly in the eye now. 'Listen, can I tell you something, Hattie? You might not like it, but I feel it's only fair you should know, because it will explain a few things. The thing is... I'm married.'

Hattie blinked at him, her brain doing its best to process this information. It certainly wasn't a surprise, but somehow still shocking to hear him say it out loud, and with almost no preamble. Reflexively, she picked up her glass and took a large gulp.

'How do you feel about that?' he was asking, his tone earnest, as he tried to make eye contact.

She shrugged, uncertain.

'The thing is, we were married very young. Too young: it was stupid. And we've both come to realise that it was a mistake. To be honest, neither of us is happy.' He looked down, twirling an onyx cufflink. 'If it were down to me, I'd leave, you know?' He raised his unsettlingly beautiful grey eyes and locked them on hers again. 'Even more reason to do so now, since you and I got together.'

He let that statement hang in the air for a few seconds, before pressing on.

'But my wife doesn't want to. Her parents... well, they've invested a lot in the marriage. Bought us a place and so on. So there's pressure to make it work.'

'But you don't want it to work?' Hattie was having to focus very hard in order to get a whole sentence out. Out of the corner of her eye, she saw Casper topping up her glass, but resolved not to drink any more.

'No, believe me, Hattie, I don't. Especially not now I've met you.'

Hattie's brain raced as she tried to process this news. She had been attempting to deny and suppress the overwhelmingly strong feelings that she was developing for Casper. After all, it was very early in their relationship. They barely knew one another. And yet, shockingly – thrillingly – he had been feeling the same way.

'So are you going to leave her?'

'Do you want me to?'

Instead of answering this tantalising question, she leaned forward and started kissing him. She felt curiously light-headed and off balance, knocking her glass off the edge of the table and onto the floor. It shattered, and splashed wine over her skirt and bare legs. The bar was busier now, and heads turned in their direction.

'Easy tiger!' Casper muttered. 'Let's not put on a floor show, eh?'

Hattie didn't really know how, but suddenly they were on the street. Hattie pulled Casper against her greedily, her mouth pressed on his neck. 'Come back to my house,' she whispered. 'Come back with me now.'

'It's not even ten o'clock yet, won't your parents still be up?'

'Yeah, so? You can meet them.'

Casper was shaking his head. 'That wouldn't be a good idea, I don't think. Not the way the situation is at the moment. I'm sure they won't exactly be thrilled to find out their daughter's seeing someone who's already married.'

'But where can we...? How can we...?' Hattie's voice came out as a croak. She was vaguely aware of grabbing Casper by the

belt on his jeans and dragging him, stumbling, into a narrow
ginnel off the main street: the place where the bar had its side
entrance, and its wheelie bins and empty crates were stored.
She felt suddenly dizzy, and leaned back against the brick wall.
Her skirt was around her waist and she was shakily unzipping
Casper's fly and trying to get him to penetrate her, whimpering
with frustration when it didn't really work. And that was the
last thing she remembered, because, only seconds later, she
blacked out.


'Hattie!'

It was her father's voice. What the hell was he doing here?

She somehow forced her eyelids open and took in her
surroundings. She was lying on top of the bed in her room at
home, still dressed in her miniskirt and boots. A trail of watery
vomit was next to her on the duvet cover, trickling over the edge
of the bed and pooling on the carpet. Sun streamed through the
window.

Her heart lurching with panic, she snatched up her phone –
08.19. So it was the next day. How did she get here, after being
in the bar with Casper?

'I thought I'd better wake you,' her father was saying. 'Since
you've got that interview to get to.'

*Oh God. The interview with Saints & Sinners. It was at ten
o'clock.*

Her father was looking down at her with disapproval. 'Harriet Claire Sewell, how on earth did you get yourself into this
state? We heard a car dropping you off after we'd gone to bed,
and you going upstairs, so you must have let yourself in.'

Hattie ignored him, jumping off the bed and pulling frantically at her clothes. 'I've got to change,' she groaned.

'I'll put the kettle on—'

'No, Dad, I haven't got time! I can't afford to miss my train!'

'Well, at least clean your bloody face up,' he said drily, before retreating.

The mirror in the bathroom reflected a pasty face streaked with vomit and panda eyes from what had been eyeliner and mascara. Retching slightly, Hattie scrubbed at it ineffectually with a wet wipe, sprayed her head with a few gusts of dry shampoo and tugged on the white shirt, pinstriped trousers and chunky loafers she had laid out the day before.

Her father wordlessly held out a mug of tea as she thundered to the foot of the stairs and she managed to gulp down a couple of mouthfuls before pushing it away, shaking her head and running out of the door.


There was a fast train to Waterloo at 08.47, and Hattie's scattered brain somehow managed to calculate that if she succeeded in catching it and got straight onto the tube, she could just about make it to the Saints & Sinners offices in Hoxton at around 10 a.m. If she was five or ten minutes late, it wouldn't be a disaster. More than that, and it would look flaky.

Her head was pounding and her stomach was churning as she ran onto the platform at Summerlands at 8.45, just as the Waterloo train was approaching. She bent to catch her breath and as she did so, a tidal wave of nausea swept over her body, making her knees shake violently. She tried to swallow it down again, pressing her lips closed, but the vomit surged out as an unstoppable force, splattering the toes of her loafers and leaving a pungent smear on her clean white shirt. The people around her leapt back in shock, as though they'd been scalded. Gasping, she straightened up and lurched towards the train, but the doors were already closing.

Suddenly, someone grabbed her by the back of her shirt and tugged her through a set of carriage doors which were being wedged open by a well-positioned shoulder. She staggered and grabbed onto the back of a seat as the 8.47 pulled out of Summerlands station with her safely on board.

'You're welcome,' said a familiar voice.

Hattie opened her eyes and saw Lewis Handley, one eyebrow raised, smiling down at her.

# ELEVEN

## HATTIE

Lewis guided Hattie to a seat.

'Wait there,' he told her, disappearing from view and returning a few minutes later with a cup of black coffee and sugar sachets, a second cup of warm water and some paper napkins.

He tipped the sugar into the coffee and pushed it towards Hattie, indicating with a nod that she should drink it. Then, with surprising gentleness, he cleaned up her face, wiped her shoes and dabbed at the front of her shirt. The stain remained clearly visible over her bust.

'I can't go to my interview like this,' Hattie wailed, pointing down at the shirt. 'Just when things were finally going my way... I'm going to have to cancel.'

'No,' Lewis told her firmly. 'You're not doing that. You can have my shirt.'

Under his leather jacket, he was wearing a pale grey flannel shirt, and he pulled it off now, revealing a plain white T-shirt. 'You can have mine. Go and change in the toilet.'

Hattie did as she was told, throwing her own stained shirt in the toilet cubicle bin before putting on Lewis's grey shirt. By the time she had returned to her seat and finished the sweet coffee, she felt a little better.

Lewis rummaged in his rucksack for a bottle of water and some paracetamol tablets and handed them to her. 'Heavy night, was it?'

Hattie shook her head. 'That's the weird thing, I only had a couple of glasses of red wine. Two and a half, maximum.'

'Are you sure?' Lewis looked sceptical and with reason: he had seen her excessive social drinking first-hand on a couple of occasions.

'Positive.' Hattie opened the bottle of water and used it to swallow two of the pills. 'Because of the interview, I was being extra careful.' She wondered whether to tell him she had been out with Casper Merriweather, but decided against it.

'In that case, I think you must have been spiked. Could someone have put something in your drink without you noticing?'

Hattie thought back. She had been looking at her phone when the barman poured that first glass she ordered, and there were a couple of other people at the bar. 'I suppose so,' she conceded.

'It's surprisingly common, unfortunately,' Lewis said, with a sigh. 'But the good news is, the effects should have worn off by the time you get to your interview. Have you thought about what you're going to say?'

Only then did Hattie realise that the notes she'd made were on her laptop, which was still on her bedroom floor. Lewis made her pull up the job description on her phone and – as she applied the make-up she'd had the foresight to put in her bag the day before – helped her think of some questions the interviewers might ask and questions she might ask them.

'Thank you. You've been incredibly kind,' Hattie managed

a smile as the train pulled into Waterloo and she gathered up the blusher compact, mascara and lipstick. 'I'll wash your shirt and get it back to you.'

'No problem. Wouldn't have wanted you to miss the interview,' Lewis replied briskly, standing up and shouldering his rucksack. 'Sounds like you'd be a good fit for the role.'

'I wish there was some way I could repay you.' Hattie stood up and adjusted Lewis's shirt, which looked quite good with her fitted black trousers.

'Repay me by getting the bloody job, okay?'


As she caught the tube from Old Street back to Waterloo just before midday, Hattie put a message on the 18.53 WhatsApp group in case anyone else was travelling home early.

Straight away, she received a private message from Bridget.

*Did you make it? x*

*Make it?*

*To your interview. Only didn't you say you were going out for a drink the night before? x*

Had she said that to Bridget? Hattie couldn't remember. Her brain was still a little fuzzy from the effects of the spiked drink. Instead, her mind lurched back to a few hours earlier, when she'd come within two seconds of missing the train, and then almost been forced to attend the interview covered in her own vomit. She shuddered.

*I was a bit hungover, and I did almost miss the train,* she typed. This was a massaging of the truth, but Bridget didn't need a full blow-by-blow. *Lewis came to my rescue. He's a really decent guy x*

Bridget did not respond to this.

A few minutes later, seated on the train home, she received a message from Casper.

*How did your interview go, gorgeous? xxx*

*Pretty good xxx*, Hattie replied.

Because it had. Thanks to Lewis's intervention, she'd looked the part. Clean and decent, at least. And despite the fuzziness and her persistent headache, she had managed to give a good account of her career to that point and answer questions calmly and thoughtfully.

She then typed a second message.

*How did I get home last night?*

*I put you in a taxi, babe! Don't tell me you don't remember?! xxx*

He'd added a shocked face emoji and a wine glass emoji.

By now, Hattie felt shaky and drained, and just wanted to sleep. She was also unsure how to respond to Casper's last message. It implied she must have seemed drunk to him at the time. She composed another WhatsApp: *I think my drink must have been spiked xxx*, then deleted it without sending. He was acting as though everything was normal, so her behaviour couldn't have seemed that odd to him. And she didn't want to come across as one of *those* women; women who were addicted to drama. Messy women.

Her parents were both at work when she got home, so she ate a bowl of cereal, took a long, hot shower and sank gratefully into bed.

.   .   .

Hattie slept for over twelve hours, waking very early the next morning and checking her phone straight away. There had been no further contact from Casper, but she was not unduly put out by this, since she had not answered his last message.

At seven o'clock, buoyed up by the success of the previous day, she decided it was high time she did something nice for her parents. Pulling on her bathrobe, she went downstairs to the kitchen, made a pot of tea and carried it upstairs on a tray with two mugs and some milk.

'To what do we owe this pleasure,' her father mumbled sleepily as Hattie drew back their bedroom curtains.

'Just wanted to say a little thank you for putting up with me.' She turned and smiled at him.

'How did yesterday go, darling?' her mother asked as she poured the tea. 'We didn't want to wake you when we got back last night.'

'Pretty well,' said Hattie proudly. 'I think they liked me.'

Sure enough, waiting in her inbox was an email from Saints & Sinners' head of HR sent late the previous evening, inviting her to a second interview the following Friday. She messaged Casper to tell him and also opened a WhatsApp chat with Lewis to let him know. He was the first to reply.

*Fantastic*, he said simply.

*I've put your shirt in the wash.*

Hattie hadn't, but she intended to do so.

*Let's try and work out when we're going to be on the same train and I can give it back to you x*

He replied with a thumbs up.

Casper took longer to reply, but was effusive in his congratulations when he did so.

*So when would the job start if you got it?* he wanted to know.

*Early in the summer some time, I suppose. Haven't asked yet, but I will at the next interview.*

*Casper is typing*, the script above the chat said, for a long time. Hattie waited.

*We need to celebrate your news. Drink after work on Monday? xxx*

The message seemed surprisingly brief after all the time he took typing it. Hattie decided that he must have written and rewritten it several times, and the thought of him taking so much care touched her. Nevertheless, she would not answer it immediately, so as not to seem too keen. Instead, she tidied her room, put Lewis's shirt and her soiled duvet cover in the wash and went downstairs to make herself coffee and toast.

Casper sent a '?' and a thinking face emoji after forty minutes.

*That would be lovely*, she replied. *Where? xxx*

*Let's make it in town this time. I'll sort somewhere we can have some alone time*

On Monday, Casper was silent all day, only texting the details of their rendezvous at five o'clock, which meant that Hattie had to scramble to get to Summerlands station and catch a train into town. He told her to meet him at Tower Hill tube station at six fifteen, and when she arrived, he was waiting for her outside, sheltering from a squally March shower under the tiled entranceway.

They went to a pub underneath the railway arches: a traditional London pub with run-of-the-mill fixtures and fittings and the usual offerings in the way of drinks and bar snacks. Which was fine, Hattie told herself; what mattered was that she was going to spend private time with the charismatic handsome Casper, and this in itself was more thrilling than anything she had experienced for years. To be able to kiss that beautiful curving mouth of his and not care who might see them. But secretly she had been hoping for something a little more glamorous. A rooftop bar with views over the City and sophisticated cocktails.

After they had had a couple of drinks, Casper pulled a set of keys from the pocket of his trench coat and waggled them under Hattie's nose.

'Want to go somewhere more private, babe?'

Again, Hattie felt a twinge of disappointment. She had been hoping for a swanky hotel room, or even a suite, but that would mean a key card and not something accessed by a Yale lock. Sure enough, he led her to an anonymous post-war apartment block on Mansell Street, and they took the lift up to the fourth floor.

'This place belongs to a friend of mine who's out of town,' Casper explained. 'All I could manage with short notice.'

*But it's been two days*, Hattie thought. Easily long enough to book a hotel room in central London.

The flat had an open-plan kitchen and living space with cheap, modern units, laminate flooring and a tiny metal-screened balcony overlooking similar blocks. The bedroom was plain and anonymous, with a portable desk fan on the single chest of drawers and masculine grey bed linen. There was no clutter, and everywhere looked and smelled clean. The bathroom had only a bottle of shampoo and some shower gel on display. There was a stack of mail on the chest: circulars and bills addressed to 'N. J. Finch', and a pair of square-cut jade cufflinks that looked oddly familiar. Hattie was sure she had seen Casper wearing them. Had he left them behind on another visit? A dark thought occurred to her. Had he borrowed this flat before, to bring other girls to? She pushed that thought aside as she went to join Casper in the living room.

Nevertheless, she was grateful when he produced a screw-top bottle of white wine from his bag and found two glasses in a kitchen cupboard. Once she had drunk several glasses of wine and the flat was softened by the blanket of full darkness, she relaxed a little and managed to enjoy what turned out to be intense and very enjoyable sex.

'We have such a connection, don't we?' Casper murmured into her hair afterwards as they lay on thin, flat pillows that smelled strongly of fabric conditioner. 'I mean, we've only just met, but I feel like we've known each other forever.'

'There's still a lot we need to find out, though,' Hattie said reasonably. She stroked his back as she spoke. His skin was smooth, the colour of pale caramel.

'Well, I hope to get the chance.' Casper pulled himself up onto his elbows so he was looking at her. 'I know things are complicated and I've got some big decisions I need to make, but I really want to spend more time with you.'

'I want that too.' Hattie glanced at her watch. It was eleven fifty. She didn't want to spend the night in this flat, in this bed that smelled of whoever last slept in it, and the last train to Summerlands left at thirty-five minutes past midnight. 'But, listen, I think I'm going to get going.'

She swung her legs over the side of the bed and started to pull on her knickers.

Casper pulled a mock-pouty face, but she just patted his shoulder and reached for her bra and T-shirt.

'Look, babe, I know this wasn't exactly the most romantic

place for us to spend time together. But it's the chance to be alone with you that matters most right now. And I'll make it up to you, I promise. How about we go away for the weekend? I can take a day off on Friday, and we can head out to somewhere lovely in the countryside.'

'I can't,' Hattie shook her head as she zipped up her jeans. 'I mean, I'd love to, but not this weekend. My second interview with Saints & Sinners is on Friday afternoon.'

Casper furrowed his brow.

'Can't we leave on Saturday morning?' she asked. 'Or even last thing on Friday?'

'No.'

She couldn't tell from his tone of voice whether he was disappointed or just plain annoyed. That was the problem, she realised. She really didn't know him all that well yet.

As if reading her mind, Casper went on, 'Look, angel girl, with everything going on for me at work right now, this is the best chance we're going to have to get to know one another better. And the place I've got in mind is completely booked up every Saturday night for the foreseeable. It's Friday or nothing.'

*Angel girl.* Hattie felt a surge of pure pleasure swell through her veins. 'I suppose I could ask Saints & Sinners if they could bring it forward slightly. Maybe to first thing Friday.'

'Exactly,' said Casper, smiling again now. 'Then we could leave Friday lunchtime: problem solved.'

'I'll email them and ask.' Hattie shrugged on her coat and reached for her bag.

'No, don't ask them: that's the wrong approach. Tell them.' Once again, Hattie couldn't quite decipher the expression that crossed his perfectly symmetrical face. 'If they really want you – and it sounds like they do – they'll be happy to move it to accommodate you.'

'Okay, I will.'

'Good girl.' Casper leaned in and kissed her on the lips. 'It's important we spend some proper time together.' He looked directly into her eyes and she felt a little shiver of excitement as he added, 'We need to talk about our future.'

# TWELVE

## HATTIE

'What do you think?' Casper asked triumphantly as the car turned into a driveway of the hotel in the Surrey countryside.

'Beautiful,' Hattie murmured, looking at the sweep of the drive, and the red-brick mock Gothic façade. They'd arrived in a small rental car because Casper's own Audi was at the garage for a repair.

'Inconvenient, I know,' he'd said as they loaded up their bags in London. 'But as long as we get there, that's all that matters, right?'

They took their bags out of the car now, and walked into the reception area. The place was nice enough, Hattie thought, looking around. But it was nothing special. A lot of wood panelling and patterned carpet, staff in cheap-looking polyester waistcoats, a rather underwhelming bar and a menu unchanged since the 1990s. The bathroom was large and well fitted, admittedly, but the furnishings in the room were fusty and old-fashioned. Heavy, dark velvet curtains all but obscured the windows and one of the light fixtures was broken, flickering constantly but with an off switch that didn't work. Hattie was struggling to see why Casper had been so set on coming to this place, at this time. Her family had stayed at Cliveden for her father's sixtieth birthday, and her grandparents had once paid for them all to visit Gleneagles. She was aware that these trips made her very privileged, but Casper himself was very cultured and well-travelled, had lived and worked in New York. She had assumed he would have higher expectations himself. Or they could have gone to the holiday cottage her parents owned in Deal. It was small and homely, but at least there was some atmosphere, and they would have the sea.

Her disappointment was all the more acute because, having followed Casper's instruction and emailed Saints & Sinners on Tuesday to say she wasn't available on Friday afternoon, she had heard nothing back. Not even an acknowledgement of the fact that she wasn't attending the second interview. 'They'll get back to you,' Casper had said airily when they were driving down the A3. 'It's early days.'

But this was simply not true. It wasn't early. It was *the* day: the day of the interview. Surely if they had wanted to reschedule in order to include her, they would have contacted her by now? The thought that she might have just blown her dream job was giving her a deep anxiety, and she said as much to Casper.

'This will help you relax.' He popped open the bottle of complimentary champagne and poured her some. 'Try to put work out of your mind, at least until Monday.'

The champagne was cheap and room temperature, but Hattie drank two glasses anyway. She leaned in and started kissing Casper, and instantly his hands were roaming over her body; probing, teasing, taking charge. He really was the most amazing lover. The champagne and the sex allowed her to do as he had asked and let go of her worry about the job. She made sure they drank the whole bottle and stayed in bed for a long time. When her body was entwined with his, she felt as though she could forget anything. And for a while she did.

.  .  .

She must have fallen asleep, because when she opened her eyes, the bed was empty.

The bathroom door was closed, but she could hear Casper's voice through it, talking on the phone. She sat up and listened.

'Look, don't give me a hard time about it, okay? You know why it has to be this weekend, we've been over it a thousand times... I know... Look, what can I say? I'm really sorry, angel, but that's the way it has to be.'

Angel. He called whoever it was 'angel'. Like he had her. Hattie felt a plummeting sensation in her stomach, like a stone sinking in a pond. This had to be his wife he was talking to, surely. But why, if they no longer cared for her, was he cajoling her in this way?

As the bathroom door opened, she lay down quickly and pretended to have just woken up.

'Let's get going,' he said briskly, a little coolly even. He shrugged on his waxed jacket. 'The grounds are pretty; we ought to go and explore them.'

The 'grounds' turned out to be about an acre of lawn with a wooden pergola and a couple of bedraggled peacocks, but they completed a few circuits anyway, before returning to the room to get ready for dinner.

'We're not too far from RHS Wisley,' Casper said as Hattie sat at the dressing table doing her make-up. 'Maybe we should do that tomorrow, if it's fine? Let's see what the weather's doing...' He picked up his phone to check the weather app, then put it down, frowning at the lamp that was still flickering on and off. 'I asked reception to sort that bloody thing out. I'm going to ask them what they're doing about it, or we'll never get any sleep.'

He opened the door of the room and headed onto the corridor, leaving his phone on the TV stand. As he'd just been using it, it was unlocked. Hattie grabbed it and went straight into the call log. He'd been phoned at 16.24 by T. No name, just an initial. She opened 'Contacts' and found the stored mobile number for 'T'.

There were no social media apps on his phone that she could see, so Hattie opened Photos. There were thousands on her own phone, but at a glance, Casper hardly had any; probably no more than fifty. Had he deliberately deleted all the images of his wife, and their life together? She was about to start scrolling when she heard footsteps stop by the door, and the handle turning. Dropping Casper's phone as though it was scalding hot, she leapt back onto the dressing stool and grabbed her lipstick, using it to turn her mouth into a slash of vermilion.

'They've promised they'll sort it out while we're down having dinner,' Casper told her, inserting cufflinks into his shirt. They looked very like the vintage jade cufflinks she had seen in his friend's flat near Tower Hill. 'Let's see if they keep that promise. You ready?'

Hattie stood up and did a little twirl, showing off her deep green shantung dress.

'Beautiful,' he said, grasping her hand and kissing it. 'You scrub up pretty well, Miss Sewell, I must say.'

Hattie flushed with pleasure, pushing down the thought that Casper had called 'T' an angel. She'd been dopey with sleep; perhaps she'd misheard.

Once they were seated in the dining room and handed dinner menus, Hattie told him about her parents owning a cottage on the Kent coast.

'Really?' Casper said with genuine interest. 'Perhaps we could go down there one weekend. It would be great to have a bolthole by the sea, now that summer's on the way.'

'I'll speak to Mum and Dad.' Hattie realised as she said this that she knew nothing at all about Casper's family or his background. 'Are your parents still alive?' she asked, as they sipped on the cocktails they'd ordered.

'Father is, mother's dead,' he said, without elaborating.

'Do you have siblings?'

'One. A sister: Tabitha.'

So perhaps she was 'T'. She supposed you might call your sister 'angel', if you were close. That was the most obvious explanation, Hattie reassured herself.

'And you said you were only living in Summerlands temporarily?' Hattie continued. 'Is that right?'

'Yes,' Casper said calmly. He didn't seem troubled by her questioning, but he was clearly not going to supply more than the minimum information. 'We're staying with relatives of my wife's while the place we've bought is renovated.'

'And where is that?'

'North London. Islington. Fantastic place. But the irony is, I'll probably never get to live there.' He sipped his wine, then looked straight at her with his pale grey eyes. 'If she – my wife – and I split up, I'll have to let her keep the house.'

'I see.'

'And that's where you and I come into it.' He reached across the table and covered her hand with his.

Hattie's eyes widened. Did he mean he wanted them to move in together? Was that what he'd meant by talking about their future?

Her phone buzzed with a text. Another enquiry about how the second interview had gone. There had been several, including from her parents. She'd lied to them about where she was this weekend, telling them she was spending it with Avril. Casper frowned as she pulled her hand away from his to check the message, then put the phone back in her bag.

'People are asking about how I got on in the second inter-view.' She bit her lip. 'To be honest, I'm not really sure what to tell them.'

'You're not still fretting about the interview?'

'A bit,' Hattie admitted.

'Look, forget about the bloody job, okay? If things work out how I'm hoping they will, you won't need a job anyway.'

Hattie stared at him. 'What do you mean?' He surely couldn't be implying she'd be married to him? Apart from anything else, he already had a wife.

He took her hand again. 'You remember Van Asbeck's have got this massive auction coming up in a couple of weeks? The Hokusai geisha painting?'

Hattie nodded.

'Well, if it goes to a buyer I've brought in, then I'm going to get a big fat bonus. Enough to chuck in the job and strike out on my own. And given the state of my marriage and the fact that – as we've just discussed – she's getting the bloody house, well... I've been thinking I may as well go abroad.'

'Abroad? Where?'

'Maybe the States. I've worked in New York already. Maybe Europe somewhere. Or maybe further afield.'

'Wow,' breathed Hattie, taking a gulp of her wine.

'And the thing is, angel girl...' He squeezed her fingers. 'I want you to come with me.'

# THIRTEEN

## JULIAN

'Ernst, old man!'

Julian was in his room in chambers, taking advantage of a cancelled trial to make some calls. First on his list was Ernst Laszlo.

'Julian. Good to hear from you, again.' The Hungarian sounded genuinely pleased. 'Although it's usually your trusty clerk who organises our lunches. To what do I owe the pleasure?'

'Actually, Ernst, I'm after a favour.' Julian paused and tapped his pen against his lower lip. 'Remember that Japanese painting that you mentioned to me at Simpson's.'

'The Hokusai? Of course. I'm registered to bid at the auction next week. Not that I will be buying it, of course; my pockets are not that deep sadly. But the pressure on seats is so great you can only get in if you're a registered bidder.'

'Oh.' Julian was deflated. 'I was going to ask if you could take me as your guest, but it sounds as though the answer is no.'

'If you're really keen, I can get my contact at Van Asbeck's to register you as a bidder too. We can grab lunch beforehand, or a cocktail afterwards at least. They usually serve some sort of refreshments in house anyway.'

'Would you do that, Ernst? That's very kind. Remind me what day it is?'

'Next Thursday. The first of April. It's in the afternoon, so they can bring in phone bids from both the States and the Far East.'

*April Fools' Day*, thought Julian grimly. Some would say that was appropriate, given the highly nefarious reason for him wanting to be there. 'Hold the line a sec, Ernst.' He muted his phone, flung open the door and shouted into the corridor. 'Terry!'

Terry appeared, his starched shirt held in place with a pair of old-fashioned metal sleeve garters. 'Yes, Mr Cobbold.'

'What am I doing next Thursday afternoon?'

Terry didn't need to consult a diary of any description: the information was all held in his head. Which was why senior clerks earned almost as much as some of the barristers. 'Just a case con, sir. On the Roth case.'

'Move it,' Julian told him, adding, 'if you wouldn't mind.'

'Of course, sir.'

'You're a gem, Terry.'

Julian went back to his desk and picked up his phone again.

'Great, Ernst, looks like I can make it.'

'I'll need your full name and address to register you, and you'll need to bring either a driving licence or a passport with you. Plus details of your bankers.'

'I'll have Terry email them over to you. And thanks. I'll see you in Mayfair next week.'

The following Thursday, Julian collected his numbered paddle from the registration office at the Van Asbeck's auction rooms on New Bond Street and took his seat next to Ernst Laszlo.

The lushly carpeted room had deep burgundy walls and rows of dark wood chairs, with a raised white podium for the auctioneer, and tiered white pews for the smartly dressed men and women taking telephone bids, much like the seating on TV panel shows. To the auctioneer's right, artfully spot lit, was Hokusai's painting. Because it was only about twelve inches by eighteen, a larger digital image of it was projected on the wall to the auctioneer's right.

There was murmuring and quiet chatter as the bidders started to take their seats, with various Van Asbeck's staff members coming in and out, then arranging themselves discreetly at the edge of the room as the auction was about to start. Julian recognised Casper Merriweather as one of them, his golden blond hair swept back, dressed in an immaculate pinstriped suit and cutaway collar. His eyes scanned the room, and he looked startled when they alighted on Julian. Then he gave a smile and a brief nod. Julian went to raise his hand in response, but realised he was holding his bidding panel, so settled on an eyebrow raise instead.

A portly man with thinning blond hair introduced himself as Hugo Barker, Van Asbeck's senior auctioneer, informing the audience that in addition to the obvious interest from Japan, that afternoon there would be buyers phoning in from New York, Buenos Aires, Dubai and Hong Kong.

Ernst nudged Julian. 'I told you: everyone is after this painting,' he hissed. 'It's the novelty factor of a new discovery.'

Hugo Barker continued, 'Today's auction is something very special. To my right, you will see *The Red Courtesan*, a painting by the Edo period master Katsushika Hokusai, whose remarkable career spanned the late eighteenth century and the first half of the nineteenth. Truly a beautiful work, which until our recent unveiling had remained completely unseen for nearly two hundred years. It goes without saying that this piece has generated a huge amount of interest, and I'm going to start the bidding at one million pounds... One million I have... against you, sir... One million one hundred... On the phone: one million two hundred. One million two hundred I have, looking for one million three hundred. One million three hundred in the room; thank you, madam...'

The bidding continued briskly, with paddles discreetly raised and the telephone call handlers covering their mouths as they spoke to their bidders. There was a lull as the price reached the eight-million mark, as none of the three interested parties remaining seemed to want to budge. Then it surged on until it reached more than eleven million pounds.

'Eleven million five hundred is bid, do I have more?' Barker boomed. 'Eleven million eight on the phone... Do I have more? With you, madam... Hammer is raised.' There was a tense silence. 'Then I will sell it at eleven million eight hundred pounds sterling, that's thirteen million, nine hundred and fifty-six US dollars... At eleven million eight hundred pounds, paddle number twelve: sold.' The gavel came down with what Julian considered a disappointingly light and undramatic tap on the podium. 'Congratulations.'

'That might be a world record for a Hokusai,' Ernst grumbled as they filed out of the room. 'But, honestly, I was disappointed it didn't go even higher.'

Julian was astonished. 'But that's an absurd amount of money. More than most people will ever have in their lifetime.'

'I came to the sale of a Francis Bacon here last summer and the bidding *started* at fifteen million.'

There were drinks set out for all the auction attendees, and a chance to circulate the Van Asbeck's exhibition space and view the artworks that would be sold at upcoming auctions. Julian helped himself to a glass of champagne, then left Ernst to go and introduce himself to Hugo Barker.

'Always nice to have a representative from Her Majesty's inns of court with us,' Barker said pompously. 'Are you particularly interested in Oriental art? Only we have other sales coming up.'

'I only have a passing knowledge,' Julian said truthfully. 'But I am an acquaintance of one of your colleagues.'

'Ah, really?'

'Yes... Casper Merriweather.' As Julian said his name, he could see Casper out of the corner of his eye, pretending to circulate and make small talk while keeping Julian firmly in his sights.

'Ah, Casper.' Barker said his name almost reverentially. 'Very popular with all of us here, and of course our clients love him.' He gave a little smirk. 'Especially the female ones.'

Julian swigged his champagne. 'Been with you long, has he?'

'Not very long, no. But he came highly recommended, and with some impressive experience. Worked at Christie's in New York, and before that at Sotheby's in Amsterdam.'

'Wow,' Julian nodded slowly. 'That is, as you say, impressive. Not really a surprise though.'

*I mean look at him*, Julian was thinking. *The poise, the charisma, the movie-star looks.*

'He's just there,' Barker turned and pointed over his left shoulder, 'if you want a chat with him.'

'Yes,' said Julian. 'Yes, thank you; I do.'

'Fancy bumping into you in my workplace,' Casper said smoothly, grinning at Julian and putting his glass down on a table so as to execute a matey hand clasp and half hug. 'Welcome, welcome. What brings you here...? Stupid question, the Hokusai of course.'

'Friend of mine's a bit of a collector. He dragged me along.' Julian indicated Ernst.

'Ah, right, right.' Casper visibly relaxed.

'So what do you make of the sale price?'

'To be honest, we were hoping for nearer thirteen.' He made a rueful gesture. 'But on the other hand, it's smashed the current ceiling of two mill for a Hokusai. So I guess you could say it's a good result.'

'And your involvement is?'

'This is where my bit comes into play. Now *The Red Courtesan* is sold, it's my job to get her prepared for transportation and shipped to the buyer. Once we've received the payment for the sale price plus our commission. She's not going anywhere until the funds have cleared, obviously.' He laughed.

'Obviously,' Julian agreed. 'And who's the lucky buyer.'

'Professional rules forbid me to say.' Casper tapped the side of his nose. 'But let's just say she's going on a long journey.'

'Speaking of funds, my friend over there, Ernst Laszlo, has got money burning a hole in his pocket when it comes to Japanese art. You should go and speak to him. Let him know what's coming up.'

'Yes, of course,' Casper said, without enthusiasm.

'I'm heading off to Waterloo shortly... will I see you on the 6.53?'

'Probably not tonight. There'll be a lot of paperwork to deal with, so I'll be finishing late. See you tomorrow maybe?'

Casper strode off in Ernst's direction, leaving Julian lingering by the table. Once the two men were engaged in conversation, he pulled out his mobile, planning to let Ginny know when he'd be home.

*Missed call from Nigel H.*

Julian stepped out of the room into a carpeted corridor and returned the call.

'Julian! Thanks for ringing back, mate... Just wanted to let you know that I've followed up your query, and your suspicions were right.'

'I see...' Julian paused, glancing around to make sure no one was listening. 'And I wanted to tell you that I've done what you asked. I now have the hard evidence you need. I'll get it couriered over to you immediately.'

# FOURTEEN

## HATTIE

Saints & Sinners did not get in touch. Not at all.

Until recently Hattie would have phoned or emailed at this point to chase, and to show that she was still interested in the job, but now her head was elsewhere. Nor did she look at any other job sites, or respond to emails from recruitment agencies. What was the point? She was going to be leaving London and moving abroad. Starting a new life with the man of her dreams. The time she had once spent searching for jobs she now spent looking at beautiful apartments in Miami, and Bordeaux, and Lisbon. Because the one thing she and Casper had agreed on, before they left their country hotel, was that they wanted to be somewhere warm and sunny.

'We need some city life, but access to beaches and the outdoors. That's the ideal, in my mind,' Casper had said and, although she secretly had a yearning for New York or Paris, Hattie had agreed happily enough. The most important thing was that he would be formally separating from his wife, and everything would be out in the open. Casper would be leaving the country with a clean slate, his marriage officially over. That was what mattered to her most, not where they were.

Since the hotel weekend, it was proving difficult for the two of them to see each other, but that was understandable. He was in the process of dismantling his marriage, and distracted by the demands of the big Hokusai auction. When they spoke on the phone, Hattie tried asking how his wife felt about what was happening, only to be met with a curt, 'I don't want to talk about her, okay? Just believe me when I say it's over.'

On the one night they did manage to meet for a drink, she succeeded in smuggling him into her parents' house afterwards, but first their giggling and then their lovemaking had woken her mother, who confronted her furiously the next day about her lack of consideration.

'Well, you'll be glad to know I'm about to move out anyway,' Hattie had spat back.

'You're moving back to London? When did this happen?' Susannah Sewell had demanded.

'Not London. Abroad.'

'Abroad?' Her mother had been astonished. 'Where?'

She was even more astonished and disbelieving when Hattie had explained that she was going to be moving in with a man she had met on the train from Waterloo to Summerlands, and that not only did she not know how they were going to make a living, she didn't even know which country they were going to be living in.

'We're in the process of discussing it,' Hattie had said hotly. 'There's a lot to sort out.'

'And are we going to be allowed to meet this man who's whisking you off to God knows where?'

'Yes. Soon.' Hattie did not know if this would actually happen. Casper was still reluctant to meet her parents, claiming it was unfair to do so before he'd told his wife their marriage was over.

'Well, I think you've taken leave of your senses. You can't just uproot your life for someone you've known a few weeks.'

Her mother was wrong, Hattie knew that. But still she yearned for someone to talk to about the situation. There was her sister, Beth, but the two of them were not especially close, and besides, what she needed was someone who also knew Casper.

She got her chance when, about two weeks after the weekend away, she agreed to do a couple of days' temporary work at a branding agency. She was getting low on spending money, and the day rate for this job was pretty good. It was the day of the Hokusai sale, and Hattie knew that she would not be able to travel with Casper, who had to be at the auction house early and stay there late. But it did at least mean she would have the chance to catch up with Bridget. She sent a WhatsApp asking her to meet at the station coffee kiosk before they caught the train.

'So you're working again, then?' Bridget asked, taking in Hattie's tidy hair, smart trousers and clean shirt.

'Just a very short-term thing,' she told Bridget, as she took her cappuccino from the barista and turned back towards the platform. 'But I'm glad I've seen you. I need to tell you what's happened.'

Lewis appeared, backpack dangling from one shoulder, and gave them both a little wave.

Bridget put a hand on Hattie's arm. 'No wait, let him go. I don't want to sit with him.'

Hattie complied, but pulled a face. 'He's really sweet, honestly.'

'No,' Bridget said firmly. 'There's something off about him. Something that doesn't add up. Have you noticed how he never talks about what he does for a living? And I know he claims to be a single dad, but how can that be true? He's in London until seven o'clock every evening, and he goes out drinking afterwards, or to dinner like that night at Carmen's. So who's looking after his child?'

'Or children,' Hattie pointed out.

'Exactly. We don't even know how many there are. Because he never talks about them.'

They settled in their seats, with Lewis a bit further forward in carriage 3.

'So...' Bridget took a sip of her tea. 'How are things with Casper?'

'That's why I wanted to talk to you,' Hattie lowered her voice confidentially. 'They're going really well. So well, we're going to move in together. Once he's officially left his wife, obviously.'

Bridget's reaction was obscured by the lenses of her glasses. 'So he is married,' she said neutrally.

'Yes.'

'Well, you did say you thought he might be. Do you think he's really going do it though? Leave his marriage for you?'

Hattie nodded, unable to prevent her mouth stretching into a beatific smile. 'Yes, I'm one hundred per cent sure. I mean, I don't know all the details, obviously. He doesn't like talking about her, and I don't want to pry.'

'It's not going to be easy for you both.' Bridget cupped her small hands round her tea in a prim fashion. 'Setting up home with the ex-wife... well, current wife, strictly speaking, given they're not divorced... being around.'

'Ah, but that's the thing.' Hattie leaned forward excitedly. 'We've decided we're going to move abroad. He'll have a big bonus from the Hokusai sale to fund it. We're just trying to decide exactly where.'

'Goodness!' Bridget blinked, her eyes huge behind their lenses.

'The thing is though, it's such a big step.'

'Obviously.'

'I mean, I've lived with a guy before. With my ex, Leo. But we were in London, so we had friends and family nearby. This will be different. Do you think I'm being completely crazy? D'you think it's a terrible idea? I want you to tell me if you do. My parents think it's a stupid idea.'

Bridget was shaking her head. 'I disagree. I think it's a wonderful idea. I mean, who ever gets to do that? To go off on a romantic adventure with a handsome stranger they've met on a train.'

'Really? You really think that?' Perversely, Hattie felt her confidence diminishing rather than growing. Bridget was making her life sound like the plot of a black-and-white movie.

'Absolutely. I've seen the incredible chemistry the two of you have, and if it's that strong, then surely the sky's the limit.'

'So I should go for it?'

'One hundred per cent.'

Hattie caught the 18.53 home.

She knew that Casper wouldn't be on the train, but on the WhatsApp group the others had all pledged to try and sit together and have a drink. Sure enough, when she boarded and headed for the central carriages, Carmen, Julian and Lewis were all congregated around one table, with Bridget at a table on the other side of the aisle. Hattie squeezed in next to Lewis, opposite Julian and Carmen

'Great to have the gang back,' Julian bellowed. 'Apart from Casper, of course, who I know is detained at work... more on that later.' As the train started moving, he stood up. 'Drinks on me. Any requests?'

He returned ten minutes later with the usual assortment of cans, miniature bottles, plastic cups and ice cubes. Hattie grate-fully accepted a gin and tonic with ice. The temporary work, organising a digital campaign for a large supermarket chain, had been bitty and frustrating.

'So,' Julian announced with satisfaction as he opened a mini bottle of cava. 'Interesting day for me today. I attended the sale of Hokusai's *The Red Courtesan*. Invited along as a guest by an acquaintance of mine.'

Bridget's eyes widened. 'You mean...? Did you see Casper there?'

'I did. Briefly.' Julian tipped more of the cheap fizzy wine into his plastic cup. 'The stuff they were serving at Van Asbeck's was a cut above this, I can tell you.'

'So what happened?' Bridget demanded.

'What happened was the painting sold for nearly twelve million dollars to an overseas buyer. Which everyone seemed pretty happy with, though I understand they were hoping for even more. It's still a seven-figure commission for Van Asbeck's. Or the buyer's premium, as they prefer to call it. I suppose it sounds less mercenary.'

'And a bonus for Casper,' Hattie blurted out without thinking. She blushed, realising everyone would want to know how she knew this.

'Really?' said Lewis, who had been silent to this point. 'I didn't think individual employees got their hands in the pot after an auction.'

'What would you know?' Bridget demanded, in a manner that Hattie found overtly rude. 'I mean, what is it you do for a living again? Oh, that's right, you never said.'

Lewis looked at her sharply, then just shook his head and took a mouthful from his can of lager.

But Bridget – nondescript little Bridget – was on the attack. 'Oh, and you're a single parent too, aren't you?' she spat. 'At least that's what you say.'

Carmen turned her head away as though she didn't want to listen to this exchange, and Julian murmured, 'Come on now, Bridget, this isn't the forum for personal attacks. If people want to keep certain things private, then that's up to them.'

Bridget gave a sour little shrug and went back to sipping her water, and the subject was changed to people's Easter plans.

It was drizzling as they disembarked at Summerlands and Hattie readily accepted a lift from Julian.

'What on earth was all that about from Bridget?' he asked, as soon as they were in the Jaguar and fastening their seat belts. 'She seems so meek and mild most of the time, and there she is laying into poor Lewis. Who's always seemed nice enough to me.'

'She has a bit of a thing about him,' Hattie admitted. 'She thinks he's dodgy in some way. That he's hiding something, or lying about who he is.'

'I see...' Julian nodded slowly, keeping his eyes fixed on his rear-view mirror. 'That's... interesting.' They pulled up at traffic lights and he turned to look at Hattie. 'And young Casper. What do you make of him?'

Hattie tried, and failed, to suppress her smile of pleasure at Casper's name. 'I think he's great. Actually...' She hesitated a beat, then went on, sure she could trust Julian. 'He and I have been seeing a bit of one another. You know: dating.'

'Really? Goodness.' Julian's eyes flicked back to the mirror, his expression indecipherable. 'And has this... this liaison been going on for long?'

'A few weeks.'

'Hattie...' They had pulled up outside the Sewells' house now, and she was reaching for the door catch, but Julian placed his hand over hers, stopping her in her tracks. 'Listen...' He hesitated, as though unsure of what he wanted to say. 'Just be careful, won't you? Be very careful.'

# FIFTEEN

## HATTIE

The next day dragged, as Hattie had known it would.

It dragged because the work she was doing was uninspiring, and because she already knew that she wouldn't be seeing Casper on the 18.53 that night. Things were still frantic, he'd told her, following the successful auction of the Hokusai, with a lot of sale paperwork to process, plus arranging for the painting to be inspected, insured, packed, and shipped. As soon as things were quieter at work, they would spend some time together, he assured her, and make a concrete plan to leave London.

As she was walking to Holborn tube to catch the Central to Bank line, her phone buzzed with a message. It was from Ethan, her one-time hook-up.

*What happened to you? Still want to get together?*

This was followed by a tongue out emoji.

Screwing her face up with distaste, Hattie replied *I'm seeing someone now, and it's serious* before blocking Ethan's number.

As she emerged from the underground onto the Waterloo

concourse at six thirty, there was another message, this time from Casper.

*How was your day, gorgeous? xxx*

She replied with a grimacing emoji
*Casper Merriweather typing...*

*I think we should aim to get away next weekend... things should be quieter my end by then. How about we go to your folks' place by the sea? xxx*

*Let me check xxx*, she replied.

Her parents drove down to the Deal cottage at least once a month, and Beth occasionally used it, either with her boyfriend or a group of her girlfriends. Since there was time to spare before the train left, she called her mother's mobile straight away. Her mother picked up, no doubt surprised to receive a call so soon before Hattie was due home.

'Everything okay, darling?'

'Yes fine... Mum, are you and Dad going to Mariner's next weekend?'

There was a short pause, and a rummaging sound while her mother flicked through the paper calendar she still insisted on keeping pinned to the kitchen wall. 'No, not next weekend. I know we usually go at Easter, but we've got that golf thing with Uncle David this year, remember? We said we'd go to theirs for lunch afterwards.'

'How about Beth?'

'No; Beth and Jonathan are off to Croatia next week.'

'So would it be okay if I go down there?'

There was another, more pointed pause. 'This is with this new man of yours, I take it?'

'With Casper, yes, Mum.'

Her mother sighed. 'Well, I don't see why not, but on one condition. Your father and I want to meet him first. Is that going to be possible?'

Hattie hesitated. Was it? Casper had expressly said he didn't want to yet, but if they were going to be living together, surely the time was now?

'Yes. Yes, I'm sure that will be fine.'

'Great. Perhaps we can get him over for supper?'

'Let's discuss the details later, Mum, I need to go and get on the train. See you later.'

She hung up and started walking briskly towards Platform 2.

The 18.53 Crew group had been active that day, and once again the whole group was assembled in carriage 3 apart from Casper.

'Someone else mind doing the drinks run?' Julian said, tugging off his overcoat and slumping into the seat next to Bridget. 'I'm absolutely wrung out today, I don't mind telling you.' He loosened his tie. 'Bloody awful child abuse case at Southwark Crown Court.'

'I don't mind doing it,' said Lewis, who had just arrived, and was about to sit down opposite Julian.

'No, I'll go,' said Hattie, who had just been paid for her two days' work and was feeling flush.

'Let me help you.' Bridget stood up and rather awkwardly manoeuvred herself over Julian's coat and past his bulky body. 'I need the loo anyway.'

While Bridget darted into the toilet cubicle, Hattie went on to the buffet car. When Bridget joined her a couple of minutes later, she was loading up paper carrier bags with drinks and cups, just as Julian always did. 'Why don't you bring the ice,' she suggested to Bridget, who was hovering redundantly. 'And maybe some crisps?'

'Sure. Good idea.'

Bridget paid for four bags of crisps and the two of them made their way back down the swaying aisle to their seats. Lewis took the tray from Hattie and poured everyone their usual drinks.

Julian accepted a plastic cup of red wine gratefully and closed his eyes as he drank it, uttering a long, shuddering sigh. 'Bloody hell, that's better.' He fumbled in his coat pocket for his vape pen. Julian nearly always vaped in the toilet on the journey home. This was a little earlier than usual: most days, he headed off around twenty to twenty-five minutes into the journey.

Lewis started asking Hattie about her temporary work ('Finished now, thank God!') and also wanted an update on the interview process with Saints & Sinners.

'Oh, yeah...' she said vaguely, flapping a hand as she downed some of her gin and tonic. 'I'm not sure now that they're going to be the best fit.'

'Really?' Lewis did not hide his surprise. Across the table, Bridget scowled at him. 'I thought it sounded like the perfect fit for you.'

'It's complicated,' Hattie replied. She didn't want to start discussing her plan to leave London with the rest of the group. Julian had previously expressed disapproval of her liaison with Casper and when he got back from his vape break, she didn't want him weighing in on the subject, possibly asking awkward questions about whether Casper was actually single. She changed the subject to plans for the upcoming Easter break.

'Hang on,' Carmen interrupted suddenly, and everyone turned their heads, surprised. She was usually reticent, an observer. 'Julian's been gone a while, hasn't he?'

It was true: he was usually back in his seat within a few minutes, cramming his vape pen into his trouser pocket as his portly figure squeezed back past the aisle seats.

Lewis glanced at his watch. 'It's only been about ten minutes, hasn't it?'

'It's nearer fifteen,' Carmen corrected him.

'Maybe he's making a phone call,' Bridget suggested. 'Or he's gone to get something else to eat.'

'I fancy another drink; I'll go take a look,' Hattie suggested. 'Perhaps there was a queue to use the loo.'

She set off towards the toilet, which was in a separate corridor between the seating area and the doors to the next compartment. As the automatic doors slid shut behind her, the toilet door was wrenched forcefully inwards and Julian staggered out, clutching at his chest. His face, usually a florid red, was a greyish purple. His bulging eyes were looking straight at Hattie, and he seemed to be trying to speak, but couldn't get sufficient air into his lungs.

'Oh my God!... Julian!' Hattie took a step towards him.

His hand moved up from his chest to his throat and then his eyes rolled back and he collapsed on the ground at her feet. Her heart hammering in her ears, she leapt over to the alarm panel next to the carriage door, broke the glass and pressed the button. There was a screeching, wailing noise, and the sound of running feet, then the train ground to a shuddering stop.

Hattie braced herself against the carriage wall, her heart hammering. This could not be happening, could not be real. It was as though she was watching a scene from a movie or a TV drama. It felt impossible that this helpless form on the ground was Julian; Julian who was always so dynamic and assertive.

Time seemed to have slowed down, then speeded up. The guard appeared; a man in his twenties wearing the uniform of navy trousers and V-necked sweater with a grey and navy South

Western railways tie. He was followed by an older man who announced loudly, 'I'm a doctor!'

The doctor was immediately on his knees on the grubby carpet, his fingers pressed against Julian's neck.

'Is it a cardiac arrest?' the guard was asking.

'Looks like it,' the other man said. 'Stand back please.'

He attempted to do CPR, pushing down hard and rhythmically on Julian's chest, then blowing into his open mouth.

After a few minutes, he stopped his efforts, shaking his head slowly and getting to his feet with a heavy sigh. 'He's gone, I'm afraid.'

Hattie felt all the blood drain out of her head, and her legs began to shake violently. The guard was talking into a walkie-talkie, then put an arm around her and led her to an empty seat in the next carriage. The alarm had stopped and a heavy silence had fallen.

'Do you know him... the...?' He jerked his head in the direction of where Julian's body lay.

'Yes,' Hattie croaked. 'Yes, he's called Julian Cobbold. He's... he was... sort of a friend.'

'You'll need to give his details to the police, when they get here?'

'The police?' she asked stupidly.

'British Transport Police have to be called if someone dies on a train,' the guard was explaining. All Hattie could think was that the words couldn't surely relate to Julian. Not 'their' Julian. He'd always seemed so robustly alive.

She turned her head to look back to the carriage and thought she caught sight of Lewis standing up and staring in her direction. But most of the passengers were out of their seats now, trying to work out why they had stopped so suddenly in the middle of a field. It had been when the train had stopped all those weeks ago that she had got to know the others. When Julian had fetched them all drinks.

There was a wail of sirens, and then green-suited para-medics clambered onto the train, then off again. Two police officers appeared, and one of them came and spoke to her, taking down Julian's details and a timeline of what happened. Then Hattie, along with all the other passengers, was shepherded off the train down an embankment and along a track at the edge of the field, while men in white bodysuits and paper bootees appeared and climbed on board.

Hattie pushed her way through the crowd and found Bridget, Lewis and Carmen. They seemed more confused than shocked, and only then did it occur to Hattie that unlike her, they had not seen what had happened. Bridget held up Hattie's bag, which she had left on her seat.

'It's Julian, isn't it,' Carmen stated flatly.

Hattie nodded dumbly, tears spilling down her cheeks. Lewis put an arm around her, rubbing his other hand backwards and forwards over his stubble.

'Is he...?' Bridget faltered, eyes wide.

Hattie nodded. 'Looks like it was a heart attack. He came out of the loo and he just... he just crumpled.'

'Oh my God...' Carmen whispered, crossing herself. 'He was just there, sitting there with us, having a glass of wine. He was so nice. Always such a gentleman.'

Hattie just shook her head. She wished Casper was there, and that it was his arm around her shoulders rather than Lewis's. 'Why are there crime scene people here if it was a heart attack?'

'Because it's an unexplained death,' Lewis said. 'They have to be thorough and check everything, given that it's happened on public transport. On a train, it's not so easy to return to the scene later if need be, like it would be with a building. It'll just be a formality.' As he spoke, the doors of carriage 3 were opened and the paramedics emerged with a stretcher carrying a black body bag. Carmen started to cry, crossing herself again.

'Will we be allowed back on?' Bridget asked. 'Only they told us to take all our belongings.'

'No, look.' Lewis pointed to two coaches which had pulled up on the road next to the grassy area where they were standing, behind the patrol cars and an ambulance. 'They're going to bus us out of here.'

The four of them joined their fellow passengers in the queue to board one of the coaches, and ten minutes later it deposited them on the forecourt of Summerlands station. 'Pub?' Lewis asked, but Carmen shook her head and Bridget said she just wanted to rest. Hattie hesitated for a second, but all she really wanted was the reassuring atmosphere of her parents' house.

'No,' she said, feeling tears welling up at the thought that she would never again be driven home in Julian's Jaguar. 'I'm just going to walk home.'

After she had told her parents what had happened and they had fussed over her, running a bath and making sweet tea, she messaged Casper, *Call me. Urgent xxx*, deciding that a WhatsApp chat was not the right forum to break the news of Julian's death.

Casper phoned back a few minutes later. 'What's up, angel? I'm still at work. There's nothing wrong, is there?' He sounded genuinely concerned.

'Yes, there is.' Hattie swallowed the lump in her throat, before launching into a summary of what had happened on the 18.53.

'Dear God!' Casper exhaled sharply. 'It's hard to get my head around. Although...' He gave an odd little laugh. 'Maybe it shouldn't be that much of a surprise. I mean; middle-aged, overweight, partial to rich food and fine wine. He's very much the typical coronary candidate.'

'I suppose so,' Hattie said flatly. 'But it doesn't make it any less awful.'

'Agreed. And you've obviously had a nasty shock, being the one who found him. All the more reason you need to get away, babe. What's the latest on the weekend at the coast?'

She stared blankly at the handset for a few seconds, their conversation of a few hours ago having completely gone out of her head. 'Oh, you mean going to Mariner's Cottage... I asked Mum and she says it's fine, as long as they get to meet you first.'

'You told them you were going with me?' He sounded displeased.

'Yes, of course, why wouldn't I?'

There was a terse silence. 'No, you're right, of course they should meet me. If we're going to live together, then that's the next step. I'll come over or something, shall I?'

'That would be great. I'll check what time would suit the old folks.'

He gave a strained little laugh. 'Got to get finished up here. I'm exhausted. Speak soon, angel. *Bisous.*' He hung up.

About half an hour after she had spoken to Casper, Lewis started a thread on the 18.53 Crew group.

> *Guys, really rough evening. Still in shock. But I think, given Julian was the one who founded this group, and that none of us will be able to think about being on the train as a fun thing anymore, we should close down this group. Agreed?*

Bridget wrote simply *Yes.*

An hour later, Casper posted, *Agreed. RIP Julian.*

A few seconds later, 21.23 *Casper has left the group* appeared in the timeline.

*21.27 Bridget has left the group.*

*21.32 Lewis has left the group.*

Hattie looked at the messages for a few minutes, then

scrolled down to the list of participants. Carmen, it seemed, must have left the group at some point before that evening, because she'd made no comment and her name was no longer listed. Now only Julian's name remained.

With a heavy sigh, she clicked *Exit group*.

PART TWO

# SIXTEEN

## NEIL

Neil Waller positioned the picture in the beam of sunlight under the window, then stepped back and admired it.

There was something so evocative and alluring about the image of a traditional Japanese geisha. He knew from his own studies that many artists were intrigued by them: even Vincent van Gogh had painted one. But to have one painted by the master Hokusai himself was an undeniable thrill.

He stepped forward and looked at it more closely, brushing his thumb gently and reverently over the surface of the oil paint. The extreme white of the woman's face, just tinged with rouge over the cheeks, the graceful curve of her neck and coquettish glance over her shoulder. The rich crimson and blue of her formal, heavily draped kimono, the gold detail on her fan. And here it was: for him and him alone to admire.

Well, there was his partner too, still asleep in the bedroom, but she had no feeling at all for art. Her interest began and ended with what the painting of the red courtesan was worth. But Neil's relationship with this acquisition was a lot more complicated.

He'd always had a taste for the finer things in life. It started when he was young, and his father used to take him to art galleries and museums in the school holidays. They'd go to the National Gallery or the Tate and then out to lunch at the Wolseley or tea at Fortnum's. But then, when he was twelve, his father lost his job in the City, and with it his six-figure salary. Neil had to leave his private school in an affluent north London suburb and go to the local comprehensive, where he was bullied relentlessly for talking 'posh'.

His father found another job eventually, with a much lower salary, but by then his parents had separated. Most of the proceeds of the detached family home went into paying off the debts they had accrued while trying desperately to keep up appearances. His father moved out of London and in with another woman, and Neil barely saw him after that. His mother moved to Southampton to be nearer to family, and Neil lived with her in a dark and cramped maisonette on a modern housing estate. He finally lost the few friends he'd managed to keep when they were still in London. A second state school; more bullying. But he would get it back, he told himself constantly during that time. That life of comfort and ease, that ability to buy whatever you wanted, eat in the best places, travel the world. He would get it back.

To begin with, he had believed the key to escaping from the drabness of his life was through education. He had intended to win a place at a top university, leave with an impressive degree and walk into a highly paid job. By the time he'd left school, he was tall and well-built, his glasses had been replaced with contacts, his teeth had been straightened by the NHS orthodontistry his mother had insisted on. Girls had started to notice him, to declare that he was 'fit'. With a good degree and this new-found attractiveness, he would be able to ascend the career ladder with ease.

That was his initial plan. But he didn't get into either Oxford or Cambridge. Their rejection of him smarted, and he arrived at Salford University with a chip on his shoulder and a resentful attitude. Not only did he not study hard enough to be in line for anything other than a scraped third, but there was also the incident at the student union bar. Someone left a credit card on the bar and he took it and used it a few times. All just a misunderstanding, really. After CCTV had captured him removing cash from a cash machine, he'd tried to convince the university's disciplinary panel that he'd not realised the card wasn't his when he picked it up. They'd expelled him anyway.

So the education part of his plan was off the table. If he was going to regain his access to the high life, he was going to have to do it some other way. And the suspended sentence he'd received for credit card fraud, while generous on the part of the magistrate, did impede his applying for well-paid jobs. Since then, he'd had to take opportunities whenever, and however, they presented themselves. It had made for what most would consider an unconventional career.

The bedroom door opened and his partner emerged, wearing nothing but knickers and a skimpy vest. Her hair was tangled at the back and she was make-up-free. She was looking undeniably sexy, but, at this moment, staring at the painting, he barely noticed. Other people reacted to her looks, and there were times when that could be extremely convenient, but to Neil they were irrelevant. Okay, yes, he still had sex with her occasionally, if they were both in the mood. They had what others would call an open relationship. Third parties were not just desirable, but essential to them. That was how it had always worked.

'Honestly, the way you drool over that thing, you'd think it was porn,' she sneered, going to the kitchen area of the living room and putting the kettle on to boil. 'You're obsessed with it.'

'Can you blame me?' he asked her. 'I mean, look at her!'

'Newsflash, Neil: she's a fucking oil painting. I'm afraid she's not going to drool over you the way real women do.'

Such a bitch, he thought. Not really a nice person at all. But he let her get away with it because she was beautiful. Beautiful, and smart. And often useful.

She poured water over a teabag and lit a cigarette.

'Jesus, put that out! We can't get cigarette smoke on it!'

'Why not? It's not as if you're going to keep it.'

'Because we don't want to risk affecting its value, do we?'

At the mention of money, she stubbed out the cigarette.

'What are you going to do with it?' she complained, tossing her teabag into the sink next to the cigarette stub. 'I mean, you can't keep it here, can you? That's out of the question, surely? It wouldn't be safe. They might find this address, come looking. My name's on the lease, remember?'

'I'm not sure,' Neil told her. 'I'll think of something though.'

'Of course. You always do.'

The cigarette smoke was clearing, but because he was only ever going to exercise extreme caution where *The Red Courtesan* was concerned, Neil reached for the corner protectors and replaced them on the painting's frame, then a layer of glassine paper, and finally a lint-free blanket, which he wrapped carefully around it.

'You treat the damn thing like a new-born baby,' she scoffed. 'And it's not even yours.'

'Ah, but she is,' Neil grinned. 'She's mine. For now, at least, she's all mine.'

# SEVENTEEN

## HATTIE

'Fish pie!' Susannah Sewell yelled, sticking her head round the door of the kitchen and calling up the stairs to her daughter. 'I'm doing fish pie. Will that be okay? Does he like fish?'

It was Easter Saturday morning, and Hattie was upstairs throwing clothes into a weekend bag. The plan was that Casper would drive over to the Sewells' house in Summerlands, have lunch with the family and then he and Hattie would make the trip down to Deal in his car, returning on Monday.

'Fine,' Hattie shouted back, although she didn't actually know. The only times she and Casper had eaten together were during the weekend at the country hotel, when he had stuck to meat. But he seemed the sort of polite and well-brought-up person who would eat whatever he was offered.

Her father shouted up the stairs a couple of minutes later. 'Sweetie, we'd probably better not have wine with lunch if your friend's driving, but perhaps he'd like a beer?'

Just as she was about to answer her father, her phone buzzed with a message.

*So sorry, angel, I've had to go into work to sort something out with the consignment department. Meet you down there? I'll head straight there as soon as I'm done here xxx*

Hattie exhaled hard, pressing her fingers into her temples. She didn't much care if Casper was going to miss his fish pie, but she knew her parents would be unimpressed. The lunch was supposed to be transactional: they got to eyeball the man their daughter was planning to move in with, and in return she got the cottage for the weekend.

'No beer, thanks!' she shouted downstairs to her father. 'There's been a change of plan.'

She then typed a reply.

*Okay, I'll now have to catch the train from St Pancras, so you might get there before me. Mariner's Cottage, 18 Griffin Street, Deal. Spare key is under the front window box. Double yellow lines outside, but there's some parking a bit further out on Sandown Rd. Firewood in the shed in the back courtyard if you want to start the log burner. See you in a couple of hours xxx*

Then she went downstairs to break the news to her parents. Predictably, they were unhappy about Casper's non-arrival.

'Where are you off to now?' her father demanded as, with the fish pie cooling on the kitchen table, his daughter stamped back into the hall and headed up the stairs. She descended again two minutes later with her weekend tote, grabbed her handbag and headed for the door.

'I'm still going to Kent,' she replied coolly. 'You'll meet Casper another time. There'll be plenty of opportunities, I promise.'

. . .

Hattie's train arrived in Deal just after three. It was only a short walk from the station to the Regency fisherman's cottage in the old part of the town. It was a tall, narrow building with one room per floor: a kitchen diner and utility in the basement, a living room with a log burner on the ground floor, and one bedroom and bathroom on each of the first and second floors.

To her delight, Casper had not only lit a fire, but shopped for basics like milk, bread and wine, and had visited the fishmonger on the high street to buy wild sea bass for their supper.

'So you do like fish,' Hattie said when she saw them, gleaming plump and silver on the kitchen counter.

He looked at her blankly.

'Never mind,' said Hattie, smiling at him. 'I'm desperate for some tea. Want a cup?'

He grabbed her wrist as she reached for the kettle. 'Forget about tea,' he said, his voice low and husky. 'This is meant to be a romantic getaway, so...' He produced a bottle of champagne from the fridge and popped the cork with a flourish. 'Let's go and sit by the fire I've been toiling over, and drink this.'

Hattie hesitated. Before Casper, when her life had been in chaos, she regularly used alcohol consumption as a numbing mechanism, and was happy to drink whenever, wherever. Time or place were immaterial. But things should surely be different now. She didn't want to numb herself, or to blot out her surroundings with booze. She and Casper were here together in this cosy place, like a normal, functional couple. She wanted to feel that, to experience it fully.

Casper sensed her hesitation. 'Come on, babe, when have you ever said no to champers?' he cajoled. 'And it's vintage, too.'

'All right,' she conceded weakly. 'Just one glass.'

And it was lovely, she decided – and romantic – to cuddle up in front of the roaring flames, with Casper's arm around her shoulders and feel the dry, icy liquid slip down her throat. They engaged in some passionate kissing, after which Hattie barely noticed her glass being refilled for a second and then a third time.

'So, angel, I have a question,' Casper said when the bottle was all but empty.

'Hmm...' Hattie felt blissed out, her head lolling on his shoulder.

'How do you feel about Mexico?'

She felt a jolt in her stomach. Twisting her head slightly, she squinted at him. 'What do you mean?'

'As a place to live. About us going there together.'

Hattie was frowning. 'Mexico?' The mental image of their US apartment shattered like the glass in a mirror. She felt a vague sense of unease.

'No, wait... hear me out.' He held up his left hand, while pouring out the remains of the champagne with his right. 'I know it must sound a bit left field, but *The New York Times* recently named Mexico City as the world's number-one destination. There are loads of expats, an incredible food scene and, most importantly, it's absolutely saturated with art. There are so many galleries and dealers... Sotheby's even has a major office there. It would be perfect from the point of view of my work.'

'But it's such a big place.' She chewed her bottom lip. In response, Casper just thrust her glass into her hand. 'And so far away. And we wouldn't know anyone there.'

'But, darling, that's the whole point; we'd have each other. That's why we're doing this. It's an adventure. When we first talked about it, I thought you were up for an adventure.'

'When would we go?'

'Soon. No burning rush, but in the next few weeks.' Seeing the uncertainty on her face, he added, 'You're not working at the moment, so what's to stop you?'

'I suppose.' An unfocused anxiety was still swirling inside her.

Casper was trailing his fingers along her arm and up to her

breast, teasing her. 'Promise me you'll give it some thought at least. Do the research?'

Her body started to tingle with pleasurable sensations, her head muzzy from the alcohol. 'All right,' she agreed, pressing her body hard against his, reaching for the buckle of his belt. 'I promise I'll think about it. But not now.'


Hattie woke up two hours later, wearing only her bra.

She was stretched out on the bed in the first-floor bedroom. She experienced a few seconds of heart-pounding panic as her brain caught up with where she was, and why. She was at Mariner's Cottage with Casper. They had had sex in front of the fire, then retired to the bedroom, where she must have fallen asleep. It was dark outside, and from the kitchen, there were smells of cooking: a rich, buttery smell of frying fish.

Pulling joggers and a sweatshirt from her weekend bag, she went down two flights of stairs and found Casper in front of the stove, the table already set and candles lit.

'Hello, sleepyhead,' he said, kissing her on the forehead and ruffling her hair.

'You should have woken me!' she protested.

'You looked so peaceful, I couldn't bear to.'

He'd opened wine and insisted she have a glass, even though the champagne had left her mouth dry and her head pounding.

Over supper, he talked about Mexico some more, and Hattie played along obligingly, even though inwardly she was still nervous about the idea. Wasn't Mexico City the biggest metropolis in the world? That thought alone was overwhelming. And wasn't there a lot of crime, and drug cartels? But the more wine they drank, the rosier the picture Casper painted. And being anywhere with him would be amazing. *He* was amazing: the perfect man. Every time she found herself questioning the sanity of the plan, she reminded herself of that. She had the most incredible boyfriend; a sexy, successful man who just wanted to take care of her. She was lucky.

The next morning, they got up late and went to buy takeout coffees, chatting happily as they walked along the beach and up to the castle. The weather alternated between bursts of sunshine and squally April showers, but despite the rain and her hangover, Hattie felt truly at ease with Casper for what was probably the first time. For the first time, they were just hanging out together in a way that felt entirely normal.

They stopped on the sand, looking out towards the horizon, and he pulled her backwards so that she was leaning against his chest, wrapping his arms around her tightly.

'You know you really are a lovely girl.'

The tone of his voice had changed, and Hattie twisted round to look at him. She was taken aback to see a sadness in his face; sorrow even.

'You're not so bad yourself.' She reached up and kissed him on the cheek, and then he bent down to find a stone to skim through the waves and the moment passed.

They returned to the cottage, watched a movie, toasted crumpets and ate the chocolate Easter eggs that Casper had bought when he'd arrived on Saturday.

On Monday morning, after a leisurely breakfast at a café in the town, they cleaned the place from top to bottom, sweeping the back yard and watering the plants as a peace offering to her parents. Then Casper drove them back to Summerlands in yet another rental car. The Audi was apparently still awaiting a part from Germany.

'Come in and at least say hi to my parents,' Hattie cajoled

when they reached the turning to her road. 'I'm pretty sure they're in.'

'Can't, angel,' Casper said with a regretful little shrug, leaning in to kiss her tenderly on the lips. 'I've got to be somewhere.'

She put her hand on his shoulder and made direct eye contact. Again, that strange sadness was there on his face. 'Please,' she begged. 'It would mean a lot to me.'

'All right, if it matters so much,' he sighed.

She looked askance at him. 'Yes, as it happens, it does,' she said, unable to keep the sharpness from her tone.

He kissed her swiftly on the lips as if to mollify her, then switched off the engine and followed her up the drive.

Her parents were in the kitchen. 'Mum, Dad... this is Casper.' Hattie couldn't quite keep the pride out of her voice. This was the first time since Leo she had brought a boyfriend home. In the Sewells' slightly tired-looking nineties kitchen, he looked even more glamorous and handsome: larger than life almost.

'Mr and Mrs Sewell... it's such a pleasure.' Casper offered his hand with a dazzling smile.

Susannah Sewell glanced at Hattie with a tilt of her head and the faintest lift of her eyebrows. This meant she was impressed.

'Coffee, Casper? We've just brewed a pot.'

He hesitated slightly. 'Go on then, you've twisted my arm. Just a small one, mind.'

Once he had the coffee, he leaned back easily against the kitchen island and made small talk about his job, and the delights of Deal, before pulling Hattie into an embrace and announcing that he had to be off.

'What a charming chap,' Alan Sewell said, after Hattie had returned to the kitchen. 'Really delightful.'

'Yes, he seems lovely,' her mother agreed. 'And how lucky

you are to have met him. I know you've had a rough year, darling, but things are looking up for you, finally.'

Hattie spent the next few days investigating Mexico City online, and becoming more and more excited as she discovered that it was a lot more sophisticated than she had imagined.

Yes, it was a huge place, but there were plenty of neighbourhoods that seemed both cultured and accessible. She decided to concentrate her research on the upmarket area of Polanco, which had leafy parks, tree-lined streets and designer boutiques. She was beginning to envisage their life there, and lots of enthusiastic messages to Casper followed, most of them links to lovely, airy apartments that she hoped they would be able to afford. He responded occasionally with encouraging remarks like *Great!* or *Looks perfect, babe!* but for the most part was engrossed at work, making the final arrangements for the Hokusai painting to be delivered to its new owners. Very soon he would be able to leave Van Asbeck's. he told her, and they could finalise their travel plans.

She heard nothing more from the rest of the 18.53 Crew, and as her excitement about her new life grew, they slipped further and further from her thoughts.

It was on Friday, while she was indulging in one of her online fantasy house-hunts, that a news alert popped on her feed. One that made the breath catch in her chest as though she had been doused with a bucket of cold water.

## POLICE IN SUSPICIOUS DEATH PROBE

*Forensic pathologists conducting the post-mortem on London barrister Julian Cobbold, 56, have referred the case to the South London coroner and reported their findings to the police. Mr Cobbold collapsed and died while on the Waterloo to Portsmouth train on 2 April.*

*'We urge anyone who was travelling on the train that evening, or who has information that might help with our enquiry, to come forward,' said DI Mike Jevons, from The Metropolitan Police's South West command centre. 'We're now confident that rather than death from natural causes, this was a homicide.'*

# EIGHTEEN

## NEIL – 2011

Neil helped himself to the master key in the equipment store and took the service lift to the seventh floor of the Hyde Park Metropole.

Suite 714; that was where he was heading. He knew, from a visit he had instigated to take care of a non-existent leaking tap, that the occupants of that room were not bothering to make use of the in-room safe. It was surprising how many guests didn't. They were afraid that they would check out and forget the safe contents, or that they would forget the code and be unable to retrieve their valuables.

He also knew that the suite was on the chambermaids' service list for that morning, which meant that the guests had gone out. They were probably shopping in Oxford Street or heading to lunch or a West End show.

The first thing he did when he stepped out of the lift, carrying the keys and a bag of tools, was to go to the control board for that floor, located behind a panel next to the fire-exit door, and disable the CCTV monitors in the corridors. There must be no digital record of him entering and leaving room 714.

As he walked down the long stretch of carpet, he was

tugging on a pair of latex gloves. He pulled the master key from his pocket, held it over the sensor pad and watched the light turn green with a satisfying clicking noise. He was in.

His first thought was that these people were animals. They might be able to afford a £1200-a-night suite in central London, but they treated it like a pigsty. Neil himself hated mess and disorder. The elegant detached mini-mansion he'd lived in as a child had been immaculate, cared for by a pair of cleaning ladies who came in every morning for three hours. And then his mother's flat in Southampton had been quite the opposite. Depression had taken hold and with it inertia: she let dirty dishes pile up, drifts of dust and grime accumulated, heaps of dirty clothes strewed every surface. Since then, Neil had been fanatical about tidiness. He didn't need luxury, or fancy home-wares, but wherever he was needed to be clean.

Glad of the gloves, he sifted through dirty underwear, half-empty disposable coffee cups and the remains of room-service meals. Then he checked the wardrobe. An expensive-looking camel coat was hanging up and he went through the pockets. There were some twenty-pound notes – which he took – and a Rolex on the shelf next to the open room safe. That went into his trouser pocket. On one of the shelves was a tangled pile of women's lingerie; clean this time. Neil sifted through it and caught a flash of gold. There, clumsily hidden underneath it was a gold Cartier bracelet studded with diamonds. Neil knew enough about jewellery to know that this was worth at least ten thousand pounds. He was holding it up to the light to admire it when the door lock made its mechanical clicking noise, and someone came into the room.

It was one of the chambermaids, carrying a plastic trug of cleaning materials, with a pile of fresh sheets draped over her arm.

'What are you doing?' she asked sharply.

'I was... I was just checking that the room safe was working properly,' Neil extemporised. He was wearing the hotel's maintenance staff uniform of grey branded polo shirt and navy cargo trousers, so this was totally plausible. He'd started out as a pot washer in the kitchens, but quickly switched over to the maintenance side of operations when he realised the opportunities free access to guest rooms afforded.

'No, you weren't,' the girl said calmly. She had shiny brown hair pulled back into a severe ponytail and wore no make-up, but there was no hiding how pretty she was. 'You were stealing that.' She tilted her head in the direction of his gloved hand. The bracelet caught the light and sparkled provocatively.

'I was not!' he protested hotly.

But she shook her head. 'I've been watching you. I've seen you take the master key and go to rooms where there are no problems reported.' Her voice was husky and slightly accented. She raised an eyebrow, challenging him. 'Give it to me,' she demanded.

He shook his head.

'Okay then,' she said with a little shrug, 'I'll go and speak to Pablo.' Pablo Kurti was the hotel's general manager. She turned back towards the door.

'No, wait!' Neil said quickly, seeing how this could end. Reluctantly, he handed over the bracelet.

'What else do you have?'

He showed her the watch and the cash.

'Is that all?'

'That's it, I swear.'

'I'll keep this, you can have the watch. We split the cash. Fair?'

'I suppose so,' he said, too surprised by this turn of events to think clearly.

Her eyes were roving over him. 'You're going to find it hard to go under the radar: the reason I noticed you is because you're so good-looking. What's your name?'

'Neil.'

'I'm Tali.' She held out her hand and shook his gloved one. 'If we work together, we will do much better, trust me.'


And that was how it had started.

They operated a slick system at the Metropole for a while, using Tali's inside knowledge of the guests and their rooms, and Neil's cover as maintenance man. Tali already had contacts in Hatton Garden and she taught him how to sell the jewellery they stole, although in practice it was usually she who made the sales; dressed in a short skirt and high heels, since most of the jewellers were male. Don't name too low a price, Neil learned, because that will only make the dealer suspect the piece is stolen and you're desperate to fence it. Don't make up an elaborate backstory about how you came to have possession of the diamond ring/Cartier tank watch/gold chain; again, that will only attract attention.

Eventually, the system became so slick that Neil grew a little slipshod and forgot to disable CCTV before entering a room. The hotel guest complained that a large amount of cash had gone missing and the duty manager, already suspicious about the high number of items disappearing from the guests' rooms, checked the footage. Neil was fired and was lucky to get away with just a police caution and repaying the cash. There was undoubtedly a suspicion on the part of the Metropole's management that he had been involved in many other thefts, but they were unable to prove it. Tali was not implicated, but due to whisperings from the other chambermaids, she did not altogether avoid suspicion either and resigned from the hotel two weeks after Neil was fired.

Their next venture, at Tali's suggestion, was to get jobs on a Mediterranean cruise ship. Lots of rich clients, lots of opportunities. The problem with this scheme was that in the middle of the ocean, there were few opportunities to spend cash or fence stolen goods, and keeping items of stolen jewellery in a tiny crew cabin was problematic. Especially since cabins could be searched by a senior member of crew with no notice. So after one season they returned to London and, because it made sense financially, moved in together in a tiny bedsit in West Norwood.

Were they in a relationship? Neil asked himself this constantly. Yes, certainly, in the early days they had sex. There was an undeniable physical attraction between them. But as they started to realise that they were so alike they were more or less the same person, the sexual attraction faded. They became more like siblings who happened to share a bed out of necessity. And Neil found Tali's attitude to sex hard to decipher. She attached no emotion to it whatsoever, nor any boundaries. Sex with other men was fine in her eyes, or even with other women. And that was okay with Neil: he was with her for her deviant brain and her unusual set of skills, not for monogamy.

Tali had an English father and a Slovenian mother. She had grown up in London but she no longer had contact with either parent, hinting at some sort of abuse or ill treatment in her past. She had no siblings either, or cousins. Her self-sufficiency and the absence of ties made her a free creature, and the only thing that seemed to drive her was deceiving others, getting one over on them. She liked money, but much of the time it was the deception that seemed more important to her. Instinctively, they knew that the best grifters always worked in pairs. If their target was male, Tali could seduce and manipulate them: if female, then Neil could employ his own charms and the polish that he had acquired during his time as one of the privately educated elite.

After the cruise ship, they acquired a card skimmer, and for a while spent the money of other people by cloning their credit cards. These were picked up off restaurant tables and at upscale bars by one of the pair while the other distracted their mark.

But, eventually, encrypted payment technology made skimming more and more difficult, and risky. Besides, they were only making a few thousand here and a few thousand there, having to discard the credit cards before they were caught. Neil had ambitions to do something bigger, something bolder. To make a single sum of money so large that he would be able to give up the scamming.

'I tell you what we need to do,' Tali drawled one afternoon in the summer of 2015. They were sitting together at a pavement café table in St James's Street, looking for tourists to scam. Keeping an eye out for handbags abandoned during a trip to the restroom, or credit cards left on a table by mistake.

'What's that?'

'Property,' she said, narrowing her eyes as she lifted a cup of black coffee to her lips. 'If we need to go after high-value items, then what's higher value than a house, right?'

'Well, yes,' Neil answered in a reasonable tone. 'In terms of cash value. But they're also not portable. You can't just take a house.'

'Ah, but you can,' Tali insisted. 'I've read about it online. All it needs to make a house yours is paperwork, right? And paperwork can be faked.'

While they sat there drinking coffee, Tali laid out her plan. She proposed that they set up a fake Airbnb account and use it to take out a long-term rental on a holiday home. Then they would sell the property without the owner's knowledge. When the peak rental season came to an end in late September, they found the perfect place; a farmhouse in Pembrokeshire that was never visited by the owner, and sufficiently isolated that there would be no nosy neighbours to interfere. They researched how to do the conveyancing themselves, then listed the property with a small and sleepy firm of estate agents in Milford Haven, using a counterfeit passport they'd bought in the name of the house's owner and bank details from statements in a locked desk drawer at the property. All they needed to do was create a fake identity for the owner's non-existent solicitors, complete with associated bank account, and the prospective buyer's cash would be transferred into it. The house was beautifully appointed and priced for a quick sale, and within days of it being listed, there was a cash offer on the table.

What neither Tali or Neil had reckoned with, however, was the Land Registry's new alert scheme, set up to prevent just such property fraud. The searches carried out in good faith by the buyer's solicitor triggered a notification that was sent directly to the property's registered owner. And so, just as Neil and Tali were packing their suitcases to leave the farmhouse and return to London, a police patrol car arrived at the property. This time there was no escaping the full force of the law, since the scale of the fraud merited referral to Swansea Crown Court.

They were sentenced together, standing side by side with a glass partition between them. Tali, dressed in a plain white shirt and tailored black jacket, remained expressionless as she was handed down a sentence of three years and nine months. Neil's was five years, eight months.

'Wait!' he shouted as one court security officer led Tali out of the courtroom and another motioned for Neil to go with him. 'Tali! It's not over, right? I'll see you again.'

But she shook her head, lifting her fingers to her lips, then holding them up in his direction. He couldn't hear her, but he saw her mouth the words, 'It's over.'

# NINETEEN

## HATTIE

Only minutes after she'd read the article about Julian's death, Hattie received a message from the detective investigating it. Would she please call back so that they could organise a time to take a statement from her. Before she had the chance to phone the number back, her phone pinged with a WhatsApp message from Bridget.

*Need to talk to you! Can we meet? B x*

Hattie replied immediately.
*Is this about Julian?!! I've just heard from the police about it.*
She added a shocked face emoji.

*Yes, but we really need to talk face to face ASAP.*

Hattie tried phoning the number for DI Mike Jevons, but it was engaged. She then replied to Bridget's message, saying that she would fit in around her plans. They agreed to meet at a café at five o'clock. Hattie would have preferred a pub, but Bridget didn't drink alcohol. She didn't even drink coffee, always sticking to tea when the two of them bought drinks at the station kiosk. Bridget was there on time; Hattie – who had no good excuse – was late.

'So, tell me, what's so urgent?' she demanded, tugging off her body bag and sliding onto the banquette opposite her friend. Bridget was dressed in a plain beige shirt dress with her hair scraped back into its mousy ponytail. She had already ordered a pot of tea.

'You've seen the news about Julian Cobbold, right?' Her eyes behind the lenses of her glasses were unusually bright. Rather than the distressing event it had been for Hattie, she seemed to view Julian's demise as a source of intrigue and gossip.

Hattie closed her eyes briefly, reliving the moment of finding the body. The shock of it assaulted her every time she thought about it. 'Awful,' she muttered. 'The whole business was dreadful enough already, but now this.' She waved over the waitress and ordered a glass of wine. 'The police want to speak to me again. Because I was the one who...' She inhaled before going on. '...Who found him, I suppose...'

'Really?' Bridget leaned forward on her elbows so that her voice wouldn't carry outside of their booth. The café was busy with teenagers hanging round after work, shoppers stopping for refreshment on their way home and a few young mothers with buggies. 'Well, this is my theory about what happened...'

She paused while Hattie's wine was placed on the table.

'Go on,' Hattie urged. 'You may as well tell me.'

'I've been over and over it in my mind, and I think there's only one logical explanation. I think someone put something into Julian's drink.' Bridget pushed her glasses up her nose and looked straight at Hattie, her hazel eyes huge behind the thick lenses. 'And I think it was Lewis Handley.'

'Lewis!' Hattie spat wine down her chin. 'Surely not!'

'Think about it,' urged Bridget. 'Think back to what

happened that evening. You and I went to the buffet car to get the drinks. You carried most of them back, I brought the crisps, remember?'

'Yes, I remember.'

'Then when we got back to where we were sitting, Lewis took the paper bag from you and handed round the drinks to everyone. I saw him give Julian his wine, not in the bottle but already poured out. So he could have slipped something into it.'

'I suppose so,' said Hattie, drinking more of her own wine. 'But why? I mean, what on earth could Lewis have had against Julian? They barely knew each other.'

'Who knows?' asked Bridget, her eyes still huge and bright. 'But if you think about the sequence of events, it's the only thing that makes sense. Plus, we've already established that there's something about Lewis that doesn't quite add up. That we don't know what he does. That his backstory doesn't make sense.'

Hattie thought about it, and she had to concede that Bridget was right. This theory did fit the facts of what happened on the 18.53 that evening, even if it didn't quite fit with her own personal experience of Lewis.

'So what do you think we should do?' she asked Bridget. 'Should we try to talk to him?'

Bridget shook her head. 'I think you should mention him to the police when you go and talk to them.'

'Maybe you should come too?' Hattie flagged down the waitress again and ordered a second glass of wine. She needed it. 'I mean, wouldn't it be better if we both went together? That way we can corroborate each other's story.'

But Bridget was shaking her head. 'I can't. My fibromyalgia has been terrible lately. Really terrible.' She pressed her fingers to the sides of her neck as if to demonstrate. 'Actually, I've been to my GP this afternoon, and he's signing me off sick. He said to avoid any stress, because that could cause a more serious relapse. And obviously getting involved with a murder investigation would be super-stressful.'

The waitress returned with the second glass of wine and Hattie lifted it to her lips, scrutinising Bridget over the rim. She did indeed look pale and washed out, with bruise-like shadows magnified by the spectacle lenses.

'So will you do it?' Bridget was asking, insistently. 'Will you mention Lewis's behaviour to the police?'

Hattie hesitated.

'Please, Hattie! Don't you realise how important this could be?'

Hattie drained most of the second glass of wine, feeling the familiar hit of confidence as the alcohol hit her bloodstream. 'Okay, sure,' she said boldly. 'Consider it done.'

As she walked back home, she messaged Casper.

*Just seen Bridget for a drink... she thinks I should report Lewis to the police for possibly poisoning Julian.*

She added a brain exploding emoji, then sent a second message.

*Do you think I should? xxx*

Casper replied once she was home and heading upstairs to her room.

*God yes, babe, absolutely! You have to!*

When Hattie woke up the next morning, she could certainly not be described as hungover. After all, she had only had a couple of small glasses of wine when she was at the café with

Bridget, and one more over supper with her parents. But hangover or no hangover, this morning she was much more clearheaded, especially after a strong cup of coffee, and therefore inclined to see things in a different light. Yes, she could see why Bridget had reached the conclusion she did, and logistically it had to be possible, but from her own memory of the scene, it didn't make a lot of sense. The space around the train tables was cramped, and it would have been very difficult for Lewis to produce some sort of liquid or powder and tip it into Julian's plastic cup without any of the others seeing it.

She also found herself thinking back to her own experience of Lewis. Specifically, the morning of her interview when she had been sick as a dog from drinking too much the night before. She would never have got to London in time if Lewis hadn't dragged her onto the train, nor would she have been in a fit state to attend her interview at all if he hadn't cleaned her up and lent her his shirt. Okay, so she didn't get the job because she was moving to Mexico, but the gesture still stood. And because of that, she felt she had to at least give Lewis the chance to explain himself.

She sent him a message on WhatsApp.

*Hi, could we meet for a chat sometime soon? It's important.*
*H x*

He replied a few minutes later.

*Sure – how about today? Fancy a walk?*

*Fine. Where? x*

*Bushy Park okay? And I'm afraid I won't be alone. I'm on dad duty.*

An hour and a half later, Hattie met Lewis at the gates of the park. He was dressed in a studded leather jacket, green Converse and aviator shades, and rather than being with a small child in a buggy as she had expected, he was accompanied by a large chocolate Labrador.

'This is Conker,' he said, as the dog deposited a drool-soaked tennis ball at her feet.

Hattie looked around her, expecting to find a play area where Lewis's offspring was dangling from monkey bars or shooting down a slide. 'Where's the kid?'

'It's just me and Conker. I'm a dog dad.' He had the good grace to look a little shame-faced.

'But not a human dad?'

He shook his head.

Hattie's eyes widened. This was not a good start to Operation Lewis Is A Good Guy. 'Not at all? Not even part-time?'

'No, I'm afraid not.' He picked up the tennis ball and threw it for the dog, then set off along the track towards the Heron Pond. A little cluster of deer lifted their heads to stare before recommencing their grazing.

'So, let me get this clear...' Hattie fell into step beside Lewis. 'When you said you were a single father, you were referring to... a Labrador.'

'Yes.'

'Wasn't that a little dishonest?'

'I suppose so, but I did have a good reason.'

They had passed the pond now, walking briskly to keep up with Conker, and were reaching The Pheasantry café.

'Coffee?' Lewis enquired. 'Yours is a cappuccino, yes?'

When he came out with the two takeaway cups, and handed one to Hattie, he looked her directly in the eye and asked, 'Can I trust you? I mean, *really* trust you.'

Hattie nodded, bending down to pat the dog, who had just dropped the ball at her feet again.

'I work for SO15.'

Hattie looked up at him blankly.

'Counter Terrorism Command. Used to be called Special Branch.'

'So you're a *police officer*?' The irony of this was not lost on her, and she let out a nervous giggle.

'Well, yes and no. Strictly speaking, I left the force a few years ago and I now work as an anti-terrorism consultant. But because I'm still dealing with some pretty nasty and pretty dangerous people, I can't talk about my work to people I meet.' He grinned. 'Especially not strangers on a train.'

'So is your name really Lewis Handley?'

In response, he simply smiled, picked up the tennis ball and threw it again.

They walked on in silence for a while. It was a beautiful mild spring day; the new grass a brilliant green and the trees weighed down with clouds of pink blossom. The park was full of dog walkers and young couples pushing prams or shepherding pre-schoolers on scooters. Groups of young people who were probably students at the nearby university were stretched out on the grass, talking and laughing, some of them turning their faces upwards to revel in the welcome warmth of the sun.

Hattie wondered how to broach the subject of Bridget's accusation, and as if reading her mind, Lewis abruptly asked, 'Did you read about the murder enquiry into Julian's death?'

She nodded. 'The police have asked to speak to me; I'm waiting for them to get back to me about it. Why, do you know any more about it than was reported in the press?'

'I don't, no, but I have thought about making some discreet enquiries. Julian was a really nice guy, so I'd quite like to find out exactly what happened to him.' He handed Hattie his cup and darted off abruptly to grab Conker's collar, pulling him away from a Jack Russell that was intent on starting a fight. When he came back, they sat down on a bench watching Conker run around in circles.

Keeping her eyes fixed on the antics of the dog, Hattie relayed her conversation with Bridget, and her theory that he – Lewis – had murdered Julian.

Lewis's response was to burst out laughing.

'So, it's not true?' Hattie asked, and she couldn't help smiling herself as she asked this. The whole thing suddenly seemed ridiculous.

'Do *you* believe it's true?' He turned towards her and his eyes met hers. Deep-set eyes, with irises the same shade of mid-brown as Conker's coat.

*His eyes match his dog,* Hattie thought glibly, before shaking her head and looking away. She felt suddenly uncomfortable.

'Thank God for that. Because it's not true. Bloody hell, of course it's not! And what's more, I can prove it to you.'

# TWENTY

## NEIL

Neil was in Hatton Garden, a part of London he hadn't visited for a while.

It was Sunday morning and, because many of the jewellery shops were closed, the streets were mostly empty. Which suited him just fine. He pulled his baseball cap down firmly so that none of his hair was visible and his eyes were shaded. Then he took the gold bracelet out of his baseball jacket's inner pocket and took it into a small jewellers' shop tucked away from the brash main drag, down a narrow side street. A place where he knew that fewer questions would be asked. Ten minutes later, he emerged, shoving a wad of folded twenty-pound notes into the pocket where the bracelet had just been.

And then he was making the familiar tube journey to Waterloo. He headed for Platform 2 and caught the Portsmouth train, getting off at Havant, where his mother now lived. She had swapped the dark and dingy maisonette where he spent his teenage years for a flat in a retirement complex, a home that was equally dark and dingy but even smaller. His mother spent her days alone inside its four walls, doomscrolling on her phone, falling prey to conspiracy theories and misinformation, and becoming more and more paranoid.

She didn't get up from the battered leatherette sofa when he arrived, nor did she offer him refreshment.

'No, don't!' she snapped when he tried to pull back the cheap purple curtains in the living room to admit some sunshine. 'If you do that, I can't see my phone.' Her reading glasses, secured round her neck with a cord, had slid down her nose and her greying hair was wiry and unbrushed. Underneath the shapeless clothes, she was very thin. The groomed, elegant woman he had known as a young boy was undetectable. She had vanished years ago.

With a sigh, Neil went into the cramped kitchenette and put the kettle on, washing up two mugs from the sink because there were no clean ones in the cupboard. He found a few dusty teabags and the dregs of milk that was on the point of turning sour and made them both tea. There was nothing in the fridge apart from a half-eaten Easter egg, which he guessed had been given to her by the warden who supervised the flats.

'Have you got biscuits?' he asked as he carried the mugs into the living room.

'Can't afford biscuits,' his mother replied, without looking up from Facebook.

'Here.' Neil reached into his jacket and pulled out the sheaf of notes, placing them on the coffee table. 'Three hundred quid.' The bracelet had turned out to be 18 carat gold, and Neil knew that it was probably worth nearer eight hundred pounds, but he also knew from experience that when something was stolen you took what you could get, in cash, and made a swift exit.

'Thanks, sweetheart,' his mother said, looking up briefly. 'How are things with you? How's that girl of yours? Still with the same one?'

'Still with her, yes.'

'Are you going to marry her?'

The question startled Neil. His mother took little interest in his love life, or indeed his life in general.

'No,' he replied, shaking his head and forcing down a sip of the rancid tea.

'Why not?'

'Because... our relationship just isn't like that. Marriage... it wouldn't work.'

'You don't know 'til you try.'

'Trust me, I know.'

Neil got up and went into the kitchen, tipping the rest of his tea down the sink.

'Want me to pop to the shops for you, pick up some biscuits? You need some fresh milk too.'

His mother, who hated leaving the flat, confirmed that she did want this.

Neil took one of the notes and went to the nearest corner shop, buying milk, biscuits, cheese, fruit, bread and ham. Once he'd unpacked them and urged his mother to eat something, he walked back to the station and caught the train back to London.


'Have we got any alcohol?' he asked his partner when he got back to the flat.

She was lying on her stomach on the sofa wearing just a sweatshirt and knickers, reading a copy of *Vogue* and smoking. She made a non-committal grunt.

'Seeing my mother's so fucking depressing, I always need a drink.'

He went to the freezer and pulled out a quart bottle of vodka, mixing it with apple juice because that was all they had.

'We need to get some wine and mixers for tomorrow,' he said, going back into the sitting room.

'Why, what's tomorrow?' She exhaled a plume of smoke,

then tossed the magazine to one side, and switched on the television, selecting an American reality show.

'Patsy's coming round, remember? So I'll need this place to myself. And all your stuff out of the way again. Bathroom and everything.'

This elicited a grunt of disapproval, and a turning up of the volume control.

'Look, I know you don't like it, babe, but it's important.'

'Can't you go somewhere else?'

'I don't want to risk being picked up on camera with her, not at this point in time. And we can't risk being overheard.'

There was a heavy sigh.

'You know what to do, right?'

'Okay, okay!' She reached for her packet of cigarettes and lit one.

He grabbed it and pulled it from her fingers. 'You're not jealous, are you?'

'Of Patsy?' She snorted. 'Of course not. It's just a pain having to clear out my stuff and go hide out somewhere else.'

'I know. But it has to be done. And we're so close. Hang on to that, okay? We're almost there.'

# TWENTY-ONE

## HATTIE

After their walk in Bushy Park, Hattie and Lewis had parted at Kingston station.

'I'll be in touch,' Lewis had called to her, waving as he headed down the steps to the platform, with Conker tugging on his lead. 'Meanwhile, please don't talk to anyone about this. Not a single person. And don't fall prey to any more crazy theories about me, okay?'

Sure enough, on Sunday morning she received a cryptic WhatsApp from him.

*Can we meet again in a couple of days or so? Need to set some things in motion first. L x*

Only a few minutes later, she received a message from Casper, who she had not seen in person since Easter Monday. As requested, she had not mentioned her meeting with Lewis to him, but had sent a generic message the previous evening wishing him goodnight, which had gone unanswered.

*Happy Sunday angel! Can we talk? xxx*

She phoned him straight back.

'Sorry!' was the first thing, he said. 'I know I've been neglecting you!'

'It's fine,' said Hattie, although it wasn't.

'The good news is that I handed in my notice at Van Asbeck's, and I'm about to get a very tidy little bonus for my efforts. So you and I need to get together as soon as we can to talk about next steps. I tell you, I'm so bloody ready for this. It's twenty-seven degrees Celsius in Mexico City today.'

His excitement was infectious, and Hattie found herself grinning into her handset. 'Absolutely, so am I.'

'Tonight any good for you? We can grab cocktails somewhere smart and raise a toast of farewell to grimy old London. What do you say?'

Hattie felt a shiver of excitement rush through her, a sensation she hadn't experienced since she was a child hanging up her stocking on Christmas Eve. 'I say I'm in.'

They met at the dimly lit American Bar at the Stafford Hotel in St James's.

When she saw the moody dark grey walls and chic red leather chairs, Hattie was glad she'd decided to wear a silk shift dress and vertiginous heels. She was more than ready to make a night of it. But after drinking just one expensive cocktail – something blue with dry ice swirling around it – Casper leaned in and whispered, 'Shall we get out of here?'

'It's only early yet,' Hattie protested. 'I fancy one of those pink ones next time.' She pointed to the drink on an adjoining table. 'I'm just getting into my stride here.'

A frown flitted across Casper's face briefly, but he picked up her hand and kissed her fingertips, pulling them into his mouth and flicking his tongue over them provocatively. 'But, baby,' he murmured, 'I can't wait to get you on your own. It's been a whole week since I've seen you, and a chap has needs, you know?'

Hattie felt the answering surge of desire snake through her own body, and it suddenly occurred to her why Casper had picked a bar in a five-star hotel. She leaned closer herself so that her hair was brushing against his cheek. 'Have you got us a room?' she whispered.

He sat back, his thickly lashed eyes not leaving her face as he shook his head. 'Afraid not, babe. I asked at reception when I got here, of course, but they're booked solid.'

Hattie's face fell.

'But, listen, we can go back to my mate's flat. The one we went to before. I know it's not exactly the Stafford, but at least it's clean. And we can be alone. Which is what matters, right?'

'I suppose so,' Hattie pouted.

'That's my girl. I'll just settle the tab.'

As a concession to this being a special night, they caught a cab back to Tower Hill. The flat was tidy but bare, as it had been before, and smelt faintly of musky perfume and cigarette smoke. Casper offered her wine or vodka and tonic, and she chose the latter. He poured a double measure of vodka.

'So, what's happening with your wife?' she asked him. 'Is it all sorted? Does she know what's going on?'

He nodded confidently. 'I've told her, yes. I've set the divorce in motion, and she's in the process of moving back into the house in Islington. So... this will be a fresh start for both of us.'

Hattie felt a little bubble of pleasure burst in her chest. Finally, he was all hers. 'That means we can talk flight dates then, yes?' she asked, pulling her phone out and opening the calendar app. 'Which day are we going to travel? Only, I suppose we ought to get on and book them as soon as we can. I looked at some flights online, and if we want to fly in the next couple of weeks, it's going to be pretty expensive.'

'Here's the thing, babe.' Casper poured himself a beer and sat down next to her. 'We're not actually going to travel to Mexico together.'

'We're not?' The chill of anxiety immediately displaced her excitement.

'Hear me out.' He topped up her glass with more vodka. 'There's going to be a huge amount to sort out when we arrive. Finding somewhere to live for starters. It's best if I go out slightly ahead of you, and do a recce, then when you come out, we'll have a better idea of what you'll need to bring. At the moment we have no clue, right?'

'I suppose so,' Hattie admitted. The vodka was going to her head and she was starting to feel woozy, distracted.

'So I'll head out there later this week—'

'This week? Don't you have to work your notice?'

'I'm taking leave I'm owed instead... so, like I said, I'll get out there with as much as I can carry and then you can come over a week or so later and bring out anything we still need. It's a smarter way to do it, right?'

Hattie sighed. 'I don't know. I just thought it would be fun to arrive together. More romantic.'

'There'll be the rest of our lives for romance, won't there?' He put his hand at the back of her neck and pulled her towards him, kissing her deeply and thoroughly. Hattie moaned with pleasure and pressed herself against him.

Within seconds, they were in the bedroom on the unfamiliar sheets, having intense and – in Hattie's case – slightly drunken sex.

'It'll be all right,' he whispered into her hair afterwards. 'Trust me.'

She relaxed into him, the post-coital glow melting away her anxiety. 'Who's going to book the flights?' she asked him. 'I mean I've probably got more time on my hands at the moment.'

'I'll do it,' Casper assured her. 'You just need to make sure you send me your passport details, your date of birth and full name. Okay, angel?'

'Okay,' Hattie agreed, sleepily.


She spent the next few days trying to pluck up the courage to tell her parents that she was leaving for Mexico City the following week.

Because it was now official. It was happening, and in her excitement, Hattie all but forgot about Julian's death, and Lewis Handley's revelation. She had forwarded her personal information to Casper and he had emailed her an e-ticket by return. Her parents demanded almost daily to be updated on her planned move and, so far, she had always given vague replies. But she could put them off no longer. She agreed to have supper with them on Thursday evening, planning to break the news with good food and wine to soften the blow.

As she was setting the table, her father tapped her on the shoulder and shoved his copy of *The Times* under her nose.

'Here...' He pointed at an article in one of the inside pages. 'Isn't this the company that boyfriend of yours is working for?'

Hattie put down the wine glasses she was holding and took the newspaper from him. When she read the headline, she felt a quickening of her heart rate, and a dull sense of unease.

## JAPANESE MASTERPIECE GOES MISSING

*The painting by internationally celebrated nineteenth-century artist Hokusai entitled* The Red Courtesan *has been reported as stolen. An art collector based in Mexico, who purchased the painting for £11.8 million at auction, claims that the artwork*

*he has been sent by prestige Mayfair auction house Van
Asbeck's is not The Red Courtesan. A representative of Van
Asbeck's told us that they are launching an investigation into
what they are referring to as 'a misunderstanding'.*

'Well, you're on the inside track now, aren't you, with this
chap of yours.' Her father took the newspaper back, folded it up
and tossed it on to the sideboard. 'You'll be able to ask him
what's going on. All sounds a bit dodgy to me.'

Hattie picked up the bottle of wine he had just uncorked
and poured herself a glass of it, draining it in one gulp.

Her mother came into the dining room carrying a steaming
casserole dish, and placed it on a mat on the table.

'What was that about your boyfriend, darling?' she
demanded, as she started ladling out the stew. 'Have you two
finalised your plans?'

'Still working on it,' Hattie mumbled, pouring herself a
second glass of wine. She couldn't tell her parents she was
moving to Mexico now. Not after her father had just read that
article. Even so, the location of the buyer had to be a coincidence, surely?

Once she was in her room after dinner, she found the article
on *The Times* website and forwarded it to Casper, with the
simple message *What the fuck?!*

He responded with one word. *Seriously?*

She phoned him then.

'You are not seriously suggesting I had something to do with
this,' he said as he picked up. He sounded more amused than
annoyed.

'Well, you've got to admit, it looks a bit weird. *The Red
Courtesan* goes missing after being bought by someone in
Mexico the same week you leave a job at Van Asbeck's and
move to... Mexico.'

To her relief, he laughed out loud at this. 'Angel girl, what are you suggesting? Do you really think I'd be stupid enough to pinch a painting sold to someone in Mexico and then head straight to Mexico.'

'It's a bit of a coincidence, that's all I'm saying.'

'Babe, you've got this all back to front. I'm going to Mexico City because it's a hub of the art world, so I'll be well placed to get a job there. And because it is a hub of the art world, there are a lot of serious collectors there too.'

'So what do you think's happened to the painting?'

She could hear him draw in his breath. 'Look, just between you and me, the guy at Van Asbeck's responsible for shipping the lots is a useless old drunk, and this is not the first time a sold lot has gone to the wrong place. We ship dozens of artworks every week; mistakes sometimes get made. It'll all be a cock-up, and the thing is probably on its way to Buenos Aires instead. Van Asbeck's are just trying to save face by saying they're launching an investigation.'

'Oh.' Hattie's shoulders slumped with relief.

'Listen, babe, I need to finish my packing. But not long now. *Nos vemos en Mexico.*'

'*Nos vemos en Mexico,*' she repeated, with more bravado than she was feeling. What had seemed like an exciting adventure was now starting to feel like a terrifying leap into the unknown. 'See you in Mexico.'

# TWENTY-TWO

## HATTIE

'I can't say I'm happy about this.'

Susannah Sewell put down the laundry she was folding, her face contracted in an expression of displeasure. 'Please tell me I've got this wrong... you're going to live in *Mexico*?' She said the word as if it was Neptune or Mars. 'And you're leaving later this week?'

'Yep, that's the plan.' Hattie stuck out her jaw defiantly. 'I am an adult, Mum! I'm thirty in a few weeks.' She had not mentioned the fact that the police had just arranged a time to interview her about Julian Cobbold's death. Being dragged into a murder enquiry at the very moment she was planning a major move abroad would not exactly be reassuring.

'If you're so successful at being an adult, how come you've been living here for nearly a year?' Her mother sounded angry now. Softening her tone, she asked, 'And where will you live once you're there?'

'We'll rent an Airbnb until we can find somewhere more permanent.'

'But what about the paperwork: visas and so on?'

'We'll be on 180-day travel visas, and after that, if we want to stay, we just apply to the local consular office. Apparently, it's quite easy.'

Her mother shook her head slowly. 'And Casper told you that, did he?'

Hattie nodded.

'Well, can we at least see him again, and talk this through before you go?'

'No, you can't. He's already in Mexico City.'

'He's flown out there without you?' her mother rolled her eyes. 'This just gets better!'

Unwilling to be on the receiving end of further disapproval, Hattie stomped upstairs and fired off a text to Casper. She felt unsettled and in desperate need of reassurance. It was early in the morning there, so she didn't expect a reply immediately. Instead, she started going through her clothes, deciding what to pack. Some of her things were in the spare-room wardrobe, but a lot was still packed up in boxes piled high on the landing. She was rummaging through them trying to locate shorts and sundresses when her phone pinged with a message. It was not from Casper, but from Lewis, and was followed by a shared location on Google Maps.

*Can you meet me here this evening? Really important. L x*

Four hours later, Hattie found herself on a quiet tree-lined road about a mile from her parents' house in Summerlands.

The property was an impressive one, and to Hattie's mind looked like something from an Agatha Christie mystery, with its tiled gables and creeper-covered walls. It was surrounded by a large garden with formal beds and topiary.

'Whose house is this?' she asked Lewis. He was wearing

jeans and an American college sweatshirt, his undercut freshly shaved. He let out a heavy sigh before answering.

'Julian Cobbold's. Well, it used to be.'

'Oh God,' Hattie murmured. 'So, why are we here?'

'You'll see. You up for this?'

'I suppose so.'

'Come on then.'

She followed him down the paved pathway, hanging back slightly as he rang the doorbell.

The door was opened by a woman a little younger than her mother. She had expensively maintained blonde hair, and would have been pretty if her face were not so strained and tense. Her eyes seemed too big for her face, and the jeans she wore hung too loose at her waist. She managed a curt smile.

Lewis reached out and clasped, rather than shook, her hand. 'Ginny, I'm Lewis Handley; we spoke last night. Thanks so much for agreeing to see us.' He turned and gestured towards Hattie. 'This is Hattie Sewell. She was a friend of Julian's too.'

Ginny Cobbold beckoned them into a spacious hallway with oak panelling and an elaborate staircase made of the same wood.

'So you're both Julian's commuting chums?' she asked disdainfully, her accent betraying a private education and moneyed background.

'Yes,' Hattie said, twisting her hands awkwardly. 'Look, I just want to say I'm so, so sorry about... about his loss. I didn't get to know him well, but he was extremely kind to me.'

Ginny managed a glacial smile.

'I phoned Ginny because I thought she could probably help put paid to this idea that I had anything to do with Julian's death,' Lewis explained, 'And she's very graciously agreed to speak to us in person. I thought that was probably the best way to put this nonsense to bed.'

She led them into a formal sitting room which had a fireplace in the same style as the staircase, and two beautifully upholstered sofas that faced each other on either side of a large ottoman. Oil paintings and intriguing watercolours hung on the walls, and there was a grand piano covered in silver-framed family photos.

'I suppose I should offer you something to drink?' she asked, not hiding her reluctance.

'No, honestly, we're fine,' Hattie insisted, only too aware that the woman had buried her husband less than a fortnight ago.

'Well, I need one anyway, even if you don't,' Ginny said briskly, returning with a bottle of wine and three wine glasses on a tray. 'Or there's Julian's single malt in the cabinet if you'd prefer?'

'Wine is fine,' Hattie said weakly.

Once the drinks had been poured, Lewis leaned forward in his chair and addressed Hattie. 'You need to know what the inquest into Julian's death found, because for legal reasons some of it was withheld from the press.' He turned back to Ginny. 'Would it be easier for you if I explained it?'

'No, it's all right,' Ginny said calmly. 'I've been over the whole thing so many times with various people, I'm used to it by now.' She took a careful sip of her wine. 'The exact cause of death was asphyxiation due to potassium cyanide poisoning. Apparently, it dissolves into a colourless liquid in water, and someone – persons unknown, as they said in the formal summing-up at the inquest – put it in the tank of Julian's vape pen. The police went through his belongings when... after... on the train and they found the vape in his coat pocket. Handed it over to their forensics people.' She swallowed some wine and looked at the pair of them with something approaching pride at her neat summary of events. 'He's always had one of the wretched things with him, you see, since he gave up cigarettes a few years ago.' She curled her lip with distaste. 'Apparently he used to use it in the train toilet, since vaping isn't allowed on public transport.'

Hattie nodded, but her mind was racing. It wasn't Julian's wine that had been poisoned. Bridget's theory was now proved to be just that: a theory.

Lewis was turned towards her, waiting for her to digest this before he spoke.

'You understand what this means, right, Hattie? That no one spiked Julian's drink: not me or anyone else. And not only was I not sitting on the same side of the table as Julian, but he was already sitting down when I arrived in the carriage that evening, so it would have been impossible for me to tamper with his vape pen.'

'All right, all right, I'm convinced,' Hattie cut in quickly. The truth was, her mind was struggling to grasp all this new information, but she had no desire to prolong the encounter with Ginny Cobbold. She stood up. 'I really think we should go and leave you in peace now. This must have been traumatic for you and the family...' She glanced at the gleaming ranks of photos. 'You have children?'

'One: Louisa. She's at university.' For the first time, emotion flickered on her face. 'We had a son, Edward, but he was killed in a car crash nearly two years ago.'

Hattie flinched in shock, at a loss for words. Ginny's only son gone, and now her husband.

'My God, that is so terribly unfair,' Lewis said sincerely. 'Condolences from us both.' He set down his glass and stood up too. 'And we've really taken up more than enough of your time.'

'Before you go,' Ginny said, 'there is something you might be able to help me with. May I please show you something?'

Hattie and Lewis exchanged a glance. 'Of course,' Lewis said with a smile. 'We're happy to help in any way we can.'

She led them upstairs, to a door with a wooden name plaque that said 'Edward'.

Hattie's heart lurched in her chest. Their son's room. She wasn't sure what she had expected, but it certainly wasn't this. Inside, the room was tidy but painfully personal, with posters on the wall and books and trophies on the shelves.

'I don't often come in here,' Ginny said in a low voice. 'Hardly ever. Frankly, it upsets me too much, even now. But after Julian died, I felt as though I needed to.' She smoothed the duvet cover with her fingers. 'I can't really explain why. Perhaps I thought it might make things clearer.' She turned round and gave Lewis and Hattie another of her chilly smiles, before talking a book off the desk and holding it up for them to see. 'Anyway, I noticed that just before...' She paused a second, gathering herself, 'Julian had left this out on Ed's desk.'

It was a hardback entitled *Dastardly Tales for Daring Boys* and the cover was designed to look like an anthology of adventure stories from the Edwardian era, with a stylised pastiche of boats and cars and explosions and boys in heroic poses.

'This was one of Ed's absolute favourites when he was little. An aunt or one of his godparents gave it to him for Christmas when he was about eight. I believe it had been in print for many years.' Ginny clenched her lips together as if trying to quash a painful memory. 'He liked the stories to be read to him at first, over and over every night, then eventually, of course, he read them for himself.' She opened the book to a page which had an orange Post-it on it. 'When I came in here, I discovered that Julian had marked something in it. At first, I didn't give it much thought, but then a friend of his from the Met got in touch. A detective called Nigel Hayes. I knew that Julian had been to see him not long before he died, and when Nigel phoned to offer his condolences, he also mentioned this book. It turned out Julian's recent visit to him had been prompted by something he saw in it.' She handed it to Lewis, opened at the marked page, still speaking. 'Only I'm now wondering whether I should give it to the police officers who are carrying out the murder investigation.'

Lewis looked at the page, and as he did so his eyebrows shot up, and his face paled. 'Let me see.' Hattie leaned forward and took the book from him. Her eyes scanned

the paragraph in question.

*It's time to introduce you to the hero of our story. A young man with a very distinguished name. His name is...*

Her eyes came to rest on the two words that had been underlined heavily in pencil. The blood rushed from her head and she felt herself grow faint.

*...Casper Merriweather.*

# TWENTY-THREE

## HATTIE

'Christ almighty! I don't know what I was expecting, but it certainly wasn't that!'

Hattie held up a hand to silence Lewis. The two of them were in the Coach and Horses, a 1930s roadhouse on the main route to London, just round the corner from where the Cobbolds lived.

'Please,' she muttered, her head bowed over her hands. 'Just give me a minute. I need a bit of time to process this.'

It was as if every emotion she had ever experienced was coming to the forefront of her brain at once, competing for space. Fear, anger, shame, embarrassment, disappointment. Perhaps the only one not present was disbelief. Because had she ever really believed in Casper? Hadn't he always been that little bit too good to be true, this man who the very first time she saw him had reminded her of a character in a glossy Hollywood movie? But every time those concerns had surfaced she had blocked them out. Usually with alcohol.

As if reading her thoughts, Lewis went straight to the bar. He fetched a brandy and a pint of Guinness for himself and returned to the table, where Hattie still had her hands covering her face. He slid the brandy towards her. 'Traditionally good for shock, so they say.'

'I don't understand,' Hattie said eventually, lifting her head and taking a gulp of the warm amber liquid. She then repeated it over and over. 'I just don't understand.'

'What's to understand?' Lewis asked, his tone gentle but tinged with a hint of impatience. 'The man we met on the train is not called Casper Merriweather. Because Casper Merriweather is a fictional character in a kids' book. And Julian, with his forensic lawyer's brain, and his son's love of that book, picked up on it immediately.'

'But surely it could be a coincidence,' Hattie protested weakly.

'If the name was Tom Smith, or Pete Taylor, maybe. But Casper Merriweather? Come on, Hattie.'

She took another sip of the brandy, her brain still struggling to dissect the implications of what had just happened. 'Maybe he had a genuine reason to change his name, and that was just what he chose. Because he'd read the book and liked it.' It had to be something as innocent as that, surely, she told herself. The man she loved wasn't capable of anything sinister.

Lewis gave her a withering look over the rim of his pint glass.

Hattie buried her face in her hands again and rocked backwards and forwards in her seat. 'I don't know what to do. I just don't know what I'm supposed to do now.'

'What exactly was your involvement with him? You were dating?'

'More than that,' Hattie let out an anguished groan. 'Much more.'

And she told him about their plan to leave London and move to Mexico City. A plan which now sounded fantastical, but had already been set in motion. Or so she thought.

Lewis let out a whistle.

'So what should I do?' Hattie pulled a tissue from her jacket pocket and dabbed at the tears that were now welling up. 'Should I just tell him that I'm not going? Should I let on that I know he's...' She closed her eyes briefly.

'A fake?' supplied Lewis.

'Exactly,' she mumbled, drinking a bit more of the brandy.

'No,' said Lewis firmly, twisting on the wooden bench so that he could make full eye contact. 'Absolutely not. It's vital that you say nothing to him, at least until we know the implications of this piece of information. As you say, a name change doesn't necessarily have to be sinister. It could be nothing more than a crazy whim. But Julian knew about it, and he spoke to a member of CID about it. Then he wound up being killed.'

'Casper wasn't on the train,' Hattie protested, clenching her hands together to try to quell their shaking, 'Whatever he may or may not have done, we know he didn't kill Julian.'

She realised as she said this that the vape could have been tampered with on a previous occasion, but Lewis did not correct her, and she pushed the thought out of her mind.

'We need to speak to this DCI Hayes,' was all he said. Ginny Cobbold had given them contact details for DCI Nigel Hayes, suggesting they talk to him if they wanted to know more.

Lewis fetched a packet of crisps from the bar.

'You'll feel better if you eat something,' he said, pushing them towards Hattie.

She picked at them while he drank the rest of his pint.

'What did you make of her?' he asked as she ate. 'Ginny Cobbold. Bit of a cold fish, if you ask me.'

Hattie nodded her agreement.

'Didn't exactly seem grief-stricken, did she?'

'No, she didn't.' Hattie stared at him, a crisp on the way to her mouth. 'You're not suggesting...?'

'That she had something to do with Julian's death?' Lewis shook his head slowly. 'I really don't know.' He paused for a moment and then went on. 'Can I tell you someone else I've been thinking about? Carmen.'

'Carmen from the 18.53 Crew?'

'How many other Carmens do you know? She was on the train that night, wasn't she, and she seemed to be a bit on edge. It was her who pointed out that Julian had been gone a while. And then later, on WhatsApp, she makes no comment about his death; in fact, it turns out she's not even in the group any more.'

'Yes,' Hattie nodded. 'I noticed that too.' She thought for a second. 'She talked to you more than the rest of us: has she not been in touch with you at all?'

Lewis shook his head, before draining the remains of his drink. 'Come on,' he said, standing up. 'We know where she lives; we may as well go there now.'

'To Carmen's? Won't she be at work?'

'Her husband will be in though.'

They caught a cab to Carmen's block of flats and rang her doorbell, several times. There was no reply. Just as they were turning away, an elderly woman came up the path carrying a heavy bag of shopping. She dropped it at her feet while she rummaged for her keys, breathing heavily.

'Who you after?' she croaked.

'Carmen Demirci,' Lewis told her. 'Flat 53.'

'Nah,' the woman was shaking her head. 'You won't find her here no more. They've gone. The whole family; just disappeared overnight. Did a moonlight flit.'


'Well, this just gets stranger, doesn't it?' Lewis said, as they walked back to the main road.

'It does,' Hattie said. 'To be honest, I don't know what to think now. But Carmen... do you think maybe she knew something?'

Lewis shrugged. 'It has to be a possibility if she's suddenly vanished... Are you still up for talking to this Hayes guy? I can go on my own if you can't handle it; I don't mind.'

'No, it's fine,' Hattie answered, forcing a weak smile. 'I need to find out what's going on: you could say I'm pretty much invested at this point.'

'I'll reach out to him then. And in the meantime...' He drew his fingers across his lips to indicate that she should keep them zipped.

That was all very well for Lewis to say, Hattie thought, as she walked back to her parents' house, but he wasn't the one whose life had been potentially turned on its head by the strange discovery in Edward Cobbold's bedroom.

She could trust her parents, but they were the last people she wanted to share this information with. They had been charmed by Casper, certainly, but still had their doubts about their daughter moving to Central America to be with him. So, instead, once she had enjoyed a restorative soak in the bath and consumed half of her under-bed bottle of wine, she messaged Bridget. Bridget knew Casper, if only a little, and had witnessed the start of their relationship. She at least would appreciate the implications of what Hattie had just discovered.

*B, something devastating has just happened. Just found out C is using a fake name. Don't know what to do xx*

Two blue ticks eventually appeared to show the message had been read, but there was no reply.

Hattie slept badly, surfacing from sleep every hour or so to check her phone.

There were several messages from Casper, using the new number he now had with a Mexican mobile provider. Mexico City was amazing, he told her. He enthused about how she'd love it too, with all its craft breweries, salsa clubs and street art. He included details of some potential apartments to rent in Polanco, and a couple of selfies looking sleek and tanned, his shirt unbuttoned almost to his waist, golden hair slicked back, palm trees waving behind him. At least she had the time difference to rely on as a reason to cut communication.

And yet still, she could not allow herself to delete the pictures, clicking on them and looking at them over and over. Surely this was all some sort of big mistake? After all, this *was* the man she had fallen in love with, and he did have a real job working at a prestigious auction house. Maybe the name thing was something to do with his marriage, or the divorce.

His latest message asked her to phone him as soon as she woke up, however late it was in Mexico. She did not do so, because she knew she was a poor actress and that he would therefore pick up the anxiety in her tone of voice. Instead, she messaged him, saying simply *Call you later xxx*.


Lewis phoned her just as she was getting out of the shower.

'I hope you're free,' he said, without preamble. 'I've cleared it with work for me to have a few hours off. Given you're supposed to be leaving the country in a few days, I thought we'd better not waste time.'

'Good morning to you too,' she returned drily.

He laughed. 'Meet me outside New Scotland Yard in an hour? Victoria Embankment'

'Make it an hour and half.'

. . .

When she arrived, Lewis was already standing outside the glass porch of the huge white stone building, with its revolving triangular metal sign.

He had two takeaway coffee cups in his hands, one of which he handed to Hattie. 'They'll probably offer us coffee inside, but odds on it will be from a vending machine and taste like crap.'

She managed a smile, but inside she was sick with nervous tension.

'You haven't spoken to anyone, I hope?' he asked, as they headed to the lift. 'Or let on to... him... that you know?'

She shook her head.

'Good.'

They were greeted cordially by Nigel Hayes as they got out of the lift; a short, muscular man in a too-tight suit, with a thatch of wiry red hair and freckles. After introductions had been made, they were led into a carpeted room with a glass-topped conference table surrounded by office chairs.

'You've already got coffee, good...' he said, putting his laptop down on the table, before offering them paper cups and passing a jug of water. 'I gather that my colleague Mike Jevons has already been in touch. That you're both friends of Julian Cobbold?'

'Acquaintances, really,' Lewis supplied. 'We'd only known him a couple of months.'

'I was gutted to hear about his death. Completely gutted.' Hayes shook his head slowly, then interlocked his fingers and pressed his hands against his chin for a moment. 'He and I went way back. When I first started out in CID and he was a relatively junior barrister, I was OIC on some of his cases at the Old Bailey... that's officer in the case,' he corrected himself. 'We stayed in touch and met up for a drink or lunch from time to time.'

'Ginny Cobbold said you'd seen him recently?' Hattie asked.

'That's right. Must have been around six weeks ago. He said he wanted to pick my brains about something. When we met, he told me he'd met this guy on a train who was calling himself "Casper Merriweather",' Hayes made air quotes around the name, 'but that something about it hadn't felt right, and then he remembered where he'd heard the name before. Apparently, it had been in a book of children's stories that he used to read to his son when he was little. His lad...' Hayes shook his head sadly at the mention of Edward Cobbold. 'His lad loved this particular story and got him to read it over and over. So the name stuck in Julian's memory. Maybe if his son hadn't died, it wouldn't have done, but he told me that his brain clung on to every single memory he had of Ed's life. There was a special resonance, he told me.'

Hayes sighed heavily before going on.

'His criminal lawyer's brain then kicked into gear and he asked himself why this guy was using a false identity. And if he could find out who he really was. That was where I came into it. And as it turned out, it was quite simple.'

He opened up his laptop and pressed a few keys.

'He showed me a picture from the website of the company this "Casper" was working for, and I ran it through facial recognition software. Which threw up something interesting. But, just to be sure, I asked Julian if he could get me some DNA to run through our database. So he got himself invited to an event at Van Asbeck's and took a glass that "Casper" had drunk from. Had it couriered to me right away. And that confirmed it.'

Hattie felt a sharp tightening in her chest as Hayes turned the screen of his laptop to face them. Lewis glanced in her direction.

'It turned out that Casper Merriweather was an alias for this man. A man who was well known to the force.' He pointed to the screen and there he was, less tanned, hair less luxuriant, in a police mugshot.

Hattie's vision blurred, then contracted until she could only see a few square inches in front of her face.

'His name is Neil Waller.'

# TWENTY-FOUR

## HATTIE

'Are you all right?' Nigel Hayes asked Hattie.

She was hunched forwards in her seat, her lower lip caught between her teeth. She nodded slowly. Lewis reached out and touched her gently on her forearm.

'He and I were... we've been dating,' she murmured.

'I see. Well, I appreciate that this must be quite a shock,' Hayes said sympathetically, adding, 'Better to find out now, though, rather than further down the line.'

There was a knock at the door of the meeting room and a woman came in carrying a manila folder. She was in her forties, dressed in a white shirt and black trousers, and her savagely cropped greying hair was tinted a vivid shade of plum.

'This is my colleague DI Jill McElwee,' Hayes told them. 'She's from the Met's Art and Antiques unit. They're part of the Specialist, Organised and Economic Crime unit, based here at the Yard.'

The woman threw them what passed for a smile and sat down.

'Jill specialises in the theft of important cultural items. She's currently investigating the disappearance of Hokusai's *The Red Courtesan*.'

'But I thought... Casper said...' Hattie looked at the two police officers in bewilderment. 'He said it was just a mix-up with the shipping.'

'The legitimate buyer is based in Mexico City,' McElwee said coolly, 'and he did indeed recently take delivery of *The Red Courtesan*. But it was a copy. Not even an oil copy, just a framed print. The sort of thing you can buy online for about a hundred quid. This was not a mix-up, this was theft.'

'But...'

'Perhaps it would help if I filled Mr Handley and Ms Sewell in about Neil Waller?' Hayes interjected more kindly.

McElwee made a non-specific noise that managed to convey impatience, opening her file and writing a note in it.

*Good cop, bad cop*, Hattie thought grimly.

Hayes continued, 'Over the last twelve years or so, Waller's been charged with a string of offences, escalating from petty theft to major fraud. The most recent, attempting to sell a property that did not belong to him, earned him a stretch in prison. And while he was inside he made sure he didn't waste his time. He's far too intelligent for that. He took a distance-learning degree in History of Art, no doubt having realised that after dealing drugs and arms, fine art is where the big money is. And when he came out of the nick after nearly three years, his newly gained knowledge made him plausible enough to apply for a job at Van Asbeck's. Having created a shiny-looking fictitious CV and falsified his references. Anyone with a clue about digital design and layout can do that without too much trouble and make it look convincing. And Van Asbeck's have admitted that they were sufficiently impressed not to phone his alleged previous employers and make the relevant checks. Evidently it helped that he looked the part.'

Hattie thought back to that first meeting on the train, to the glamorous, perfectly groomed Jude Law lookalike. The fact that she was not the only one he'd fooled made her feel a little less gullible

'As I've said, so far his offending has been limited to serious fraud and misrepresentation. Murder is a worrying progression, but it's certainly not unheard of where big money is involved.'

'Murder?' Hattie glanced at Lewis in alarm, the blood pounding in her ears.

'Julian Cobbold had discovered his true identity. He was asking questions at Van Asbeck's. Evidently, he knew enough to expose Waller.' Hayes kept his voice calm.

'But Cas— Neil wasn't on the train!' Hattie protested.

'Obviously that is something that needs further investigation. Something DI Jevons and his team are currently looking into.'

McElwee leaned forward and held up her biro, indicating that she wanted to take over the narrative. 'Do you know where Waller was living?' she asked Hattie. 'Did he ever take you to his home?'

Hattie thought back. Casper – as she still thought of him despite this turn of events – had always been very vague about his temporary accommodation in the Summerlands area. He'd certainly never mentioned an address, nor had there ever been any question of Hattie visiting the place.

She shook her head. 'The only place we went to together, other than my house, was the flat of a friend of his, at Tower Hill. We couldn't go to his home because...' She shifted in her seat. 'His wife was there.'

'Waller isn't married,' McElwee said, with an impatient tilt of her head. 'Never has been.'

Another icy ribbon of shock coiled its way through Hattie's insides. So that wasn't true either. It was looking as though nothing she had believed about Casper was true.

'Do you remember the address of this flat in Tower Hill?' Nigel Hayes asked.

'It was in Mansell Street. Modern block of flats, on the fourth floor. I think it was Flat 16?'

McElwee wrote this down.

'But he's in Mexico City now,' Hattie added.

'So he's told you.' McElwee said waspishly.

'I'm pretty sure he is,' Hattie insisted. 'He copied the email receipt for his own flight to me when he sent my e-ticket. And he's been sending me photos.'

She showed DI McElwee the selfies on her phone.

'And in terms of the places you and Waller went together, can you think of anywhere that he might have used to hide the Hokusai painting? Because if he has flown to Mexico City, then he certainly wouldn't have risked travelling with it. Not so soon after it was reported stolen, and with Van Asbeck's having just raised the alarm about his involvement.'

Hattie hesitated, glancing at Lewis again. He gave a tiny nod of encouragement.

'We did go away together a couple of times. The first was to Oakley Grange Hotel in Surrey. For a weekend. And then at Easter, we went to my parents' cottage in Deal.'

'Was there anywhere there that he could have hidden the painting? And any opportunity for him to do so?'

Hattie thought for a moment. 'No, it wouldn't have been possible. We were together the whole time, and he just had a very small weekend bag with him.' She furrowed her brow. 'I mean, I saw it. It just had his washbag, a sweater and some clean underwear in it.'

McElwee scribbled furiously, then raised her head again and pushed her business card across the table in Hattie's direction. 'We'll need details of the property, and depending on the outcome of our enquiries, we may need access to perform a search.'

Hattie nodded slowly, her heart sinking. Her parents were going to be thrilled about this. Just thrilled.

'We're very grateful for your co-operation,' Hayes said, standing up with a smile and extending a hand. 'Your input has been very useful. And it goes without saying that if Waller makes contact with you, you must inform one of us straight away. But act normally. Don't say anything that will make him think you know his real identity. Not a word.'

# TWENTY-FIVE

## HATTIE

Hattie woke with a start just after 4 a.m.

She lay in her bed for a few minutes, feeling shaky and unsettled. Was it too early to phone Lewis? she wondered. Yes, almost certainly, unless he was an insomniac, and there was nothing to suggest that was the case.

She lay in bed listening to the radio for forty-five minutes before creeping down to the kitchen to make tea. Because there was no possibility of her getting back to sleep, not now. At five fifteen, she dialled Lewis's mobile. If he was still asleep, his phone would most likely be in silent mode, she reasoned, in which case she could leave him a voicemail.

He picked up immediately. 'What's wrong? Has something happened?'

'I was going to leave you a message,' she said weakly. 'I didn't expect you to be awake.'

'Conditioned reflexes from being in Special Branch. Always on high alert.'

'The thing is, I've just remembered something. It didn't occur to me when we were at Scotland Yard, but it came to me in the middle of the night.'

'Go on.'

'At Easter when I went down to our cottage with Casper...' She corrected herself. 'With Waller... he arrived before me, and used the spare key to let himself in. He'd made a fire when I got there, which involved him having to go out to the back yard. So he could have brought something with him... *The Red Courtesan*, I mean... and hidden it before I got there. So, we could go down to Deal and check. My parents and sister haven't been down since then, no one has.'

At the other end of the line, Lewis exhaled hard. 'You're going to have to tell the cop from Art and Antiques this. If you don't, you're potentially obstructing a police investigation.'

'But I really don't want my parents to find out,' Hattie pleaded. 'They're going to be so angry. Can't we just pre-empt the police getting involved by checking ourselves?'

Lewis sighed. 'I don't think it's a good idea, Hattie.'

'Please. If we find anything, then I promise we'll tell the police straight away. And if we don't... well, maybe the painting will turn up somewhere else and they won't need to search Mariner's. In which case my parents don't need to know I've taken a really dodgy criminal there.'

'I don't know— Not now, Conker, it's too dark for walkies!' Hattie could hear the dog's claws skittering on some hard surface in the background. 'Let me think about it, okay?'

'Beth's coming over tonight,' her mother announced when Hattie went downstairs a few hours later to get some breakfast.

'She is?' Dazed, and distracted, Hattie stared at her mother.

'If you're intent on disappearing off to the other side of the world, then of course your sister's going to want to see you before you go,' her mother said impatiently, picking up her jacket and her tote bag ready to head to her job at the local estate agents. 'So please, darling, make sure you're in. Okay?'

'Is Jonathan coming?'

'No, she wants to spend time with you alone.'

That was a relief, at least. Hattie found her sister's lawyer boyfriend hopelessly dull.

She went up to the top floor again and packed away the clothes she had been planning to take to Mexico. Her phone pinged with yet another photo message from 'Casper'. With shaking hands, she opened it.

He was wearing shades and standing in front of an obelisk in a fountain. She enlarged the photo and examined it carefully. It definitely seemed real. And that obelisk was in Polanco, she recognised it from her online research. *Not long til you're here! Can't wait!* the message read. Should she reply? Wouldn't he get suspicious if she ignored it? Deciding that a neutral response was called for, she just sent three kisses.

Her hands still shaking, she went to the Van Asbeck's company website and looked for Casper Merriweather's profile. It was no longer there: a site search for his name brought up a 'not found' message. The Instagram account she had checked when she'd first met him was gone too. Deleted. The man had been a mirage, and she had been taken in by him, building a future with him in her head that was as fake as he was. She had been prepared to ditch her career and her home for a man who didn't even exist.

The extent of her desperation started to finally sink in, and she broke down into uncontrollable sobbing. After crying for nearly an hour, she ventured down into the empty kitchen and took a bottle of wine from the wine rack. Once she had drunk almost all of it, she collapsed onto her bed and fell asleep.


'Hatt!' Someone was shaking her awake. 'Hatts, what's going on?'

Her younger sister was sitting on the edge of her bed.

Hattie glanced at the bedside clock. Six thirty. She'd been asleep for hours. But then that was hardly surprising given she'd been awake half the night. She struggled into a sitting position.

'You've been crying.' This was a statement, not a question.

'Yeah, sorry, Bethie.' Hattie dabbed her eyes with her sleeve and gave her sister a hug.

'What's going on? I thought you were about to head off on this amazing adventure.'

'Can we...?' Hattie leaned over the bed and pushed the empty wine bottle out of sight. 'Can we go out somewhere, just you and me? It's hard to talk with Mum and Dad around.'

Beth suggested the Railway Arms, but Hattie didn't want to bump into any of the 18.53 crew. Instead, they went to the tapas bar where she'd met 'Casper'.

'Is this something to do with your new man?' Beth demanded once they'd ordered a couple of sangrias. She'd also ordered several plates of tapas, but Hattie only picked at them, concentrating on her drink instead. The place was crowded, with a noisy stag party in one corner and what looked like an office outing in another.

Hattie nodded. 'It's over.' She couldn't tell her sister the truth, but the pain and disappointment weren't faked.

'Oh my God... so you're not going to Mexico after all?'

Hattie shook her head. 'But don't say anything to Mum and Dad, okay? Not yet. I'll tell them eventually.'

'So what happened? Can you tell me, at least?'

'He turned out not to be who I thought he was,' Hattie said truthfully.

'Well, it was a very big step to take, given you'd only known him, what, a few weeks? Jonathan and I knew each other years before we moved in together.'

*And that's the difference between us*, Hattie thought sadly.

But it turned out her sister's way, previously dismissed as safe and boring, was probably the right way after all.

'You should go away,' Beth urged, sipping on her punch. 'Why not go down to Mariner's?'

'I might,' Hattie agreed. 'I might well do that.'

'Well, let me know if you do, okay? I left my gold charm bracelet down there last time I went, in the top left-hand drawer of the chest in the blue bedroom. I'd quite like it back.'

Hattie's phone buzzed.

'Is that from him?' Beth asked, as Hattie picked it up.

*Please God, let it not be.*

But it was from Lewis.

*Okay, I'll do it. I'll come down to Kent with you. Sooner the better. L x*

# TWENTY-SIX

## HATTIE

It was strange, Hattie thought, but she found herself rather looking forward to seeing Lewis again. Not just because she appreciated his support, but because she found his physical presence reassuring.

When he met her at St Pancras the next day, he had his dog with him, 'Hope it's okay if Conker comes too. Only, he loves the seaside.' Lewis held up a large brown paper bag. 'Train picnic,' he said briskly. 'Can't make a train journey without a train picnic.'

'The journey time's only just over an hour,' Hattie said weakly.

'No matter: food always helps pass the time.' Lewis's warm brown eyes swept over her, taking in her pale, pinched face and the combat trousers that hung loosely round her hips. 'And you look as though you could do with a bit of sustenance. Have you been eating? Sleeping?'

'Not very much of either,' she admitted as they boarded the train and found their seats. She thought it best not to mention that almost all of her calories in the past few days had come from alcohol. That she had been drowning her intense sorrow –

heartbreak even – over the betrayal she had suffered at the hands of Neil Waller. She sat across the table from Lewis and Conker, feeling a little self-conscious. It felt strange to be on a trip with him that was not the Waterloo to Summerlands commuter route.

Lewis opened the bag and took out two sausage rolls. This immediately piqued the dog's interest, but Hattie shook her head. The sight of the greasy pastry made her feel queasy, but she did accept an apple and half a Twix.

'Has Waller been in touch?'

It took her a couple of seconds to realise who Lewis was referring to.

She sighed, nodding. 'Yes. Sent me a selfie from Mexico. But don't worry, he doesn't realise anything's wrong.' She pulled up the chat thread on her phone and showed Lewis.

'You do realise you need to show this to that DI we met. McElwee. Or at least to Nigel Hayes, although I don't think he's officially involved at this stage.'

'I will. Just as soon as we've checked out the cottage.'

Heavy rain was falling as the train eased its way out of south London, but by the time they reached the coast, a strong breeze was breaking up the heavy, purple-grey clouds to reveal bright spring sunshine. The first thing Lewis and Hattie did after leaving Deal station was to take the delighted Conker for a long run on the beach.

Then they walked the couple of blocks inland and headed to Griffin Street.

'Nice,' said Lewis appreciatively, as Hattie fumbled under the window box for the spare key. 'Lucky old you having a bolt-hole by the sea, here whenever you want it.'

'I suppose so,' said Hattie. 'I guess I take it for granted.'

Lewis glanced at her, and she felt herself colour slightly. *He must think I'm some spoilt Home Counties brat.*

He put a hand on her arm to restrain her as they headed

into the ground-floor sitting room. 'Hold on a second, let's be a bit forensic about this, before we charge in. Does everything look as it should do?'

Hattie slowly took in the room. There was ash in the grate of the burner, but that was how she and 'Casper' had left it. Otherwise, the room looked untouched: the cushions, books and ornaments all where they were supposed to be. She left Lewis to go and check the kitchen and went upstairs to the first-floor bedroom where they had slept.

'Check under the mattresses!' Lewis shouted up the stairs. 'And in the wardrobes.'

She had stripped off the bed linen when they'd left on Easter Monday and taken all the sheets and towels down to the basement utility room. The duvet was where she had left it, folded neatly in the centre of the mattress. On the top floor was what the Sewells called the blue bedroom. This too was untouched, but as she headed to the stairs, Hattie remembered her sister's request and turned back. Then her heart sank.

The top left-hand drawer of the antique mahogany dresser chest was slightly ajar. As she pulled it open, Hattie already knew what she was going to find. The drawer was empty. Beth's 18-carat gold charm bracelet had been taken. And the only person who could have taken it was him. Waller. It was easier to think of him as that now, as a little nugget of anger crystallised inside her, hardening her heart.

Closing the drawer, she went down the three flights to the basement kitchen to find Lewis, with Conker sitting patiently to attention.

'I've been through all the drawers and cupboards, and I can't find anything unusual. but I've never been here before, so you'd probably better double-check.'

Hattie did a quick once-over of the room. 'We need to check outside,' she told Lewis. 'I told him – Waller...' she still flinched slightly as she said the name out loud, '...about the log store and he lit a fire before I arrived, so he must have gone out there.'

Followed by Conker, they went out into the small terraced yard, and opened the shed. The door had a metal hasp for a padlock, which immediately attracted Lewis's attention.

'It's not locked,' he observed. 'Is that how it was left?'

Hattie nodded. 'It's only accessible from the house, so we tend not to bother locking it.'

They looked inside the shed, which smelled of sea must and wood shavings. The logs were stacked neatly along the back wall, and there was a trug with a few gardening implements for tending the window boxes and planters, a yard broom, a couple of folded deckchairs and a small toolbox.

'Does it look how it did before?' asked Lewis.

'To be honest, I'm not sure. It's ages since I've been in here myself.'

'Then we're going to need to look behind the woodpile,' Lewis said with a sigh, 'Which is going to be a bit of a pain. But it's the obvious place to hide something.'

Slowly and painstakingly, they dismantled the stack of logs, completely exposing the back wall of the shed. There was nothing underneath them, apart from a couple of disgruntled spiders. It took even longer to replace the logs, and by the time they had finished, it was starting to get dark. They retreated to the kitchen, where Hattie made a pot of tea and found some chocolate biscuits and a bowl large enough for Lewis to fill with the kibble he had brought for Conker.

'There's no loft or attic space where something could be hidden?' Lewis asked.

She shook her head. 'It's been converted into another bedroom.'

'Well, I guess that's it then. The painting's not here. You can tell DI McElwee as much, although, strictly speaking, they don't have to take your word for it. They might still want to conduct a search, but I think we've at least succeeded in delaying that. Especially as I'm ex-job, so they know we'll have done it properly.'

'He must at least have thought about it, because I think he did a recce of the place before I arrived.' She told Lewis about her sister's missing bracelet.

'Thieving bastard,' he pronounced with satisfaction.

After they had locked the door and replaced the key, Lewis said suddenly, 'There's another thirty minutes till the next train: let's go for fish and chips.'

Hattie looked doubtful.

'Come *on*,' he wheedled. 'There are few things better than fish and chips at the seaside. It's all part of the magic.'

And he was right, Hattie reflected, as they ate chips out of paper on their way back to the station, the brown Labrador plodding at their feet. Despite the oddness – and the sadness – of the day, and despite the chip shop being unlicensed and them now only having cans of cola to drink, there was a small part of it that had felt just that: magic. As the train wound its way back through the London suburbs, the image of the sophisticated Casper amid the sun and palm trees of Mexico receded just that little bit further.

# TWENTY-SEVEN

## NEIL – TWO DAYS EARLIER

Thank God his partner had found out what was going on in time, and thank God they had had come up with a last-minute plan.

'Patsy knows' was all she had said. All she had needed to say.

They had come up with the nickname 'Patsy' at the start of all this. Patsy, as in dupe, or fraud victim, or mark. He couldn't remember who had come up with it first. Him, or Tali.

*Ah yes, Tali.*

Because she had come back to him. As they were led down from the defendants' dock in Swansea Crown Court back in 2016, he had believed he would never see her again. She was almost certainly going to be released on licence some months before he was, and in his mind she would then disappear into the ether. Or to Slovenia. Or maybe she would have resolved to go straight, and to ensure success, make sure she gave him a wide berth in future.

But that was not what happened. He was released from HMP Berwyn in 2019, after serving half of his sentence, and returned to London immediately, living for a while in a hostel for ex-cons in Archway. He fell into the habit of taking the number 309 bus to Great Titchfield Street and sitting in the pavement cafés in the pedestrianised area behind Selfridges, looking for marks. He spotted people who were sloppy with their phones and their credit cards, just as he always had, but he didn't act on them. He wasn't going to risk going down for some petty fraud. Not while he was still on licence and any offence would have him back in prison serving the remainder of the five-year eight-month term. He had bigger targets in mind now, not thousands or even hundreds of thousands of pounds, but millions. Enough for him to get far away from the UK and escape prosecution for ever.

Then he saw a young woman sitting with her back to him, her shiny brown hair falling down her back. She was smoking, and there was something about the way she held her cigarette which sent a bullseye of recognition straight to his brain. His heart, normally unmoved, skipped a beat. He had thought that only happened in movies. It was her. Natalia. Tali. He got up and walked slowly over to her table.

'I saw you,' he had said, 'but you didn't see me. You're slipping, Tali.'

'Oh, I saw you,' she replied calmly, exhaling a thin plume of smoke in his direction. 'I've been coming here looking for you. I was just waiting to see if you would notice me.'

He sat down opposite her, and waved to the waitress to bring his coffee and sandwich from the table where he had been sitting.

'So, Mr Waller...' Tali said, extinguishing the cigarette, its butt now ringed with scarlet lipstick. Her hazel eyes had danced with mischief as they roved over their fellow customers. 'Spot any potential here today?'

He shook his head firmly. 'I'm not doing any more short cons. Not worth it. I'm working on something much more long term. A one and done fix.'

Tali narrowed her eyes and pulled another cigarette from the pack. 'Tell me more.'

'Why, are you interested?'

'I might be,' she replied carefully.

'Only, it's going to involve a lot of planning. And patience. And probably putting someone on the send.'

He had used the con artist's term for staging a whole invented world, created to lull a victim into a false sense of security. Tali, of course, knew exactly what he was talking about.

And she was in immediately; of course she was. And so they got back together. For this plan to work, they had to operate as a couple, but just as before, there was no emotional commitment, no monogamy. Sure, they fucked every so often. But feelings were not involved. Feelings made everything far too high risk.


And now, around a year later, here they were. Tali was still in London and he was in Mexico City, and so far, it was turning out to be fine. Better than fine. The Polanco district that Patsy had researched – doing his homework for him, which was ironic – was really rather nice. He was not going to be here very long, obviously, but for now it was all working.

That was until Tali broke the news in a panicked message that his fake identity had become public knowledge. This was hardly a shock, given that Julian Cobbold had already worked it out. But it did make their next steps a lot more complicated. And it was galling, too, given that when he had originally chosen the name, he had been so convinced no one would recognise it. He had been given a copy of *Dastardly Tales for Daring Boys* by his father when he still lived at home, and the character of Casper Merriweather had fired his child's imagination, sticking in his mind. Twenty years later, it had struck him as the perfect name for an upper-class, well-connected international art dealer. Surely, he had told himself, it was so obscure that no one would recognise it. But thanks to a chance meeting on a train, someone had. Julian Cobbold.

As soon as it was morning in the UK, he phoned Tali using one of the burner phones he had bought in Mexico, this one on the Telcel network. The SIM card from his most recent London phone had been snipped into two and flushed down a toilet at Heathrow, the handset tossed into the waste hand towel bin.

'You're going to have to move the *Courtesan*,' he told her, with more calm than he felt. 'You'll need to get it to the secondary location. And you're going to have to do it immediately. I'll send you details, but get yourself to St Pancras. Now. And take a big enough bag or suitcase.'

He had then texted her the location of the Sewells' cottage in Kent.

*They keep a spare key under the window box (pretty stupid, I know) and the package is in the wardrobe on the first floor. Call me when it's done.*

After he had sent it, Neil left the small, anonymous guest house where he was staying and headed to one of the cafés just off the Avenida Presidente Masaryk. There he whiled away an anxious two hours drinking strong Mexican coffee spiced with cinnamon.

Eventually, long after it had grown dark and the café was about to close, Tali sent him a message.

*I've got it. All okay. Heading back to London with it now. Will send new location details tomorrow.*

Neil felt a tidal wave of relief wash over him, and gestured to the waiter to bring him a glass of añejo, before replying simply: *Hope you remembered to use gloves.*

The police might make a trip to Mariner's Cottage at some

point, and while it made no difference whether Patsy couriered the package from there or another location, he couldn't risk the police getting there before she did and finding it. If a search was conducted, there was nothing to tie him to the place. He had used gloves when he'd stowed the painting, and had still been wearing them when he'd casually cased the top-floor bedroom and shoved the gold charm bracelet into his pocket.

To his mind, the plan was still viable; it just needed to be tweaked. Before things had gone awry, he had planned to tell Patsy that she needed to fetch something he'd left behind in Mariner's Cottage by mistake, and that she should bring it with her to Mexico, packed in one of her cases. There was no way that he and Tali, given their criminal records, could have risked travelling with it. But dear old Patsy was ditsy enough to do it, while still being squeaky clean in the eyes of the law. She didn't have so much as a speeding fine to her name: he had checked.

It had taken a while to work out what he was going to tell her was in this package. It couldn't look like a framed painting, either to her eyes or to the airport scanners. That was why he had chosen the *Courtesan*: for her high value relative to her size. He had had years of studying while in prison to do his research. Sure, there were more valuable paintings out there. Most coveted Impressionist paintings, for example, were worth double or even treble. The same with Modernists like Rothko. But most of them were too large to move around easily. Using the professional contacts he had made in the fine art packing business at Van Asbeck's, he had bought a hinged, clam-shell style archive box and adapted it so that it had a false bottom. *The Red Courtesan* was under the partition, in her corner protectors and glassine wrapping, and the top compartment was filled with the sort of documents people might want to take with them when they moved their life abroad: medical records, educational certificates, banking details. They were all counterfeit, naturally, but good enough to fool Patsy if she looked inside the box.

Or at least they would have been, if she hadn't already found out there was no such person as Casper Merriweather.

Would she look under the documents and find the partition? Almost certainly not: she was too scatty. Which was why she had been selected as the mark in the first place. More importantly, would she still be willing to bring the box out to Mexico with her, as he had originally intended her to do, knowing what she knew? Now that was the million-dollar question. Literally.

Like all con artists, Neil was essentially a gambler, and he was prepared to bet that she would. How was he so certain of this? Because whatever his real name was, the woman was completely infatuated with him. She adored him. She wrapped herself round him like a vine in bed, whispering in his ear that he was the best she'd ever had. That she couldn't get enough of him. And what else did she have in London? She no longer had a job: he'd taken care of that. And apart from an uneasy relationship with her parents, she had no one. She was incapable of a functional relationship with a man, because whenever she was stressed, she drank, and when she drank, she blacked out. The plan had been to push her and push her until she was backed into a corner with no way out, and it had succeeded. So, his Patsy would be on that plane to Mexico City in three days' time. He'd bet eleven million eight hundred thousand on it.

He took a swig of the amber spirit that had just been set down in front of him, and worked out what he would say in his next message to her.

# TWENTY-EIGHT

## HATTIE

When she woke up the morning after her abortive trip to Deal, Hattie felt calmer. She almost felt happy.

That was until she picked up her phone and saw a message from Neil Waller.

*All okay, babe? You've been a bit quiet! Just checking you are still coming? xxx*

Hattie copied and pasted it to Lewis in a panic.

*What should I say? Should I just ignore it?*

He replied immediately.

*Remember what McElwee told you? Act like everything's normal and your plan's going ahead. Remember, he has no idea that you know he's not Casper.*

Hauling herself to a sitting position, Hattie typed a message to Neil.

*Of course, can't wait to see you! xxx*

She climbed out of bed and went downstairs in search of tea, taking her phone with her. Before she had even reached the kitchen, Neil messaged her again.

*Great! Need you to pick up some stuff I left behind and bring it with you in your case (not in the hold). Here's the address xxx*

He had attached a location pin and a key code for a Mail Boxes Etc. just behind Waterloo Station, offering short-term luggage storage. Hattie set the kettle to boil and then phoned Lewis. She heard his intake of breath.

'This could be really huge, Hattie. Save everything he's sent you and show it to McElwee as quickly as you can. Phone them and let them know you're coming.' Despite his calm demeanour, the urgency in his voice was unmistakeable. 'You should try to get over there this morning.'

'Okay, sure,' Hattie told him. She poured boiling water into the teapot. 'As soon as I've got dressed, I'll head to Victoria Embankment, I promise.'

There was a slight pause, then Lewis said, 'Do you want me to come with you?'

'Yes.' She found herself smiling with relief. 'Yes, please.'

When DI McElwee saw the communication from Neil Waller, she became fractionally more animated, although still far from friendly.

She handed Hattie's phone to a detective constable who was with her, and instructed him to perform a trace on the number Waller was using. 'You'll get it back as soon as they've copied the details,' she told Hattie, with what almost looked like a smile. Then she stuck her head out into the corridor and barked at another constable to organise a pool car to take her and her sergeant to Mail Boxes Etc.

'It shouldn't take us long. We'll go on blues. Not much point you coming with us since we're only going to put what we find into an evidence bag and bring it straight back with us, but you're welcome to wait here.'

'Here' was the same meeting room where they had been a few days earlier.

A shy-looking young female PC appeared with a tray. There was a certain amount of fiddling around with coffee cups and saucers and fetching first milk, then biscuits. By the time they had been served and consumed their drinks, it was only a few minutes more before DI McElwee returned with one of her sergeants, carrying a large brown paper bag. She was followed by a smiling Nigel Hayes in another equally tight suit, his laptop tucked under his arm.

'I'm now officially assisting DI Jevons' team with the enquiry into Julian's death,' he told Hattie and Lewis. 'So Jill thought I might like to be here for this bit.'

McElwee set the bag down ceremoniously at the centre of the table and pulled on latex gloves. Then she slid out a matt black archive box that was about nine inches deep. Nigel, Hattie and Lewis all leaned forward to get a better view of what was inside. Hattie's heart dropped. It was just a pile of papers: what looked like certificates and bills. McElwee held up and examined each one, before handing it on to the DC to place in a separate clear plastic evidence bag.

Hattie exhaled and sat back. 'So no painting?'

'Wait!' McElwee barked, holding out her hand palm side up to the DC. He obediently placed what looked like a Stanley knife into it, and she slid it down the side of the empty box, wiggling it carefully along all the edges. Then, with a gesture of pure triumph, she lifted out a cardboard partition with the same dimension as the base of the box.

'The old false bottom trick,' she said drily. 'Hardly original.'

And then, with a flourish, she lifted out a paper-wrapped bundle, about twelve by eighteen inches. With exaggerated care, she unwrapped the paper and slipped off the cardboard corner protectors. And there it was. *The Red Courtesan.*

There was a communal exhalation of wonder.

'Oh wow,' said Lewis. 'It's so beautiful.'

The graceful geisha, her face powder white, looked coquettishly over the shoulder of her sumptuous red kimono as she fluttered a gilded fan. Hattie had seen images of the painting before – Neil had shown her the auction brochure – but the real thing was breath-taking.

Once they had all taken a good look, being prudent not to actually touch it, McElwee wrapped the painting carefully and told her DC to log it into the on-site evidence store. 'And put in a call to the auction house to let them know. See if you can get one of their experts over here to authenticate it. Quickly as possible.'

'Wow,' Hattie said, leaning back in her chair. 'So he really stole it.'

'Since his role at Van Asbeck's was to oversee the shipment of sold artefacts, then I imagine it would have been pretty straightforward for him to switch it with a copy,' McElwee said, adding drily, 'Especially for a man of his talents.'

'And he expected me to take it out to Mexico for him.' Hattie tipped her head back and stared up at the ceiling for a few seconds, blinking back tears. 'Do you think that was always his plan?'

Hayes pushed the plate of biscuits towards her. 'It's very likely, yes. He probably realised that by the time he boarded a plane, Van Asbeck's would likely have pointed the finger of suspicion at him, possibly even have found out who he really was. If he was going to have any chance of leaving the country scot-free, there was no way he could risk travelling with *The Red Courtesan* in his possession. You, on the other hand, well look at you...' It was obvious he was trying to make Hattie feel less awful, and she couldn't help liking him for that. 'There's no reason you'd be suspected, or searched.'

McElwee, on the other hand, was clearly not worried about how Hattie felt. 'Am I right in thinking Waller purchased a flight for you?' she demanded brusquely.

'Yes. But obviously I'm not going to be on it.'

'Here's the thing, Harriet—'

'Hattie,' she corrected him.

'The thing is, Hattie,' Hayes continued, 'We would very much like you to make the trip as planned. I have no doubt Waller does not plan to stay in Mexico longer than he needs to, because it has an extradition agreement with the UK. Not only do we want to charge him with the theft of the painting, but now that the investigation into Mr Cobbold's death is making headway, there are still questions for him to answer over that matter.'

Hattie frowned. 'Even though he wasn't there?'

'I can't say too much at this point,' Hayes said, assuming a professional poker face, 'but we now have reason to believe Waller was not working alone.'

She glanced at Lewis, but he remained impassive.

'What Waller wants – what he needs – is *The Red Courtesan*,' said McElwee. 'We suspect he's promised it to another collector in Mexico City. Now, we don't know what identity he's using, or where he is. In a city of twenty-two million people. That's almost equal to the entire population of the Australian continent. Even with the co-operation of the Mexican authorities, we're talking needles in haystacks. Yes, we have a mobile number for him, but that will be a temporary phone that he'll no doubt ditch when the pressure's on. However...' She tapped her fingers on the table in front of her. 'We have you. And if you have the painting, then you can lead us to him.'

Hattie glanced around her in bewilderment. 'But I'm not going to take it with me, surely, not now you've recovered it?'

'Yes, you are,' McElwee contradicted her, icy calm. 'You're going to fly to Mexico, and you're going to take *The Red Courtesan*.'

# PART THREE

# TWENTY-NINE

## NEIL

'It's a bit early,' Tali complained, when Neil FaceTimed her from Mexico the following morning.

On his phone screen, he could see a rumpled mess of bed linen and an equally rumpled Tali at the centre of it in vest and knickers, her face free of make-up and her hair looped up on her head in a wispy topknot.

'Jesus, we don't exactly have time to waste,' he said without sympathy. 'You really need to get packed up and get out of that place, before anyone comes calling. If Patsy's in the know, then how long before someone joins the dots and comes calling?'

'I told her it was Lewis Handley who finished off Cobbold, remember?' Tali said calmly. 'And I reckon she believed me.'

'That might buy us a bit of time, but no more than that.'

Tali climbed out of the bed, still holding her phone, and walked into the kitchen corner of the living room to switch on the kettle. The flat looked a lot more untidy than it did when Neil had been there. Not that it had ever been exactly homely, but it had served a purpose for a while. He and Tali had moved in there together when she had first reappeared in his life, so he would always look back on it with a certain nostalgia. But they were moving on to bigger and better things now. Much better things than a nondescript rented flat in a nondescript street near Tower Bridge.

Tali propped the phone on the worktop while she filled the coffee machine with water and reached into the fridge for milk.

'You need to get yourself on a plane to Mexico City as soon as you can, okay?' Neil told her. 'But not the British Airways one leaving Heathrow at around nine pm. Patsy's flying on that one with the package, and we can't risk you being on the same flight. If she sees you, it will blow the whole thing right out of the water.'

'Right, I've got it,' Tali said impatiently. He could hear a teaspoon being stirred vigorously in a mug, then she picked up the phone again. 'I'm just not quite sure what I'm supposed to do with all the stuff here.'

She had returned to the bedroom and flung open the doors of the fitted wardrobe.

'Obviously, the priority is to make sure there's nothing left behind that can identify us,' Neil said, exasperated. 'Other than that, just pack the absolute minimum. You'll be able to get new stuff here. Everything else, you can just bag up in bin liners and chuck in the dumpster round the back of the building.'

Tali had flipped the phone camera around so he was now looking at the contents of the wardrobe with her. She pulled out a dowdy dark blue raincoat on a hanger. 'Well, this is going straight in the dumpster,' she said with a little laugh. 'And so are these.'

She was pulling things off hangers now: shapeless calf-length skirts and suit jackets, cheap chain-store blouses that buttoned all the way to the neck. She reached onto a shelf and grabbed a spectacles case, giggling as she took out some thick-lensed glasses. Putting them on, she tied her hair back at the nape of her neck and flipped the camera to face Neil again. 'You always did fancy me like this, didn't you?' she smirked.

'That stuff's got to be the first to go,' Neil said, laughing back. 'You won't be needing any of it now. You don't need to be Bridget Dempsey ever again.'

# THIRTY

## NEIL – SIX MONTHS EARLIER

They had discussed at length what their perfect 'Patsy' would be like. They had even turned it into something of a game, discussing it as they lounged half naked on rumpled sheets after they had had sex, with Tali blowing cigarette smoke at the ceiling.

'It needs to be a female, don't you think?' Neil had said. 'They're generally easier to manipulate.'

Tali had pulled a face at this, but he ignored it and went on, 'Someone I can seduce and you can befriend. Ideally, they'll be fairly young, but not so young they confide everything to a parent or a sibling. Someone who's at a crossroads in their life, with no fixed direction.'

'A rudderless ship,' Tali had suggested.

'Exactly.' Neil had thrown her an admiring glance. She instinctively understood the assignment; of course she did. That was Tali. Her feel for these things was unparalleled.

They had agreed that they would keep their eyes open for the perfect target but take their time. It was important not to rush these things. The set-up had to be just right.

In the end, it was Neil who spotted her. He was doing the

rounds of the bars in Hoxton Square during the Christmas office party season: a rich hunting ground. He was in a basement bar fittingly called Oblivion when he saw her. 'Mixed Drinks and Mischief', the cocktail menu bragged, and it was clear that most of the punters were indulging in both.

This girl was very pretty. Her colouring was also similar to Tali's, which he instinctively sensed could prove useful. But it was not her looks that caught Neil's attention. Central London bars were full of pretty girls. No, it was her demeanour, which was both untrammelled and helpless. She had her back against the bar and some guy who appeared out of nowhere and clearly didn't know her was pressing himself against her and kissing her neck. She arched her back and giggled, but it was clear from the glazed expression in her eyes that she didn't really know what was happening. He slid his hand up her leg and under the hem of her skirt and she laughed uncertainly and made a half-hearted attempt to brush it away. It was obvious to the casual observer that she was already pretty drunk, but she accepted another drink just prepared by the barman: a violet-coloured concoction of some sort.

The man she was with watched her drink it, then steered her off in the direction of the bar's toilets. Taking a baseball cap from his pocket and pulling it low over his face, Neil followed at a discreet distance. The girl was led into the disabled cubicle and emerged a few minutes later, looking dazed and tugging up her underwear. The man followed and they exchanged a few words, after which she handed him her mobile and he entered his number into it. He then appeared to be trying to persuade her to have another drink, but she was shaking her head in an unfocused fashion. She retrieved her coat – a bright pink fake-fur number – from the cloakroom and staggered out into the street alone. Or at least, she was alone apart from Neil, who managed to stay out of sight. She swayed into the wall of the building, then doubled up and vomited a stream of violet-coloured liquid into the gutter, splashing her tights and shoes.

After this she must have sobered up slightly, because she managed to walk in a reasonably straight line to Shoreditch High Street, where she hailed a 26 bus. She climbed unsteadily onto the top deck, while Neil remained on the lower level. The bus took thirty minutes to reach Waterloo, where the girl clambered off. Since it was the last stop on the route, all the remaining passengers disembarked at the same time, allowing Neil to blend into the group as he followed his target into the station.

She stared blurrily at the huge departures board on the concourse before heading for the Portsmouth train on Platform 2. Neil swiped his Oyster card on the barriers and did the same, making sure to sit in the same carriage a few seats away. She got off at Summerlands, where the southern fringes of London merged into leafy Surrey. After walking straight out of the front of the station as though she was continuing on foot, she doubled back abruptly and jumped into a taxi waiting at the rank.

Frustrated at having lost her, Neil went to check the times of trains back to Waterloo, and seeing he would have to wait twenty minutes, crossed the road to buy himself a drink and a snack. As he emerged from the mini-mart a few minutes later, he spotted the same taxi the girl had hailed returning to the rank to pick up another fare. If it was back already, she couldn't have travelled very far. Reaching back into his pocket for his wallet, he tapped on the driver's window.

The window rolled down. 'Where to, guv?'

Neil explained that he didn't need a cab, just the address where he had taken his previous fare. The cabbie's reluctance was quickly overcome by two crisp twenty-pound notes pushed through the open window.

'12 Warner Avenue. But you didn't hear that from me.'

As he waited for the train back to London, Neil looked up

the address on Street View. A substantial but unremarkable family house. Did she live there with a husband? Seemed very unlikely given her age and the frankly sloppy way she had just behaved. Much more likely she still lived with her parents, and given her lifestyle choices, that was probably not a very comfortable arrangement on either side.

He typed a message to Tali.

*I've just found our Patsy. She's perfect.*

A period of concerted surveillance ensued.

They followed Patsy to work out her daily routine, starting early in the morning at the address that the taxi driver had given Neil. Two older adults would emerge around the same time, almost certainly the parents, and drive off in different directions. Patsy herself would walk to Summerlands station and catch a fast train into town, usually the 7.48. From Waterloo, she caught the tube to St John's Wood, where she was working in the offices of a construction company.

Her evening routine was a lot more unpredictable. In fact, you couldn't really call it a routine. She went out frequently and chaotically, to bars and clubs, occasionally meeting girlfriends, but more often a sequence of men on what appeared to be blind dates. Sometimes she would disappear with them to hotels or their flats, often staying out all night. At other times, she would weave her way back to Waterloo and take a late train. What eventually emerged after a week or so was that if she was going straight home from work, she almost always caught the non-stop 18.53 Portsmouth service.

It was on one of these evenings, in mid-February, that Neil and Tali arranged the 'meet cute'. Neil had by now been employed at Van Asbeck's using the name Casper Merriweather and falsifying his references, and Tali had dreamed up the persona of mousy civil servant Bridget Dempsey, who only drank tea, did not date and had chronic health problems. They waited near Platform 2, and, sure enough, 'Patsy' appeared, looking frankly rough. She was obviously hungover after one of her casual encounters the night before. Following her into the third carriage of the train, they waited until she had found a seat and took up two of the free seats nearby, with Neil – irresistible as the suave, urbane Casper – opposite her.

The plan had been that 'Casper' would strike up a conversation and 'Bridget' would arrange to bump into her later once they arrived in Summerlands and were leaving the station. Once they had been introduced, she would make sure that she encountered Hattie on the way to work in the morning and strike up a friendship, gaining her confidence and pushing her to take a romantic interest in Casper. This was not as straightforward as it sounded, because in order to join Patsy for her morning commute, Tali first had to travel down to Summerlands from Tower Hill. This involved a very early alarm and a Waterloo train leaving no later than 6.15.

As it turned out, they had some good luck on their side that night when the train stopped for a while because of a sick passenger. They all fell easily into conversation over drinks, and Casper officially began his wooing of Patsy. Or Hattie Sewell, as they discovered she was really called. They also found themselves with a ready-made villain in the shape of the tattooed and somewhat taciturn Lewis Handley. He would come in useful as a misdirect.

But there was also some bad luck in the mix that evening. Because among their number was one Julian Cobbold QC. And Julian would become a problem. A big problem.

# THIRTY-ONE

## HATTIE

'Hold on: let me get this straight.'

Lewis looked across the boardroom table, from DCI Hayes to DI McElwee and back again. There was a challenging tone in his voice that Hattie had never heard before. For the first time, she saw him as the Special Branch officer rather than a hip, tattooed guy with a photogenic dog.

'You expect Hattie here to fly to Mexico City alone and meet with this man to lure him into some sort of fine art honey trap?'

'Exactly,' McElwee was deadpan.

'Isn't that putting her at risk?'

'Waller is a prolific conman, but he's never been involved in any sort of violence.' Hayes said patiently. 'As you said your-selves, there's still no direct evidence to link him to Cobbold's death. Trust me, he's just interested in the money.'

McElwee managed a regretful shrug. 'My unit is only six people strong, and I can't spare anyone from other active enquiries at such short notice. Not given you're due to travel tonight. Ideally, yes, we'd have someone accompany you, but we can't raise suspicion by delaying your travel, and it takes time to free up an officer.'

Hayes gave Lewis and Hattie what he clearly hoped was a reassuring smile. 'What DI McElwee's team has managed to arrange is for someone from the local equivalent of the FBI – the Policia Federal Ministerial – to make contact with you as soon as you arrive and tell you exactly what you need to do. Not, as I've said, that I believe you're in any danger. You're just the intermediary who's being used to courier the painting. Once you've handed it to Waller, he's not going to be interested in you anymore. Remember, he still believes he's Casper Merriweather to you. Just behave as you always have done towards him, and you'll be fine. Okay? As long as he believes you've been taken in, you're not in any danger.'

'Okay,' said Hattie, with more confidence than she felt.


Hattie had told her parents she was leaving for Heathrow at seven, and they both planned to be home from work in time to wish her bon voyage.

But after her meeting at New Scotland Yard, she decided she would need to sneak away earlier and avoid an in-person farewell. She had never been any good at concealing her feelings or pretending, and they would quickly realise from her demeanour that something was very wrong when it came to her glamorous new life abroad with her boyfriend. They would try to stop her from going. And how on earth could she explain to them that she had a priceless Japanese masterpiece surrounded by her underwear at the centre of her hand luggage?

A uniformed officer in a police squad car dropped off the painting at her house about three hours after her return from Victoria Embankment, with instructions from McElwee to leave it in its black cardboard archive box when she packed it. By then it was five o'clock, and Hattie left a note for her parents and caught a cab to the station, taking a train to Hounslow and then the tube to Terminal 5. Feeling queasy with nerves, she checked in her large suitcase and, pulling her carry-on case containing the painting, queued to get through security. She headed straight for a bar in Departures, where she ordered a double brandy.

'Room for a little one?'

A shadow fell across the table, making her jump. She looked up into the face of Lewis Handley.

'What the—?' Her voice came out as a squeak. 'Why are you here? Did DI McElwee send you?' Her heart started to pound. Perhaps the police had decided she was not up to perpetrating this deception, even though *The Red Courtesan* was a few feet away in her cabin bag.

Lewis dropped his backpack on the ground and sat down opposite her, picking up her brandy glass and sniffed at it.

'I don't like flying,' she said defensively.

He raised an eyebrow, before taking in a long breath. 'Listen... I suppose you could say that indirectly McElwee's responsible for me being here. I know the Met is struggling with understaffing, and I know there's law enforcement on the ground over there waiting for you, but even so... I just didn't feel comfortable with the idea of you going out there by yourself. We've no idea what Waller will do.'

'He would never hurt me,' Hattie insisted.

'You could argue that he already has.'

'No, he hasn't. Trust me, I'm fine.' She jutted her chin, giving him a forced smile.

'How about the time he spiked your drink?'

'What do you mean?' Her expression changed abruptly.

'Don't tell me you've already forgotten. The night before your job interview when you went out with him. And I scraped you up off the station platform the next morning covered in your own puke.'

'We don't know that was him.' Hattie knew what Lewis was saying was logical, yet still she couldn't bring herself to believe him. 'It could have been anyone in that bar.'

His response was just to shake his head.

'He's not who you think he is.' Realising this sounded absurd, she corrected herself: 'He's not how you think he is. When he was with me in private, he was so...' She let her voice trail off, taking a sip of the brandy and enjoying the way it burned the back of her throat.

Lewis flung her a sceptical look, but said merely, 'You shouldn't drink that on an empty stomach. I'll get you something to eat.'

He returned a few minutes later with sandwiches for them both and sat down again, removing the denim jacket he was wearing. As they ate, Hattie stared at the tattoos on his forearms, trying to decipher the intricate design of birds and flowers. By the time they had finished, the departure board was telling them that their gate was open, and they walked there together. Assuming they were a couple, the cabin crew member in charge of boarding switched the seating assignment so that they were next to each other.

'So has he made contact since I saw you earlier? Waller?' Lewis asked as he pushed his backpack into the locker and took his seat.

Hattie buckled her seat belt. 'I haven't heard anything since he sent the location of the storage locker. I don't even know for certain that he's still in Mexico City.'

Lewis was glancing around the cabin, taking in their position in relation to all the other passengers.

'What's wrong?' Hattie asked him.

'It's just occurred to me that we should probably have turned down the kind offer of seats next to each other. If Waller's there to meet you, then it's probably not a good idea for us to be disembarking together. I mean, if he sees me, then he's almost certainly going to twig that you know something.'

'I suppose so.'

He looked at her intently. 'Look, Hattie, you haven't told anyone what's going on... your parents or your sister or anyone?'

'No, no one. Oh no, hang on,' she said abruptly. Despite eating the sandwich Lewis had bought, the brandy had gone to her head, making her feel muzzy and muddled. 'Yes. Yes, I did tell someone. When we first found out, I did send a WhatsApp message to Bridget.'

'Bridget?' Lewis snorted. 'The virgin spinster? I guess she's pretty safe. I mean, who the hell is she going to tell? Her cat?'

'I don't think she has a cat.'

'You know what I mean. She's a semi-recluse who doesn't drink and rarely goes out. I think we're safe.'

After sitting on the stand for some time while a delay over someone's luggage was dealt with, the aircraft finally pushed back and started its long, steady cruise to the start of the runway.

Hattie looked out of the window at the traffic flashing past on the M4. 'I'm still going to have to pretend to Casper though. Waller. You know, that everything is fine. And I'm a rubbish actress.' She took the heated towel she was being offered and wiped her sweaty hands.

Lewis laughed, then his face took on a more serious expression. 'Look: painful as it might be, Waller isn't really interested in you. All he wants is the painting. And that's exactly what he's going to get.'

# THIRTY-TWO

## NEIL

Neil walked the still dark streets for nearly half an hour before he found a café that was open at 5 a.m.

Having downed a strong black coffee and eaten some *pan dulce*, he caught the metro into the city centre, changing onto Line 5, which took him straight to the airport. Hattie was on the British Airways flight which had recently landed. Not that he was going to meet her: quite the opposite. He needed to avoid her. But he calculated that by the time he reached Terminal Aérea, she would have cleared passport control and collected her luggage. Only when he was sure she had done that would he risk contacting her.

And she would do what he asked of her, he knew that. She might know who he really was, but she would be prepared to pretend she didn't. She would play the game. And as long as she was playing the game, she could be manipulated. She still wanted him, he was sure of it.

At the beginning, she had wanted him very much. Her desire for him, in combination with her tendency to messiness, had made her very easy to seduce. And much as he had pretended to Tali that it was all part of the job, he had really enjoyed the physical intimacy with Hattie. She was both passionate and abandoned, and he found this abandon intoxicating, especially in contrast to Tali, who was so controlled at all times. The irony was that Hattie was usually so drunk she had no idea how good the sex between them really was. The next day she usually couldn't even remember it.

That was one of many reasons he hadn't been prepared to throw away money on the girl; not more than was strictly necessary. He'd already been forced to invest money on Casper's wardrobe; clothes that made him look like a man of means. There was not much cash left over to spare on fancy hotels and cars. He'd told Hattie that he drove an Audi, but conveniently when he was with her it was always in the garage being valeted or having work done on it, and he just hired a car when he needed one. Again, she wasn't sober enough most of the time to pick up on this.

It had also been highly satisfying to discover that she had lost a good job as a direct result of her flakiness and was reduced to doing temporary work. This reinforced her profile as the perfect candidate to do *his* bidding. But then she had a fit of either conscience or maturity and started hunting for another permanent position. This risked her becoming rooted to a normal London routine and unable or unwilling to courier the painting he had planned to steal. He and Tali had their mugshots on the police database, so it was too risky for them to do it.

That was where 'Bridget' had proved especially useful. She had found out the date of the all-important job interview, allowing him to take Hattie out for drinks the night before. And yes, for once she had vowed to be sensible and stick to a minimal amount, but a few drops of GHB in her red wine was all that was required to render her incapable of getting herself into town on time the next day.

Annoyingly, she had made it on time, aided by that irritant Lewis Handley. He clearly fancied her, though she was too ditsy to see it. No matter, there was still a second interview to screw up. It had been simple enough to arrange a weekend away to clash with it. As Neil had pointed out to her at the time, if the employers were keen, they would reschedule it. It turned out they were keen, because they emailed to offer an alternative time while he and Hattie were on the A3, en route to Oakley Grange. Seeing the notification flash up on her phone, which was resting in one of the cupholders in the car's cockpit, he had announced that they needed to fill up with petrol. He made sure to pull in with the fuel pump positioned on Hattie's side of the vehicle, and because she was an obliging sort of girl, she offered to fill the tank. He'd overheard her drunkenly repeating her phone passcode out loud several times, so it had been easy enough to unlock the phone and delete all trace of the email. Job done. Or rather, job over. Back to temping, which Hattie hated. Not difficult to sell the delights of Mexico City to someone working in a third-rate branding agency in some down-at-heel part of London.

She could easily have got herself a much better job, if only she'd had the chutzpah to embellish her CV a little. God knows, that strategy had worked spectacularly for him. When he was in HMP Berwyn, he'd mugged up on Photoshop and InDesign while studying for his History of Art degree. It was the easiest thing in the world to mock up some fancy-looking references, complete with fake email accounts for the referees, which in turn would generate glowing testimonials for Casper Merri-weather in the event that Van Asbeck's made further enquiries. He'd been to private school after all, if only briefly, so he knew how to dress the part, how to talk. Easy enough to invent some shiny-sounding experience in New York. And the role could not have been more perfect. As consignments manager, he was in charge of the coming and going of massively valuable works of art. It also meant that he was line manager to Phil Simmons, the registrar in charge of the shipping of all sold lots.

And Phil Simmons, a man on the verge of retirement who was fond of a tipple, was a piece of cake to manipulate. After a few fingers of the single malt Neil plied him with, he would fall asleep at his desk. Simple enough then to replace the packaged *Red Courtesan* with a copy and take the original home with him in a large backpack he had bought for the purpose. The copy was shipped off to Mexico with Phil Simmons none the wiser. By the time the theft came to light and the finger of suspicion turned inevitably towards 'Casper', he had left the job and thrown away his phone. The home address on his CV had been fake too, of course. Embarrassingly, the management at Van Asbeck's were forced to admit that they had no idea who this man was or where he had gone.

Once he was in Terminal 1, Neil put on one of his many baseball caps and a set of shades. And it was just as well he took this precaution because there, walking out of the Arrivals doors, was Hattie. Her flight must have been delayed, or there must have been a problem with the unloading of baggage, because by his calculations she should have already cleared the airport by now. He tugged the hat down more firmly and turned at an angle so that most of his face was obscured.

Then he spotted another familiar figure walking out of the sliding doors a few metres behind Hattie, and his heart rate quickened. Lewis Handley. What the fuck was he doing here? Were the two of them an item now? And if so, who the hell did they think they were fooling by keeping their distance like that?

Neil retreated to one of the coffee concessions in the arrivals hall, and waited until the coast was clear. Taking out one of his phones, he composed a message. Only then did he check the arrivals board again, and position himself by the doors. Tali's flight was about to land.

# THIRTY-THREE

## HATTIE

Despite Lewis's warnings about dehydration, Hattie drank all the wine that was offered with the in-flight meal.

She did so because she was desperate to sleep and, eventually, a few hours before landing, she fell into a shallow doze. The next thing she was aware of was Lewis nudging her arm and saying, 'Wake up! We're in Mexico.'

A few minutes later, they stood, groggy and disorientated, by a baggage carousel in the cavernous terminal building.

'Anything?' he asked

Hattie checked her phone. 'No messages yet. I don't think I have service yet.'

'Try phoning him.'

She did as she was told, only to be greeted by a message telling her '*numero fuera de servicio*'. She handed her phone over to Lewis, who frowned.

'Waller's probably switched phones to remain untraceable. Let's hope he breaks cover soon, or we're going to end up with crashing jet lag for nothing.'

Sure enough, just as they had walked through the arrivals

hall and headed for the taxi queue, her phone pinged with a message from an unknown number.

*Sorry, angel, lost my phone! This is my new one. I've got a reservation at the Intercontinental in Polanco. Head there and I'll catch up with you shortly. Hope you remembered to bring my document box! xxx*

Hattie showed the message to Lewis, who held it up in front of his own phone and took a photo of it. 'Old cop habit,' he told her. 'We're taught to have a record of everything. Anyway,' he added drily as he handed Hattie's phone back, 'at least we'll have an address to give the taxi driver. Right now I just want to have a nap without my knees being up around my chest.'

'Should I reply?' she asked as they reached the front of the queue and climbed into the back of one of the city's distinctive bright pink and white cabs.

'Definitely,' Lewis told her. 'McElwee said you need to behave as if everything is completely normal. And, presumably, if you didn't know what you know, you'd be desperate to see "Casper" at this point.' He put sardonic air quotes around the name.

Hattie sighed, and closed her eyes briefly, before beginning to type.

*Yes, I have the box. Hope you won't be long: can't wait to see you xxx*

As the taxi merged onto the city's inner ring road amid frantic, honking traffic, another text arrived.

*Just got to take care of a bit of business. See you soon, babe xxx*

'Probably best not to say anything else,' Lewis told her when he'd read it. 'Let's keep our tinder dry until at least we've spoken to your Mexican police contact.'

Hattie checked in at the Intercontinental and after she had collected her key for room 904, she and Lewis got into the lift.

When they reached the ninth floor, however, Lewis beckoned her away from the door marked 904, and jerked his head in the direction of the emergency exit.

'You're not staying here,' he said firmly. 'It's much too risky for him to know where you are.'

'So I'm checking out?'

Lewis shook his head, helping her wheel her case onto the staircase. 'No. We still need Waller to think you're staying here. We'll go and find a room somewhere else. We passed a place a few hundred yards back that looked okay.'

Too tired to argue, Hattie dragged her case all the way down eighteen flights of stairs and they walked in blindingly bright morning sunshine to the Contempo Suites Hotel. It was a stolidly three-star place: clean and corporate with box-like rooms furnished in shades of grey and brown. Lewis checked in too, requesting to be put on the same floor as Hattie. They agreed that they would shower and try to get some sleep before doing anything else.

'Put the chain on, and don't open the door to anyone, okay. Not without phoning me first,' Lewis instructed her. 'And once you've checked that the painting's okay, hide it somewhere: in the room safe if it's big enough and if not, under the mattress or something.'

It was bizarre, Hattie thought as she unpacked, that along with her knickers and toiletries her cabin bag contained a painting worth nearly twelve million pounds. The sum was difficult for her to get her head around. Not that it seemed possible that Waller would be able to realise the value of *The*

*Red Courtesan* now, since it was far too well known to put up for sale.

She asked Lewis about this a few hours later when they met in the hotel bar.

'Yeah, I've been thinking about that too,' Lewis said as he downed a bottle of beer and ate a handful of salted nuts. 'One thing we do know about Waller is that he plans ahead. A long way ahead. I reckon he has something worked out already when it comes to realising the painting's value. Or something close to it.'

'Okay, so what happens now? Look...' Hattie showed him a series of missed calls from Waller. 'I'm just pretending to be asleep, but at some point soon he's going to go to room 904 at the Intercontinental.'

'Exactly.' Lewis flipped a few nuts into his open mouth. 'He's desperate to get his hands on the painting, which means we don't have time to waste. I've told Hayes I'm here with you now, and he's made contact with the guy from the Policia Federal Ministerial. He should be here any minute now.'

Sure enough, a few seconds later, a handsome, well-dressed man came into the bar and walked straight over to their table, introducing himself as Hector Mejia. He had soulful dark eyes, black hair swept back off a square forehead and a neatly trimmed goatee. He took off his dark green bomber jacket, draping it over the back of his chair, and pushed up his shirt-sleeves to reveal deeply tanned forearms.

'Okay, so this is where we are.' Mejia's English was fluent, with a faint American accent. 'Our target does not know you are both here at this hotel, correct? You are sure about this?'

'Waller doesn't even know I'm in Mexico City,' Lewis explained. 'And he thinks that Hattie is staying in the room he reserved for her in the Intercontinental, here in Polanco. She checked in there, just to be sure.'

'Good,' Mejia nodded. 'I'll arrange to get the Intercontinental under surveillance straight away.' He pulled out his phone and spoke rapidly into it in Spanish, before turning to Hattie. 'Do you know if he has a key to the hotel room himself?'

'I don't think so.' Hattie thought back. 'I filled out a new registration form, and the desk clerk offered me two keys.'

'If he has a key or does not have a key, we will still be aware if he goes there now my men are in place,' Mejia said, with a little shrug. 'But what we need to prosecute him for grand theft is to catch Waller in possession of the painting. And, with no key, he has to be sure you are already in the room.'

'He's been trying to call me, several times,' Hattie said. 'If he could get into the room, he would probably just show up.'

'Hang on though,' Lewis held up a hand. 'Waller might be able to persuade the reception desk to give him a key to the room, given it was him who made the reservation. And if he goes up and finds it empty, he's going to know he's been stung. He might run.'

Mejia frowned, stroking his beard. 'Okay, so we can't afford to waste time. This is what we will do... call him straight away and speak to him. Arrange to meet him there, at the other hotel, at a specific time. Assure him he can have the painting. And then let me know immediately. By then, we will have the relevant agents in place. Okay?'

'Okay,' Hattie said weakly, glancing at Lewis.

'But whatever you do, don't see him alone, not without informing me first.' Mejia pushed his business card across the table. 'You must let me know what is happening, every step of the way. This is most important.'

# THIRTY-FOUR

## NEIL

'Not exactly what you were expecting?'

Tali curled her lip and gave a little shudder. They were sitting on the tiny balcony of a run-down building in the impoverished barrio of Tepito, overlooking streets strewn with rubbish and a crowded open-air market packed with stalls shaded by ragged canvas awnings. There was a smell of cooking onions and bad drains. It was only a few kilometres south of Polanco, but it might as well have been a different country. But this, as Neil explained to Tali, was the whole point.

'That's one reason for coming here to Mexico City. To a metropolis the size of a nation state. They'll never find us here. And in a place like this...' he pointed back into the dirty, two-room apartment he had rented, 'whatever we do, nobody's going to ask any questions. Or if they do, a few hundred pesos will shut them up.'

'But we're not staying here? In Mexico?' Tali frowned at him.

He shook his head. 'No way. Too dangerous. We're only here because our buyer is here. As soon as we've offloaded the *Courtesan*, we're heading straight to Honduras. Great climate,

Caribbean sea and – most importantly – a totally inefficient law and order system and no extradition arrangement with the UK. We're untouchable once we get there.'

'I see,' Tali said coldly. 'This is what you've decided?'

'Babe, we don't really have an option. We have to go somewhere the British authorities can't pursue us, and trust me, Honduras is the best option. They have offshore islands with beautiful white sand beaches and loads of water sports. With the money we're about to make, we'll be able buy a great property and live like kings.'

'*If* we get the money.'

'We'll get the money. Now go and put on something sexy, and let's get going. The soon-to-be owner of *The Red Courtesan* is expecting us.'


The house was an extraordinary edifice of wood, steel and stone, like a modern imagining of a Japanese samurai castle. A swimming pool completely encircled the structure like a moat, and was surrounded in turn with lush green tropical gardens.

'Wow!' Neil said simply when he saw it. He had parked his rental car at the kerb of a broad, tree-lined avenue in Lomas de Chapultepec, an affluent neighbourhood that bordered Polanco. At first, the building was hidden from view behind a large metal security gate, but when Neil pressed the intercom buzzer and announced himself, it slid back to reveal a home that must have been worth many millions of dollars.

'Have I got this right?' Tali asked as they stood taking in their surroundings. She was dressed in a blue silk shift dress and long gold earrings, her hair freshly washed and curled. 'The guy who lives here is the one who made the successful bid for *The Red Courtesan* in the London auction? The one who paid for it?'

'You have,' Neil said. He sounded calm, but his pulse was

racing and he was sweating, despite being dressed in a white linen shirt and lightweight cotton chinos. They were close to the end game now, but there was so much at stake. So many things that could go wrong. They walked up the drive, watched closely by an armed security guard. 'He's called Ricardo Velasco. One of the richest men in Mexico. His family own copper mines and a railway company, and he's worth about twenty billion US dollars.'

'But if he's already paid nearly twelve million for the painting, why would he buy it all over again?' Tali asked.

'It's simple,' Neil smiled smugly. 'To save face. The guy at Van Asbeck's who dealt with him directly told me he was buying it as a surprise gift for his much younger third wife. She's obsessed with Japanese art, and with Hokusai in particular, and he'd already bragged about how he was going to acquire it for her collection. I also happen to know from handling the sale that he took out worldwide all-risks insurance cover prior to it being shipped. "All risks" includes theft. So he will have got a good chunk of the twelve million back from his insurers anyway. And as we're going to sell it back to him for a lot less, he won't have lost much. It's pocket change to him, and he gets to make his wife very happy.'

They climbed a flight of wide, pale stone steps to a huge vertically panelled door. Modern sculptures hung in front of it, and to either side were double-height screens of glass. A maid admitted them through a long hallway that featured some exquisite Japanese art and into a large, open room with enormous windows and fitted ebony bookcases. The only furnishings were oversized sofas covered in tan suede.

'Are you sure he doesn't know who you are?' Tali whispered, as the maid poured them glasses of water and retreated.

Neil shrugged. 'I suppose by now he may have been told that I'm the prime suspect in the theft. But look, the terms of the insurance policy will have been that if *The Red Courtesan* is officially recovered, he has to reimburse the pay-out it if he wants to retain the painting. Otherwise, the insurers are the legal owners. We're allowing him to keep it at a healthy discount. So why should he care?'

There were footsteps on the sculptural ebony and steel staircase, so Neil lowered his voice. 'Anyway, men like him don't like getting the police involved in their affairs. They've always got far too much to hide.'

Right on cue, a short, heavyset man of about fifty entered the room. His grey hair was slicked back with gel, and he wore bulky gold chains and an enormous gold watch. He gave Tali a courtly little bow and extended a thick-fingered hand to Neil.

'Mr Smith.' The tone of his voice implied quote marks around the surname.

'Good to meet you,' Neil said smoothly. 'Can I just say what a wonderful home you have.'

'Let's cut the bullshit,' Velasco growled. He had the unidentifiable accent of someone with an international lifestyle. 'I want my painting back. That's all I want to talk about. If you're straight with me, I'm happy to overlook exactly how it came into your possession. If you're not...' He simply glanced in the direction of the security guard, who had appeared in the hall and had his hand on the gun in his holster.

'Ten million US dollars,' Neil said crisply. Despite the fierce air conditioning, he could feel sweat prickling at the back of his neck. 'Directly into my numbered account. I think that's more than fair.'

There was a coffee table measuring about eight feet square in the centre of the room. Velasco stood up and took a cigar from a box on its glass surface and lit it. 'And you've got the *Courtesan* with you?'

'It's arrived here in Mexico City, yes.' Tali smiled at him with a warmth that bordered on coquettishness and was intended to mask the half-truth.

Velasco gave a non-committal shrug. 'Without it, we can't take our discussion any further. Obviously, I'll need to see it in person before we agree on a sum. Bring it here, and let me have my art broker examine it, and if I'm happy, I'll transfer the funds.'

As soon as they were out of sight of the house, Tali gave a little whoop and held up her hand for a high five. 'So all we have to do is get the painting from Patsy and bring it here.'

'I'll message her when we get back.'

'And don't forget you still have to come off all lovey-dovey. We know that she knows you're not Casper, but she doesn't know that we know she knows.'

Tali laughed at this tongue-twister, as though she relished the multiple layers of deceit, adding cheerily, 'When you said that art theft was where the money was, back when I got out of HMP Eastwood Park, I never realised it would be this easy.'

'Hardly easy,' Neil reminded her darkly. 'Remember what we had to do to get to this point.'

No one was supposed to get hurt.

That was what everyone committing crimes always said, wasn't it? But in Neil's case it was true. After being bullied and beaten up as a posh kid in a rough comprehensive, he was repulsed by violence of any sort.

But after months of painfully planning and executing their plan, there seemed to be no other solution to the problem that was Julian Cobbold. The problem had become apparent when he spotted Julian at the auction of the *Courtesan* . A coincidence, surely, Casper reassured himself. The barrister was successful and well-connected, and undoubtedly had wealthy friends. There was nothing too surprising about him coming along to a high-profile auction in Mayfair. People often treated them as a spectacle, and attended without any intention of making a bid. It was sheer coincidence that he happened to turn his head at the exact second Julian took the empty champagne glass Neil had been drinking from and slipped it into his jacket pocket. And there was only one reason he could possibly have wanted to do that. To have it tested for DNA. DNA which would be identified on the police database as belonging to one Neil Waller, convicted criminal.

By way of confirmation, only a couple of hours later, Hugo Barker – the senior partner who was conducting the auction – stopped him in the corridor.

'Nice chap, that contact of yours. QC chappie.'

Neil had plastered on a smooth smile. 'Julian? Yes, yes, he is a nice guy. Not that I know him all that well.'

'Yes, that's what I thought. He was asking a lot of questions about you; where you come from and your experience and so on. Things one assumes he would have known if you were more than passing acquaintances.'

Neil didn't have time to worry about the veiled accusation in what Barker had just said. Because a thought had just occurred to him. He remembered Julian mentioning that he'd had a son who would have been in his twenties if he'd been alive. A boy who could very easily have had a copy of *Dastardly Tales for Daring Boys*: he was the right age. Was it a memory of the name from that book that made Julian suspicious? Very possibly. But it was the secreting of the champagne glass in his pocket that was the definitive proof. Julian Cobbold knew too much.

Neil's plan had been to try to find something he could use to blackmail Julian with, but Tali dismissed it. They didn't have time for that, she had insisted. There was only a small window before Neil's true identity was discovered. Julian had to go before he had the chance to raise the alarm. Putting potassium cyanide in his vape pen had been her idea. Before she met him, Tali had had a temporary job in a hospital pharmacy, and she and one of her colleagues used to steal restricted drugs and sell them on the street. She contacted the former colleague now, and within hours – for a sum that cleared out nearly all the cash they had – acquired a small vial of cyanide.

Julian was overweight and unfit: in a man of his age, it would just look like a heart attack, Tali had assured Neil. Her confidence throughout had been unnerving. The vape would have to be doctored by her, in case Julian had already voiced his concerns about Casper. So Neil had been 'working late' on that day at the beginning of April, and Bridget had been sitting next to Julian on the train. It was easy enough for her to lift the vape pen from his coat pocket where he always kept it, and drop it into her bag. Then when she and Hattie went to fetch drinks from the buffet car, she had claimed the need to use the toilet, and poured a few drops into the liquid chamber of the pen. Then it was only a matter of slipping it back into Julian's pocket and waiting for him to use it, which he invariably did at some point during the evening journey.

It went like clockwork. Julian was dead, apparently of a cardiac arrest, and Casper Merriweather was nowhere near him when it happened. By the time the post-mortem had been formally reported, an inquest held and the findings passed from the British Transport Police to the Met, Neil had been en route to Mexico. And Bridget – mousy unassuming Bridget – had vanished into thin air.

# THIRTY-FIVE

## HATTIE

Once their meeting with Mejia was over and they were back at the hotel, Hattie tried to phone Waller's new number. There was no reply. But minutes later, she received a text

*All sorted! Will be with you in time for breakfast tomorrow morning. Keep the bed warm! Can't wait, angel girl xxx*

As instructed, she phoned Mejia as soon as she received it.

'This is good. Tell him you'll see him in the morning,' Mejia told her. 'Did he say what time he would be at the Intercontinental?'

'He just says "in time for breakfast". I guess that could mean anything from seven to ten.'

There was a silence the other end, and Hattie could sense Mejia thinking.

'Okay,' he said eventually. 'I think you need to go over to there tonight. We can't afford to make the mistake of arriving too late. Get together whatever you need just for tonight, and my officers will come and fetch you from your current hotel in a few hours. The tactical team will stay in position at the hotel and wait for Waller to arrive. As soon as you hand over the painting, they'll arrest him. Clear, yes?'

'Yes,' Hattie agreed. She made herself sound calm, but as she cut the call, her hands were shaking. She walked down the hall and knocked on Lewis's door. He was wearing boxers and a T-shirt, and had a toothbrush in his hand.

Hattie gave him a hurried update. 'Fancy a margarita? I need one to settle my nerves.'

'One second.' Lewis pulled on his jeans, grabbed his room key and they took the lift down to the bar. While they were waiting for the barman to mix their cocktails, Lewis rested his hand briefly on hers. 'Want me to come and wait in your room for the Policia Federal to show up?'

Two icy glasses were set down in front of them, and Hattie took a long, grateful draft of the sour liquid. She shook her head. 'No, it's all right. You were obviously on your way to bed. Hector and his men will take good care of me, I'm sure.'

'I doubt you'll get much sleep.'

'Probably not.' Hattie took another gulp of her margarita and tried to sound cheerful. 'But look on the bright side: this will all be over in a few hours. We'll be able to get a flight back to London tomorrow night and get on with our lives. I, for one, can't wait.' Her glass was almost empty, and she waved at the barman to make her a second.

'Want another?'

Lewis shook his head. 'They taste like they're pretty much all tequila. One is plenty for me.'

Hattie swallowed down the fresh drink in a few gulps, and they headed back to the lift. He was right: the margaritas were extremely strong, and by the time she reached her room, the combination of alcohol and jet lag was making her woozy and un-coordinated. All she wanted to do was to lie down on the bed, but she couldn't. She had to stay awake for a little while longer. She pulled the painting in its black box from the top shelf of the wardrobe where she'd hidden it under spare blankets, and placed it on the bed in readiness. Then she pulled out her small carry-on bag and tried to decide what she needed to put in it.

*Focus*, she told herself sternly. *You can do this. Not much longer.*

She tried to stay awake, she really did, but after a couple of hours, it was impossible to fight off sleep any longer and she dozed off on the bed next to her packed bag, fully dressed.

A loud rap on the door woke her with a start. Hector Mejia and his agents were here to escort her to the Intercontinental. Still in a daze, Hattie stumbled to the door and tugged it open.

Without giving her time to collect her thoughts, two people rushed into the room dressed in dark clothing and with faces obscured by what looked like rubber Halloween masks. Combining force and the advantage of surprise, they knocked Hattie backwards onto the carpet. Half asleep and slightly tipsy, she couldn't even open her mouth before a gloved hand was clamped firmly over it to prevent her from crying out, and handcuffs were snapped round her wrists.

The second, smaller figure picked up her cabin bag and started going through it, pulling things out and tossing them onto the floor. Finding her wallet and her passport, he pushed them into the pocket of his trousers. Was that what this was about? Hattie thought, straining against the first man's hand. Was she being robbed?

Then a familiar voice hissed, 'Make absolutely sure you leave her phone here. And better check the bathroom. Make sure Handley's not in there.'

It was him. Of course it was.

She tried to protest, but her mouth was roughly prised open and a cloth gag forced into it. He snatched up the black box containing *The Red Courtesan* and then hauled her to her feet, pushing her out onto the corridor and propelling her towards the fire escape door. From there, she was half pushed, half pulled down to the basement parking garage and shoved onto the back seat of a car. It screeched out onto the darkened street at high speed and took off at speed. Everything had happened so fast. If only, Hattie thought, bitterly. If only she had accepted Lewis's offer to wait in her room with her. But it was too late. Far too late.

Raising her cuffed hands to her face, Hattie managed to tug the cloth gag from her mouth and wrench her legs round so that she was in a half-sitting position. 'Neil,' she gasped. 'What the fuck are you doing? You were supposed to come to the Intercontinental.'

'What, and be picked up by the Mexican police?' He laughed bitterly. 'You surely don't think I'm that stupid.'

'But how did you know I was at the Contempo?'

Neil pulled off his mask and as he turned to face her, he was smiling that charming smile of his. 'Seriously, babe? I've had a geolocation app tracking your phone for weeks.'

The other person, who was driving, said nothing. After they had been driving for about fifteen minutes, through successively grimier and more run-down neighbourhoods, the car came to a stop in a narrow alley next to a row of rickety buildings. Hattie was dragged from the car and up two flights of stairs before being pushed into a dark, foetid-smelling room and onto a mattress on the floor. A bottle was pushed to her lips and she was forced to drink what looked like water but had a bitter, metallic taste to it.

Only now did the second person pull off their mask, slowly and deliberately while looking straight at Hattie. A sharp stab of adrenaline surged through her as she recognised the face, jolting her – if only briefly - into the present moment. Goosebumps stood up on her arms and she shivered, despite the hot, stuffy room. 'I don't believe it,' she said, not managing more than a hoarse whisper. 'It's you.'

Then there was a ringing in her ears and a buzzing behind her eyes and she passed out cold.

# THIRTY-SIX

## LEWIS

Lewis was woken from a deep sleep by his mobile ringing loudly.

He usually put his phone on silent when he went to bed, but tonight, in case Hattie needed anything, he'd left it not only switched on but with the ringer at full volume.

'Hi,' he said, snatching it up and accepting the call without even looking at the screen. In his Special Branch days, he had frequently been summoned to a case in the middle of the night, and that conditioning never quite left him. He was instantly alert.

But it wasn't Hattie.

'Lewis? Nigel Hayes here. Look, I know it's really late your end, but this really couldn't wait.'

Lewis pulled himself up on one elbow and switched on the bedside light. Outside on the street, there was a faint roar of traffic: a city as big as this one was never at rest. 'Go ahead.'

'Have you got a laptop with you? It would help if I could show you something.'

'No laptop, no, but I do have a tablet. You could FaceTime me on this number.'

He hung up and rummaged in his backpack for his tablet. Sure enough, a few seconds later, a FaceTime call came through. Lewis smoothed down his hair, pulled on a T-shirt and sat down at the table before accepting it. Nigel Hayes appeared on screen looking fresh-faced in a crisp white shirt, a coffee cup next to him on the desk. A quick glance at the clock confirmed that it would be early morning in London.

'Hi,' Hayes held up a hand in salute, but he was not smiling. 'Like I said, there's something urgent I need to speak to you about.'

'Go ahead.'

'It concerns the murder of Julian Cobbold.'

Hayes was on his phone handset, but he opened his laptop, tapped a few keys and then angled the screen so that Lewis could see it clearly. There was an arrest photo, similar to the one he and Hattie had been shown of Neil Waller, but this time it was a woman. Lewis leaned in, so that he could see more clearly. The person he was looking at was familiar and yet strange at the same time.

'Jesus Christ!' He exhaled noisily. 'It's bloody Bridget. Without the glasses.'

'I believe this woman was on the train the evening Julian Cobbold was killed?' Hayes asked. 'That she frequently travelled with you and Ms Sewell. Is that right?'

'Yes, but...' Lewis leaned back, dragged his hand over his forehead. 'I'm sorry, I don't understand.'

Hayes' demeanour was still serious, but he raised his eyebrows slightly to acknowledge that Lewis's confusion was justified. 'Okay, let me try to explain. CCTV picked up images of this woman sitting next to Cobbold on the evening of the second of April. We've run facial recognition analytics and, lo and behold, she's one Natalia Jade Finch. Former accomplice of none other than Neil Waller. She was in on the property theft scam that Waller dreamed up. He got nearly six years for it; I believe she was sentenced to around three.'

'So... hold on... she's not called Bridget Dempsey?' he asked incredulously. 'She never was?'

'Just one of many aliases she's used over the years. I don't suppose you happen to know where she might be now? Or where she was living at the time?'

'No. No, I don't think she ever told me. I mean, I hardly knew her. It was Hattie who was chummy with her.' Lewis leaned forward again, staring at the photo, and felt the blood drain from his face as the implications of what Hayes was telling him sank in. 'So Waller wasn't on the train when Julian died, but his criminal accomplice was? Bloody hell. That puts the whole thing in a different light.'

'I've liaised with Inspector Mejia, and I understand Ms Sewell is about to do her bit and help entrap Waller?'

'That's right,' Lewis said. He was still slowly shaking his head, shocked. 'Any minute now, if all goes well. The officers will keep an eye on her until Waller appears for his liaison with her in the morning.'

'Once we've got Waller, things may become clearer, of course, but in case he goes silent on us, I may need to speak to Ms Sewell and see if she can help us shed light on Finch's whereabouts. You'll update her as soon as you can?'

'Sure,' said Lewis. 'Leave it with me.'

After he had hung up the call, he sat staring at the wall of his hotel room for a few seconds, while above him a ceiling fan circulated lazily. What was it he had called her? Bridget the virgin spinster. And he couldn't have been more wrong. She was a cold-blooded killer. What was more, Hattie had innocently told this woman that she knew about Casper's true identity. She had confided this to a criminal who was in league with Neil Waller, so he would be aware that Hattie knew the truth. And Hattie was due to meet with him. Very soon.

Suddenly fearful, he leapt to his feet and ran down the corridor to her room, banging on the door and shouting her name. There was no reply. Racing to the lift, still in his bare feet, he ran down to reception and demanded that the night manager fetch the master key and let him into the room.

Her small carry-on case was next to the bed, half packed. Some of her clothes were strewn over the floor, as though she had either been interrupted or decided to go without them. There was no sign of the box containing the painting either. Perhaps when Mejia and his men had arrived to collect her, they had been in a hurry and there hadn't been time for her to pack properly.

It was entirely possible, and yet Lewis's instincts told him otherwise. They told him that something about this wasn't right.

He returned to his room long enough to grab shoes, key and phone, and set off at a fast jog to the Intercontinental Hotel. It was nearly midnight, and, although the streets were far from deserted, they were quiet enough for heads to turn curiously as he ran past.

Once in the lobby of the much larger, grander hotel, he headed for the bank of lifts and pressed the button for the ninth floor. The carpeted corridor was silent and empty apart from a few room-service trays that had been left outside the rooms for collection. Lewis hammered on the door of 904. There was no reply.

He was back on the street in less than a minute, heading straight for the unmarked car that was waiting outside, its occupants watching the front door of the building. He rapped on the passenger side window, and it was wound down.

'Are you with Inspector Mejia?'

The two men nodded.

'Can you get him on the radio. It's urgent.'

One of the men spoke in rapid Spanish into his airwave set and then handed it to Lewis.

'It's Lewis Handley. Is Hattie Sewell with you?' he demanded as soon as the call was answered. 'Have you come to collect her yet?'

He was breathing so heavily by now that Mejia, whose fluency in English had so far been excellent, seemed confused. Lewis repeated himself more slowly this time, and the short silence that followed told him all he needed to know.

'My officers are at the Intercontinental, but they have not seen the suspect. I myself am on my way to the Contempo Hotel now. Miss Sewell is not there right now?'

'No. So, to be clear, she's not with you?'

'No, she is not.'

Lewis buried his face in his hands. 'Oh, Christ. He's got here before you, and taken the painting. And he's taken Hattie too.'

# THIRTY-SEVEN

## HATTIE

It was daylight when she woke.

Or, more accurately, came to. You could only wake up if you'd been asleep, and it didn't feel like sleep if you'd been drugged. Hattie's mouth was dry and foul-tasting and her head was pounding. She was lying on the floor on a dirty mattress, her hands no longer in cuffs, and sunlight was seeping through shutters that opened onto what looked like a small balcony.

The room was poorly furnished, with a small table and a very grimy green sofa. There was a makeshift kitchen in one corner with a portable stove, a cupboard and a sink. What little air there was in the place was stale and very, very hot. There was no sign of the painting, or Neil. Or Bridget.

*My God, Bridget.*

It all came back to her in a sickening rush. The terrifying car journey and the mask being lifted by the second, smaller man, who wasn't a man at all, but Bridget Dempsey.

Hattie pulled herself up so that she was sitting, and found a bottle of water next to her. She opened it and drank all of it greedily. She immediately felt slightly better. But then it occurred to her that perhaps this was the only water she would have for a long time, and she should have saved some of it.

Now that her head was clearer, she was able to think properly. Her current predicament was her first thought. She staggered over to the door of the room, but it was locked. She rattled it and tried to shout for help, but her voice came out as a weak, ragged yelp. The glass door to the balcony was also bolted, but through it she could see a bustling street, and what looked like an open-air market. She wrestled with the bolt, and when she couldn't release it, tried banging on the glass. Although a couple of heads turned, people just went about their business as though she was invisible.

Sinking back onto the mattress, her thoughts now went back to London, and to that first meeting. She had met Neil and Bridget – or whatever she was called – on the same night, on the 18.53. It had never occurred to her that this was anything but a coincidence, but clearly it was not. They had known each other, and been working together. Were they boyfriend and girlfriend? Husband and wife even? No, McElwee was insistent that Neil wasn't legally married. Now she was remembering the night of Carmen's dinner party when she had removed Bridget's glasses and put make-up on her. She had looked so pretty: like someone entirely different.

*An entirely different person.*

And now her brain was working overtime, replaying those scenes when they had been together, and piecing clues together to give the narrative a whole new meaning. The way 'Casper' and 'Bridget' never spoke to each other when they were all in a group. Bridget's determination to push Casper as a suitor, insisting he was interested in her, when – looking back – how could she possibly have known this for sure. Her irrational dislike of Lewis, and insistence there was something untrustworthy about him. Of course, the two of them would not have wanted her to get too close to Lewis. He was analytical and intuitive. They might even have done some digging and discovered that he was an ex-police investigator.

There were voices on the other side of the door now. Hattie pushed the empty water bottle out of sight and lay down, closing her eyes and opening her mouth slightly in what she hoped was a convincing facsimile of sleep.

Two sets of footsteps came into the room and stopped close to the mattress.

'Looks like she's still out cold,' Neil's voice said. 'How much of that stuff did you give her? It should be wearing off by now.'

'Just the standard dose. But when we picked her up last night, she'd had a skinful, remember? Wasted, just like she always is. So maybe the alcohol has increased the toxicity.'

The voice of Bridget, so familiar and yet now sounding so cold, so detached.

'Hold on, let's get some air in here, it smells rank.' Neil dropped something onto the table, then strode across to the door to the balcony. Hattie heard it being unlocked. Now there was more air, admittedly still hot air, and the noise level from the street increased.

'What did you do with her passport?' he demanded.

Hattie felt her pulse quicken, but forced herself to remain immobile.

'Don't worry about that, it's safe.'

'You can't just hang on to it, Tali; it's far too risky. If we get stopped, how's that going to look? It's incriminating.'

'The way I see it, it's a hell of a lot riskier to travel out of here as Natalia Finch.'

Natalia. Tali. Was that Bridget's real name? Then surely this was the mysterious 'T' that Neil had been speaking to when they were together. Not his sister Tabitha, as she'd assumed – he probably didn't even have a sister – but Natalia.

And then another memory came back to Hattie. Finch. Yes, that was the name she'd seen when she first went to the flat in

Tower Hill. There'd been a letter there addressed to N. J. Finch. She had assumed it was the name of the friend who had let him use the place. But, it seemed, 'Bridget' had been living there all along.

Hattie's brain was reeling now, making it even more difficult to lie still. There had been the jade cufflinks she'd spotted there too and wondered where she'd seen them before. She had been right: they *were* Neil's. Or more accurately 'Casper's'. He'd favoured the old-school button-free shirt cuffs designed to be worn with links.

'Now we've got the painting, we need to get it to Velasco as soon as we can,' Neil was saying. 'In fact, we should probably go and see him now, while Patsy's passed out.'

*Patsy? Was that what they called her? Because she was a fool?* Fury surged through Hattie, but still she couldn't move a muscle.

'We're one step ahead right now, but it's not going to stay that way for ever.' He stopped, and there was a heavy pause. 'Tali, you didn't leave it in the car?'

'Well, I couldn't exactly carry it up here last night, could I? Not when we had to get *her* up here and give her the sedative. It's okay, it's in the boot, and I made sure I locked it.'

'But we're in one of the poorest barrios in the city!' Neil had raised his voice, was almost shouting now. 'What if someone steals the fucking car?'

Hattie could almost hear the sharp intake of breath. 'For God's sake, calm down, okay? Let's go and check now, and then we'll drive straight to Velasco's house.'

There was a scuffing of the wooden floor as Neil darted over to the balcony door and bolted it again. Then her two captors hurried out, banging and locking the door. A second door then slammed shut, which must have been the front door to the apartment. So clearly there was another room in addition to this living space, a bedroom perhaps.

Hattie waited until she was sure they were not returning, then opened her eyes. The extreme heat was making her thirsty, so she retrieved the empty water bottle from where she had hidden it under the mattress and limped over to the tiny sink in the corner to refill it. She leaned her weight against the sink as she drank, still feeling dizzy.

And that was when she saw it.

A mobile phone, there on the table. Neil must have put it down there because he needed both hands for the bolt on the balcony door. And then, in his panic about *The Red Courtesan* being left in the car, he had forgotten to take it. Her hands shaking, Hattie snatched it up and stared at the screen. It was locked, but surely it would still be possible to make an emergency call? Yes, there at the bottom left corner of the screen below the number icons for the passcode, it said 'Emergencia'. She pressed it.

She was connected immediately, and met with a volley of rapid Spanish.

'Hello?' Hattie croaked. 'Can you help me?'

This was met with an aggressive, 'Allo?' and more Spanish.

'Do you speak English?'

'What service you require?'

'Police.'

'Where is your address?'

'I don't know.'

'You do not know where you are?' the operator demanded impatiently.

'No, I don't know. I don't know where this place is.' Hattie suddenly realised she must sound as though she was drunk. 'I was brought here by two people... I was given something. Drugs.'

The call was cut. She had clearly been dismissed as a time-waster who had spent the night partying. She wondered if she could phone the Mexican officer they had met, but she could only remember that his first name was Hector. His surname was gone, wiped from her memory. And without unlocking the phone she couldn't find his number anyway. The same applied to Lewis's mobile number and the number for the reception desk at the Contempo Suites. Even if she could have got through to him somehow, what could she tell Lewis that would enable him to find her? She had no idea where she was.

And then it came to her. When she had received her first message from this phone, at the airport, Lewis had taken a picture of the text with the sender number displayed above. He knew that this was the number Neil Waller was currently using. And with the number, he could trace the phone, as long as it remained switched on. So all she needed to do was to hide it so that Neil didn't have the opportunity to switch it off.

After searching the room carefully, she found a loose piece of flooring, just where it met the skirting board. She checked that the phone was in silent mode, then hid it under the floorboard.

Then she drank some more water, lay down on the mattress and waited.

# THIRTY-EIGHT

## NEIL

The door of the fabulous Lomas de Chapultepec house was opened by a housekeeper.

She did her very best to turn Neil and Tali away, claiming they couldn't possibly see Mr Velasco unless by prior arrangement. But then Ricardo Velasco himself appeared at the top of the dramatic floating staircase and, as soon as he saw the black archive box in Neil's hands, said something in Spanish that clearly meant he would speak to the intruders. They were ushered into a smaller room this time: a study or library that featured the ubiquitous ebony panelling. There was a baronial desk and behind it, a huge, squashy leather chair. So huge that when Velasco sat down on it, and rested his elbows on its arms, he looked for all the world like the villain in a James Bond movie.

With a curt little nod, he indicated that the archive box should be placed on the desk in front of him. Without uttering a word, he took a pair of white cotton gloves from a drawer in the desk and pulled them over his thick, gold-ringed fingers. Then he opened the box, removed the padding and the glassine paper and took out the painting. Under the room's artfully directed lighting, it looked more impressive than ever; its colours positively glowing.

'I think you'll find—' Neil started, but Velasco held up a white-gloved hand, silencing him. He turned the painting over and looked at the markings on the back, then held it up under one of the lights, closing one eye as he examined the paintwork closely. After fitting the corner protectors again, he wrapped the paper around it and laid it down carefully in the box. Only then did he speak.

'It is very beautiful. Very beautiful indeed.'

'So... you're going to buy it?' Tali asked.

'I would indeed like to buy it,' Velasco said, his tone giving nothing away. 'If it is the real thing. Only the last time I bought this painting, what was in the crate shipped from London was nothing but a fake.'

He directed his gaze directly on Neil's face now.

'Oh, I can assure you this is the real thing,' Neil said smoothly. 'I can absolutely guarantee it.'

'Excellent.' Velasco removed his white gloves and steepled his fingers. 'Then you won't mind me having my expert authenticate it.' He gave a little shrug. 'Nobody buys important art these days without having it forensically tested. The age of the paint, the type of canvas; that kind of thing. I'm sure you both know this.'

Tali shifted impatiently. 'How long will that take?'

'My man is on his way here from New York. I think he will arrive tomorrow. And I must also arrange for the ten million dollars to be available.' He gave a wry little smile. 'Even men with my resources don't have that sort of money just sitting around. I have to move some things around to liquidate a sum that large.'

'So if we come back tomorrow?' asked Neil.

But Velasco shook his head and held up two fingers. 'Two days. Bring it here the day after tomorrow.'

. . .

'Two days!' Tali snarled, as they drove away.

Neil was driving, and the black box containing *The Red Courtesan* was on Tali's lap. She picked it up now and slammed it down hard on her thighs in an angry gesture.

'Careful!' Neil glared at her.

'D'you think he's deliberately stalling us? Because I think there's something else going on here. I think he's going to get the police involved, and set a trap for us.'

'No. He's not going to do that.' Neil kept his gaze on the car's satnav, trying to negotiate the city's over-congested roads. 'He wants the painting; I told you that.'

'Okay, so even if he does, what are we going to do for the next couple of days?'

'We stay put, and we wait.'

'But what do we do with *her*? With Patsy? By the time we get back to Tepito in this traffic, she'll probably have come round and called for help. And even if she hasn't, we can't keep her drugged for the next forty-eight hours.'

'We could,' said Neil, in a reasonable tone. 'You could get some more of that stuff from that dodgy pharmacy in Tepito. Seems they don't ask questions.'

'I could get more, but it's risky,' Tali insisted. The car was crawling bumper to bumper now, with nothing visible in front of them but clouds of dust and more cars in an endless queue. 'It's not possible to predict how long the sedation will last each time, so she could wake up and shout through the balcony door at any point. In the night, while we're asleep.'

'Then we'll just have to watch her all the time. We'll do a shift system: take it in turns.'

But Tali was shaking her head slowly. She placed her hands palms down on the box, set her jaw, and turned away so that she was looking out of the passenger window.

Neil recognised that look. Over the years, he'd seen it many times. 'What?' he asked sharply, 'Tali?... what?'.

It was nearly a minute before she answered. 'I think we need to get rid of her.'

Neil braked hard, turning his head so that he was looking directly at her. 'What are you talking about?'

'I think we should kill her. She knows far too much. Even if we get the money off Velasco, she's going to go to the police with what she knows. We'll never get away with it.'

Neil felt his hands begin to shake. He gripped the wheel hard, and shook his head slowly but firmly, from left to right. 'No. That's why we're going to Honduras, babe. They can't get us there.'

Tali kept her face turned away from him. 'I'm not going to Honduras with you.'

The car almost collided with a truck in front of them, making Neil slam his foot on the brake. A horn sounded loudly in protest, and others joined in. 'What do you mean?' he asked in a low voice.

'What I said. I'm not going with you. I don't want to spend the rest of my life hiding out in some beach colony for ex-pat criminals, never able to go anywhere. It doesn't matter if the weather's lovely, or we've got an expensive house, we'll still be like prisoners. We'll have no freedom. And I can't live like that.'

'But what option do you have?' Neil was forcing himself to sound calm, but he did not feel it. 'The name Natalia Finch will soon be on an Interpol red notice, if it isn't already. Not for stealing a fucking painting, but for the murder of Julian Cobbold! You won't be able to go anywhere anyway.'

'Natalia Jade Finch won't, no. But Harriet Claire Sewell will.'

They were in Tepito now, on the side street that ran behind the block where their rented apartment was. Neil brought the car to a halt and switched off the engine. He unclipped his seat belt and pulled Tali round so that she was facing him.

'Are you saying...?'

She nodded, and there was a gleam in her eyes, the same gleam she always got when she was planning a long con. 'I've already got her passport. If the police think she's gone abroad of her own free will, they won't look for her. And if she's dead, there's nothing to stop me taking her identity too. I can *be* her.'

# THIRTY-NINE

## LEWIS

The headquarters of the Policia Federal was a few kilometres north-west of Polanco, in a vast grey concrete building behind barbed wire.

Lewis had been driven there by Hector Mejia several hours earlier and was sitting miserably in a corner of the open-plan office space with a plastic cup of machine coffee. It was bitter and not particularly hot, but it was something. And at this point, it was about the fourth cup he had drunk.

A tired-looking Mejia was standing near a huddle of his colleagues, most of whom were gathered around a bank of flickering computer terminals.

A young man in a leather jacket pushed the swing doors open with a sense of palpable urgency and walked quickly towards Mejia. A plain clothes officer, Lewis guessed. There was a hurried, urgent conversation, then Mejia broke away from the group and headed towards him.

'Anything?' Lewis asked wearily.

Mejia nodded. 'That is one of my officers. He's been to the Contempo Suites to check their CCTV. They've found images of a car leaving the underground car park at the relevant time.'

Lewis's eyes widened, but Mejia's expression immediately became apologetic. 'The numberplates had been obscured in some way: some... how do you say... crude covering with tape, or something like that.'

'So you have no idea where it went?' Lewis's shoulders dropped.

'It was picked up by the camera outside the exit to the garage, so we do know that it headed south. But after that, the numberplate recognition cameras can't detect it, so it's very difficult. There will be many other street cameras between there and where they were headed, but it would take days, or even weeks, to look through all their footage for a car with a blacked-out numberplate.'

'So where does that leave us?' Lewis asked, tossing his cup into the bin. 'Because after what my colleagues in London have told me about Waller's sidekick, I genuinely believe that Hattie Sewell's in danger. Or why else would they take her? They would just have snatched the painting.'

Mejia shrugged heavily. 'I really don't know what they would want with her. It doesn't make sense. Having a hostage only makes things more complicated, more difficult.'

'And you can't track her phone?'

'She didn't take it with her. We found it in the room when we searched it. I think this was... what is the word... deliberate. They didn't want to risk us tracking her location.'

And then it came to Lewis. He inhaled hard, slapping his forehead with the flat of his hand. 'Oh God, I've just remembered. Waller had just switched out his burner phone for a new one when we landed here in Mexico City. When he messaged Hattie from it, I took a photo of the message. It was identified just by the phone number, since it wasn't a saved contact. Copper's instinct, you know.'

Mejia looked blank.

'I used to be in the Specials. It's a bit like you lot.' He

gestured round the room at the FMP offices with one hand, digging in his jeans pocket with the other. He pulled out his phone and touched the screen to unlock it. It remained blank. The battery was flat.

Mejia gestured to his colleagues with loud, barked instructions in Spanish. A flurry of activity followed, which resulted in a phone charger of the relevant spec being produced. Lewis's phone was plugged in, and as soon as the battery had the minimal charge, he went into his photo album and pulled up the image of the text message to Hattie.

'Of course, he might have moved onto another burner already, in which case this isn't going to help us. Or it could be switched off or uncharged. But it's got to be worth a try, surely?'

Mejia took the phone from him. 'I'll give this to one of our digital forensic guys right now.' He hurried away to another part of the building.

The room became warmer as the sun's rays filtered through the slats in the blinds at the window, and an exhausted Lewis lay down on a padded bench by the vending machines, trying to fight off sleep. Eventually he lost the battle, and drifted off.

He was eventually woken by Mejia gently shaking his shoulder.

'Mr Handley?'

Lewis pulled himself up, blinking groggily. 'What time is it?'

'Just after midday.'

'Shit.' He must have been asleep for at least two hours.

'I have some news.'

Lewis's face fell.

'Please don't be worried. It's good news, I think. With some help from the cell service provider, we've managed to track the phone Waller's using. It's at an address in the south of the city. In Tepito.'

Lewis straightened up. 'So are we—'

'I am going there with an armed team now. But you must stay here, I'm afraid. We are not permitted to bring civilian personnel.' He gave a half-smile. 'Insurance indemnity or something.'

Lewis sighed, shaking his head. He wanted to be there. It felt entirely wrong to sit by and do nothing.

Mejia produced Lewis's phone, which he handed back to him. 'You are going to need this. And don't worry, I will contact you as soon as there is news.'

He squeezed Lewis's shoulder briefly, then walked away.

Lewis raised one of his hands to show that his fingers were tightly crossed. There was really nothing else he could do.

# FORTY

## HATTIE

After what felt like hours, Hattie heard a slamming sound, then footsteps.

A few seconds later, the door to the room was unlocked, and just one person came in, standing only inches away from the mattress. She parted her eyelids just enough to see a pair of man's shoes. Neil – or Casper, as part of her still wanted to think of him. Instinctively, she allowed her eyes to open.

'How are you feeling?' He looked around for the bottle of water, and refilled it from the tap before handing it to her.

'I really need the loo,' Hattie croaked, without making eye contact.

'Sure. Sorry. I should have thought of that.'

Neil held out a hand and pulled her to a standing position, before leading her through into the adjoining room. There was a small double bed, and at the centre of it the black box that housed *The Red Courtesan*. A couple of suitcases lay open on the floor, their contents spilling out haphazardly. There were two doors, a heavy one which must have led out of the apart-ment and a small, more flimsy one which revealed a tiny, ramshackle bathroom with toilet and shower cubicle jammed in next to each other. As Hattie emptied her aching bladder, with Neil standing waiting for her by the door, she was suddenly transported back to their hotel stay in Surrey, and the large comfortable en suite bathroom they had shared then. Another continent, and what felt like another lifetime away.

'Where is she?' Hattie asked, as he escorted her back into the second room and locked the door behind them, pocketing the key. 'Bridget. Or whatever her name is.'

'Tali,' said Neil heavily, and there was a strange inflection in his voice. Silence hung between them, and then eventually, without looking at her, he said, 'She's gone out. To... On an errand.'

'Is she your girlfriend?'

Still avoiding eye contact, he shook his head. 'No. Not anymore. She was once. We've known each other a long time.'

'From before you went to prison?'

He looked at her sharply now.

'Yes, I know all about that,' Hattie said simply, rubbing her wrists where the cuffs had chafed them. Her skin was sticky with sweat and dirt, and she wished she had asked if she could have a shower. 'Julian Cobbold worked in the legal system, remember, and he had friends in the police.' She was looking at him directly now, challenging him. 'They did some digging, and apparently it wasn't hard to find out that you're Neil Waller. You shouldn't have chosen an alias from a successful children's book. Turns out it wasn't that obscure.'

Whatever Hattie had been expecting from a hardened conman like Waller, it wasn't what happened next. He sank down onto the grimy sofa and buried his face in his hands, his whole body shaking. 'I expect you think I'm a total shit,' he said eventually, looking up. The distress he was feeling was clear from his expression. 'And you have every right.'

'It's a bit bloody late to be worrying about that.' Despite herself, there was some gentleness in her voice.

'Hattie, it's important that you know I didn't fake all of it. I was attracted to you, and I did enjoy the time we spent together... Well, some of it.' He gave a rueful smile. 'When you were sober.'

'Was that why you chose me?' she demanded. 'Because I liked to go out and have a good time? Because whatever my life-style choices, it doesn't justify what you've done.'

'I know that, I know that.' Neil buried his head in his hands again. 'You're still a good person; I'm aware of that. In a way, I'm jealous of you.'

'Jealous? Of me?' She stared at him.

'Of everything you have. A happy, stable upbringing. Parents who love each other, and love you. That's worth so much.'

Hattie felt her resolve crumbling at the mention of her parents. How appalled they would be if they could see her now. Appalled, and terrified.

'You just don't seem to understand how lucky you are,' he went on. 'I need you to really think about that. Appreciate it.'

'I do,' Hattie said quietly. 'I've been guilty of taking my family for granted, I know that. But I also know I'm lucky.'

'That day we came back from Kent. On Easter Monday. And we stopped off for coffee with your family. I hadn't planned on meeting them, because... well, you know.' Neil's voice trailed off for a second. 'But I enjoyed it so much. Just hanging out in the kitchen, talking. It was so normal, and so lovely. I felt this overwhelming sense of envy, I suppose. I always wanted to have a family like that.'

'Was yours very different?'

He gave a wan smile. 'It started off pretty well. I was a product of privilege, just like you. We had money. A nice home. I went to private school, had holidays abroad. But it didn't last. My father lost his job, and my parents got into debt. Then they split up, and I barely saw Dad after that. He has a whole other family: half-siblings I haven't even met. My mother moved into a small place in Southampton, and developed all sorts of mental health issues. I never settled there. The perpetual outsider: that's how I felt. You know something...' He gave a bitter little laugh. 'I don't have a single photo of my father. Not one. The only way I know what he looks like now is from his new wife's Facebook.'

'You could still have had a good life. You didn't need to get into all this.' Hattie gestured around the hot, dusty room.

'Maybe.' He shrugged. 'I just never seemed to get the right break.'

'You had a job at one of the most prestigious auction houses in the world!' Hattie said angrily. 'You got that by using your own knowledge of art. Okay, probably your charm and your looks too. But the point is, you have plenty going for you.'

'I got that job by pretending to be someone I wasn't,' Neil said flatly. 'That's been the story of my life. As myself, I was nothing. Anyway... no turning back now, eh?' He smiled, and there was a flash of that animal magnetism that had drawn her in.

'If you let me go,' Hattie urged, 'and hand back the painting, then maybe they'll give you a light sentence and you can start over.'

He shook his head. 'Not now. Not with Julian dead. Julian getting involved was where it all went wrong. He's why you're here now, in this room.'

'But you didn't kill Julian. You weren't there!' Hattie protested.

He looked straight at her with those mesmerising grey eyes, and her heart sank as she realised that the police had it right: that Neil had been involved.

'It's too late, can't you see, Hattie?' His tone was pleading, desperate. 'If you and everyone else had gone on thinking I was Casper Merriweather, you would have brought the painting out here to me, handed it over and that would have been that. Even if Julian died but you still never discovered who I was, you wouldn't be sitting here now. We wouldn't have taken you from that hotel room. But that wasn't how it happened. You did know who I was, and you told "Bridget" as much.' He made air quotes. 'And if you knew, the odds were pretty high that it was because someone in authority had worked it out. And because of that, you wouldn't be flying out here alone just to give me a twelve-million-pound painting. Or live happily ever after. And you didn't, did you?'

His voice had changed, grown colder, and Hattie's heart started to pound. 'Didn't what?'

'You didn't come alone. You came out here with Lewis Handley.'

There was no point denying it. 'How do you know that?'

'I saw him at the airport when you arrived. So, we knew that any arrangement to meet up was going to be a honey trap. We weren't going to be stupid enough to show up at the Intercontinental and walk straight into the arms of the Federales. We needed to get you first.'

'And now?' Hattie asked, her voice breaking. 'What's going to happen to me now? You've got the painting, so why keep hold of me?'

Neil looked swiftly away, unable to meet her eye. Nor did he answer, and from that silence she knew. She knew that they were planning to kill her.

# FORTY-ONE

## HATTIE

Neil came towards her, his arms extended, and Hattie shrank back, terrified.

But he simply placed his hands on her shoulders and gave her a long, lingering look. 'Look, this wasn't what I wanted. This whole thing has become...' He flapped his arms wide in a gesture of helplessness. 'This was never the plan. I just wanted to resell a valuable piece of art, bank the cash and use it to fund a quiet, crime-free life. Maybe one with a family of my own. It was supposed to be a fool-proof plan, this time. One and done.' He sighed heavily. 'One that would leave me so well set up I'd never, ever run the risk of going to prison again.'

'And you never intended for me to start a life with you here, in Mexico?'

He shook his head sadly. 'No. But it would have just been a case of thank you and goodbye. Not this.'

'It still could be. I'll walk away from here and give you a head start. You can be gone before there's any possibility of the police finding you.'

But Neil stayed rooted to the spot, as if unable to make a decision, and it came to Hattie then.

'It's her, isn't it? Natalia? It's her who wants me dead.'

He closed his eyes, nodding.

'But why?'

There was no answer.

'Why complicate things so much? You'll have to get rid of my body, somehow. And people will come looking for me.'

'That's the thing,' Neil said falteringly. 'They wouldn't. Because she's going to be you. She's got your passport; with a few tweaks to her appearance, she could travel as you, no problem. And then, as far as the authorities are concerned, you've taken off abroad to be with me. So they won't even be looking for a body. Immigration control and a flight manifest will show that you've left Mexico.'

Hattie was shaking her head slowly. She was so stunned that she didn't even have the capability to feel frightened. Her brain was taking a while to catch up, but when it did, she had a moment of powerful lucidity. Neil didn't want her dead. And Natalia would find it very difficult to kill her if he was gone. 'Bridget' was a lot smaller than Hattie was, and not particularly fit. Even in Hattie's weakened state, it would be a challenge for Natalia to overpower her. With Neil gone, she stood a chance. Against the two of them, it would all be over very quickly.

And then she thought about the burner phone, secreted under the floorboard. It was the last, and only, card she had to play. Even so, it was a gamble. She moved closer to him, and took hold of his hand. Instinctively, their fingers intertwined. That magnetic connection was still there, even now.

'You left your phone in here, and I've hidden it. With it switched on. And Lewis knows the number. There's absolutely no doubt that the police are already tracking its location. They could literally be here any second.'

His eyes widened in shock. Good, she thought, he was not expecting this roll of the dice.

'And if they find you here, you'll be locked up for the rest of your life. There'll be no crime-free life of leisure, no family. Just a six by nine cell.' She squeezed his fingers, letting go of his hand but keeping eye contact. 'Casper,' she said quietly, because now, in this final moment, this was how she thought of him. He flinched as she used the name. 'Take *The Red Courtesan* and go, while you have the chance.'

He stared into her eyes for what felt like an endless moment, then turned and left the room. Seconds later, she heard the door to the apartment slam shut.

It took a few seconds for the shock to recede.

Only then did Hattie realise that Neil had left without locking the door behind him. And if she was not locked in, she could escape. She was barefoot, since when Neil and Natalia had taken her from the hotel room she had not been wearing shoes. But that hardly mattered now. She took a quick gulp of water and went into the bedroom. The black archive box was gone from the bed. Neil had taken it with him: of course he had.

She hurried to the door of the apartment, but it was already too late. There were footsteps on the stairs and the door opened. Natalia stared at her, caught off guard by finding Hattie in the bedroom.

'Where's Neil?' she demanded. Instead of the combat trousers, man's T-shirt and baseball cap she had worn when she abducted Hattie, she was dressed in a silky red slip dress and strappy sandals, with a designer bag over her shoulder. She looked for all the world as though she had come from a cocktail party, but there was a wildness in her eyes, and spots of colour on her cheeks. There was no trace at all of the meek and mild Bridget.

'He's gone.'

Hattie tried to push past her, but Natalia ducked to one side, blocking her path.

'Let me go, Natalia,' Hattie said, in a low voice. 'Neil's gone, the painting's gone. It's all over.'

'No,' Natalia hissed. 'No, not yet. I'm not finished yet.' The prominent canines looked like fangs now, sharp and vampiric. Before Hattie could even draw breath, she reached into the bag and brought out a hard, shiny object. 'It's not over yet,' she repeated, 'But, trust me, it soon will be.'

And then there was a click as the safety catch was released and a gun was pointed directly at Hattie's chest.

As a strong survival instinct took hold, Hattie's mind whirled forward, like someone scrolling through a reel of film at top speed. The phone. This was her first thought. *I could tell her I have Neil's burner phone.*

But then, no. Immediately, her brain corrected her. *If I mention that they're tracking the phone, then she might panic and fire.*

She needed something else. Some delaying tactic. She forced herself to try and see this wild-eyed woman as Bridget. Loner Bridget, who only drank tea because coffee was too exciting. That helped, the image calmed her.

'If you leave now,' she said, unable to keep the tremor from her voice. 'You've still got a chance to go with him. To be with Neil. Isn't that what all this was about, after all? Isn't that what you want?'

Natalia just laughed. 'No way. Spending the rest of my life sipping cocktails on some remote tropical beach? I'd be bored to death. I need to be in a city, where things are happening. Where there are people. New York, maybe. Or Los Angeles.' She prodded Hattie's ribcage with the gun. 'Hattie Sewell can start her new life there. Because that's who I'm going to be from now on.'

'Don't you love him?'

A firm shake of the head.

'Did you ever love him?'

Natalia tilted her head as she considered this. 'No,' she said airily. 'I mean, I enjoyed sleeping with him, sure. You know as well as I do, that's where he excels. And he was useful to me. We were useful to each other. Made a good team. But love, no. I don't believe in it.'

As Hattie opened her mouth to ask another question, there was a faint wail of a siren, becoming stronger, more urgent.

Natalia whipped her head in the direction of the sound, genuinely shocked. Her voice emerged in a hoarse whisper. 'What? How do they—?'

Car doors slammed, and then several pairs of boots thundered up the stairs of the apartment block.

Panicked, Natalia stepped backwards, then levelled the sights and squeezed the trigger. There was a loud crack, then pain, then blackness.

PART FOUR

# FORTY-TWO

## HATTIE – FOUR WEEKS LATER

Hattie stood on the platform at Summerlands station.

Her heart was pounding, and she swayed slightly as she clutched her takeaway coffee cup. This was the first time since her return from Mexico that she had travelled on the train to Waterloo, and strangely it was this, rather than the ambulance ride to Hospital Angeles Mexico, or the flight back to Heathrow, that was giving her PTSD.

The events of the past three months swarmed her brain. The 18.53 crew having drinks that first night. Julian Cobbold's dead body. Embracing 'Casper' on Deal beach. Being driven handcuffed through the back streets of Mexico City. Natalia Finch squeezing the trigger of a revolver. The burning pain that followed.

With one hand, Hattie now tentatively touched her left ribs where the bullet had hit her. She had had just enough presence of mind to throw her body to the right when Natalia pulled the trigger, and it had grazed her side, causing what turned out to be a superficial wound instead of a life-changing injury. It still felt tender and sore when Hattie touched it, but she was grateful for the scar. Because the bullet hitting her had disorientated

Natalia, making her hesitate just long enough for Hector Mejia's armed officers to reach the first floor of the building and burst through the door, their own weapons raised.

Natalia had been arrested and was still in jail in Mexico City, awaiting repatriation to the UK and trial for Julian's murder. Hattie was rushed to the emergency room for treatment, where she was later joined by a very concerned Lewis Handley. As for Neil Waller, he and *The Red Courtesan* had vanished, flying out of Mexico City that night using – irony of ironies – a passport in the name of Casper Merriweather, just before Interpol had got round to raising red notices on all of his many aliases. Talk about having the last laugh, Hattie thought grimly. And yet a small part of her was glad he had escaped, and that it was Natalia who would be carrying the can. As the sting of heartbreak had receded, and she had adjusted to the fact that 'Casper' didn't exist, Hattie felt almost sorry for Neil Waller. Yes, he had deceived her, but, ultimately, he had not wanted her to come to serious harm. And finally, he had got what he wanted.

The train pulled into the platform, the doors slid open and Hattie climbed on board. She instinctively looked around her for familiar faces, but this was not a commuter train. It was eleven in the morning. She was not going to see any members of the 18.53 Crew.

She looked out of the window as the train sped towards the city. It was late May now – almost summer – and the leaves were at their most brilliant green, the sky the brightest possible blue, the roses in the suburban back gardens coming into bloom, lawns freshly mowed. Despite the warmth of the train carriage, Hattie shivered. It still felt strange to be making this journey, even though it was important.

At Waterloo, she caught the Edgware branch of the Northern line, getting off the train at Hampstead. When she reached the ticket hall, she spotted Nigel Hayes straight away, wearing one of his shiny suits and bouncing impatiently on his heels.

'Ms Sewell, lovely to see you.' He shook her hand with genuine warmth. 'We just need to wait for your friend, and then we'll set off. It's not far from here.'

Hattie turned back towards the ticket barriers and there he was, taking the steps two at a time. Hair freshly shaved; tattoos revealed by the short-sleeved T-shirt. Lewis Handley.

Hayes had a patrol car and uniformed driver outside the tube station. Hattie noted that it was parked on the double red 'no stopping' lines, but supposed that if you were a police officer, this was okay.

With Hayes in the front next to his constable and Lewis and Hattie in the back, they were driven into the heart of Hampstead village, pulling up outside a prosperous-looking red-brick mansion block. The path that led up to the shiny black front door was fringed with lilac bushes, their scented flowers in full bloom.

From the carpeted lobby, they took a lift to the top floor and were greeted at the door by a spry, long-limbed man in his seventies. Hayes introduced him as Victor D'Onofrio, and they were led through the apartment to a large room with sloping ceilings and skylights that had been set up as an art studio. At the centre of the room was an expansive horizontal easel covered in white linen, and to the side of it a trolley crammed with paints, brushes and bottles of liquid. There were canvases leaning against the wall all around the room, some of them – Hattie realised – Hokusai oils.

'Victor here is an art forger,' Nigel Hayes said, not without a hint of admiration. 'One of the most successful in the world. His imitations of the great masters have been sold as the real thing in auction houses all over the globe. His

Matisses and van Goghs and Dalis have all fooled the experts.'

'And I've paid the price for it,' Victor said ruefully, his accent revealing that he was American. 'Once the FBI finally caught up with me. Twelve months in Otisville Correctional Institution.'

'Only, these days, Victor makes an honest living by selling authentic reproductions, or recreating them for film and TV,' Hayes grinned. 'And sometimes he's called in to help our colleagues in the Art and Antiques Unit at New Scotland Yard.'

Lewis and Hattie exchanged glances, still unsure why they were there.

'Victor has agreed to give us a little tutorial in art forgery, which I thought the two of you would find useful.'

'First of all,' Victor spread a piece of canvas over the white cloth. 'You have to be confident of the medium that the artist in question worked in. Not just what colours, but what type or even brand of paint he or she used. Then you have to make sure your canvas looks right. Best of all is to find an old painting of the correct age and clean the paint off it completely. If you can't do that...' He spread out the canvas with his fingers and looked at it thoughtfully, 'There are ways to fake antiquity.'

As Lewis, Hattie and Nigel Hayes moved closer to watch, he dipped a brush in a clear liquid and painted it all over one side.

'This is a solution of bleach, which – when it dries – will make the canvas feel dry and brittle to the touch.'

He then reached for an ashtray, containing a foul-smelling soup of cigarette butts in water. This, too, was painted over the back of the canvas, leaving a faint brown-ish wash.

'This can be used on the wooden frame of the painting too.' He turned the canvas over, revealing an Impressionist-style painting in primary colours, then washed a different solution over it. 'Oil and water will leave faint cracks when it dries. And this,' he brandished a tube of brown umber paint, 'when it's diluted, can be added on top to create the illusion of dirt in the cracks. I can't show you just now, because the canvas is too wet, but you get the picture. Literally.' He grinned.

'This is fascinating,' Lewis said. 'I mean, genuinely, it is. But what...'

'You remember that morning when the two of you came to see DI McElwee and I, and we retrieved *The Red Courtesan* from where Waller had left it in the storage locker?'

'I do.'

'Well, that painting was held in our evidence store and Victor here was urgently commissioned to make a forgery of it. That forgery was in the box that one of McElwee's officers dropped off with you, Hattie, at your parents' house. The same box that you flew over to Mexico City for us...'

'And that Waller took from my hotel room,' Hattie filled in, her eyes wide with shock. 'And he had no idea?'

Victor interjected at this point, filling the stunned silence. 'Fortunately, as you can see,' he waved at the canvases round the edge of the room, 'I'd already mastered Hokusai's techniques. And because of the publicity about the auction of *The Red Courtesan*, I'd already done some preliminary work on reproducing it. So I didn't have to start from scratch. Which would have been a tall order in just the few hours I was given. I normally work on a reproduction for a lot longer than that.'

'Wow,' said Lewis simply, putting his hands on his hips as he looked around the room.

'And I'll be honest with you, it wasn't as good as I would have liked. I need more time to perfect something like that. But it was good enough to pass cursory inspection, even if it wouldn't have fooled an expert.'

.   .   .

They said their goodbyes and went out to the street, where the squad car was waiting.

'You realise why we couldn't risk telling you at the time,' Hayes said to Hattie, his tone suitably apologetic. 'Need-to-know basis, and all that. But there was no way McElwee and her colleagues were going to let the real *Red Courtesan* board a plane to Mexico and fall into the hands of a convicted fraudster.' He held the rear door open for Hattie to get in.

'So what happened to the real painting?' Lewis asked.

'Ah,' said Hayes, tapping his nose. He wasn't even trying to conceal his pleasure at his big reveal. 'If you come with me now, there's someone else I'd like you to meet.'

They were driven back into the centre of London, heading down Edgware Road and along Park Lane.

The car finally pulled up in a Mayfair side street, outside the chic magenta and gold frontage of Van Asbeck's London auction room. They were ushered inside, where they were greeted by a tall, self-important man in a pinstriped suit.

'Hugo Barker,' he introduced himself. 'And you must be DCI Hayes? And Mr Handley and Miss Sewell. Lovely to meet you all. Delightful. If you wouldn't mind coming this way.'

They were led down a carpeted corridor and into a spacious, artfully lit room lined with glass-fronted display cases. A large floor-standing display easel stood at its centre, and sitting on a velvet chair next to it was a tanned, heavyset man with a thick neck and gelled-back hair. His open-necked linen shirt revealed chunky gold chains, and he wore suede Gucci loafers with no socks.

'May I present Mr Ricardo Velasco,' Hugo Barker said. 'He's just flown over from Mexico City to be with us.'

Hattie was a little confused, until she saw Velasco's Chopard watch when he shook their hands. She knew they cost so much that only an extremely wealthy man could buy one. So this must be the man who had bought *The Red Courtesan*. The real *Red Courtesan*.

Sure enough, Hugo Barker was saying in reverential tones, 'We thought that given the part you played in getting it back, Miss Sewell, you should be here to witness this moment. Mr Velasco is about to see his acquisition for the first time.'

There was a hushed pause while the door opened and two staff came in wearing khaki warehouse jackets and white cotton gloves, carrying a paper-wrapped package. It was laid on a table and unwrapped, and then Hokusai's work was set on the easel under a carefully directed spotlight. Velasco stood in front of it without speaking, his arms crossed, his chin resting on one hand.

'It is our pleasure to present you with *The Red Courtesan*,' said Barker obsequiously. 'Quite spellbinding, isn't she?'

One of Barker's assistants stepped forward with a camera and snapped a photo of Velasco looking at the painting.

'They may well be grovelling,' Lewis muttered in Hattie's ear, 'given it was stolen while Van Asbeck's were still responsible for it.'

Once Velasco was satisfied, Barker nodded at the two men in khaki jackets, who packed up the painting again.

'I will, of course, have my forensic expert look at it before I leave London,' Velasco told Barker, 'but I'm certain that this is the genuine work. And this time it will be travelling with me, and a security guard, on my private plane.'

Barker muttered something about how this was his choice, but had the grace to look embarrassed.

'I was almost sure that the painting Mr Waller brought to me was a fake,' Velasco went on, 'but, of course, I didn't let him know this. I told him to bring it back so I could authenticate it, but instead of my expert, he would have found a member of the Policia Judicial waiting with me. But, as I think you know, he did not return.' He turned to Hattie with a little bow, 'And may I thank you for your part in getting it back. I am very grateful.'

He was escorted out of the building and into a waiting chauffeur-driven limousine, which purred off into the West End traffic.

Nigel Hayes, Hattie and Lewis were ushered into a side room where they were served tea in proper china cups, and a selection of fancy biscuits. There was a glossy Van Asbeck's brochure on the table, and Hattie picked it up and flicked through it. There were several pages under the heading 'Our Team', with formal black-and-white headshots of all the sales directors, fine arts specialists and administrators in the London office. Of Casper Merriweather, there was no mention. According to this, he had never existed.

But then, as she and Lewis followed Nigel Hayes back to the front entrance of the building, they passed a large, framed photograph clearly taken at some Van Asbeck's social event. And there, in the middle of the front row, Hattie spotted a familiar face. Her breath caught in her throat as she recognised him. His golden blond hair swept back, his skin glowing with health, his smile disarming. Just as he had been on the day she had met him.

Only the person in the photograph didn't really exist. And nor did the man she had encountered in carriage 3 on the 18.53 from Waterloo.

# FORTY-THREE

## HATTIE

Mon, 1 June 08.39
From: Tasha Newbold
To: Hattie Sewell

Re: Role of content strategist

Hi Hattie,

Sorry to be contacting you out of the blue, but the whole team at S&S was very sorry when things didn't work out back in the spring. I just wanted to let you know that our plans haven't gone as we hoped with the person we recruited for the role, and the position has become vacant again.

I realise things may have moved on for you in the interim, but if you're interested, give me a call, and perhaps you can drop by for another chat?

Best wishes,

Tash

Hattie let out a whoop of joy as she read the email, leaping out of bed and performing a little dance in her underwear.

Within two hours, she was showered and dressed and on her way to Hoxton, barely registering the fact that this meant a commute on the Summerlands to Waterloo line. An hour after that, she emerged from the Saints & Sinners Hoxton office with a firm offer of a job. She phoned her parents to relay the good news, then made a tour of the local estate agents, registering her interest in rentals of one-bedroom flats in the Old Street, Islington and Shoreditch area. With her new salary, she would be able to afford somewhere pretty nice on her own, but she told the agents she would also consider two bedrooms. She could sublet the second room, maybe to Avril, who was talking about wanting to live more centrally. Then, feeling highly delighted with herself, she bought a frappuccino and strolled back down Bishopsgate to Bank, where she caught the Waterloo and City line.

She was on the train back to Summerlands when the text arrived.

*Want to meet up later? L x*

She'd had a feeling that it was only a matter of time before this happened and now, with serendipitous timing, it had.

She texted him back, suggesting a walk. The weather was beautiful, and in the evening it would still be light enough to head for the park. And a park was a neutral, impersonal space.

*Okay.* A single word, that hinted at the sender's disappointment. He'd clearly been hoping for something more intimate.

They met in Bushy Park, at the Diana Fountain.

Lewis was wearing his trademark tight T-shirt, and had Conker with him.

'The Pheasantry closed at six,' he told her. 'But they're not licenced anyway. We could always go to the pub?'

Hattie shook her head, pulling a bottle of water from her bag and brandishing it. 'No, it's okay, I'm not drinking at the moment.'

He raised an eyebrow, and let Conker off the lead. The dog trotted away over the open grassland, and Hattie and Lewis strolled behind him.

'So, no more alcohol, eh? Is this the new and improved Hattie Sewell?'

'It is,' she replied, with a smile. 'And I've got a new job too. Well, not exactly new.'

It was, she explained, the role she had been interviewed for that morning when he found her on the platform at Summerlands.

'I suppose I have you to thank, since I wouldn't even have got as far as meeting them if you hadn't rescued me. Although...' She turned to face him. 'They told me today that they did want me to go for a second interview, even though I couldn't make the first time they suggested. Only I never got that email.'

'That's strange.' Lewis put his fingers in his mouth and whistled for Conker to come back. The sun was sinking towards the horizon, bathing the whole park in a warm golden haze.

'I'm not sure it is, actually. Because the morning it arrived I was with him. With Casper. Waller.'

'You think he deleted it somehow?'

'It would make sense, wouldn't it? Because if I'd taken the job, I wouldn't have been available to act as his mule.'

'That does makes sense. And that reminds me, there's something I wanted to show you.' Lewis pulled out his phone, pulled up a message thread in WhatsApp and handed it to Hattie to read. It was from Carmen Demirci.

*Hi Lewis, hope you're okay? I've been wanting to drop you a line because I feel a little guilty about just disappearing. I won't go into all the details, but after Steve lost his job, we got into a lot of financial problems. We had credit card debt and we owed back rent. So we decided we would pack up and leave the flat and come out here to Turkey, to stay with my family while we get ourselves straight. The boys love it here and both Steve and I have found work, so things are a lot better now. Take care, C x*

'Ah, I see, that all makes sense now.' Hattie handed back his phone and shook her head, feeling a little silly that she had thought that Carmen could be involved in Julian's death, even if only for a brief moment. 'So, how are things with you?' She linked her arm through Lewis's companionably. 'You still travelling on the 18.53.'

'When I work in town, yes. I'm working from home a fair bit now. How about you? Are you going to be back on the commuting treadmill now you've got a job?'

She shook her head firmly. 'I'm going to be moving out of my parents' house and back into town. Hopefully somewhere within walking distance of my new office. That's the plan.'

'So this really is a new Hattie.' Lewis sounded wistful.

'It is. It's going to be a bit of an adjustment, going out with friends and not drinking, but I'm going to try. I'm planning to join a gym, and lift weights instead of wine bottles. And...'

His warm brown eyes were on her face now, and she knew she had to do it. To quell any hope he might have. She liked Lewis: she liked him a lot. He was a great guy, he made her laugh, and more importantly, she trusted him. He even had a cute dog. But now was not the right time.

'...And no dating,' she said, with what she hoped was conviction.

'None at all?'

'No. Not for a while, at least. Not until I've got life – and my head – properly straight again.' She smiled at him, feeling suddenly a little shy. 'But in a few more months, who knows?'

They walked in silence for a while, as the golden glow of the sun turned first to coral pink, then to burning amber.

Lewis flung her a curious look. 'Do you still think about him? I mean, obviously you think about what happened in Mexico. I do too: it's all still pretty fresh. But do you think about *him*. In a romantic sense.'

There was a heavy silence, dragged out over several seconds.

'No,' Hattie said eventually. 'I mean, I sometimes think about Casper Merriweather, the glamorous Jude Law lookalike. But he wasn't real. And no, I don't think about Neil Waller.' She sighed heavily, casting doubt over the truth of this statement. 'I don't think about him at all. I don't know where he is or what he's doing, and I don't want to know.' She turned to him. 'Come on, let's go to the pub after all. I can have a ginger beer.'

Lewis called the dog, and with him trotting at their heels, they walked slowly back towards the setting sun.

# EPILOGUE

## NEIL

The beach at Turquoise Bay, lived up to its name. The sand was a startling white, and the ocean shaded from jade green in the shallows to a dark aquamarine as the sea bordered the coral reef. A wooden boardwalk snaked out over the sea, punctuated by stilted, over-water bungalows with thatched palm-leaf rooves. Neil watched as a dive boat prepared to go out, with resort staff loading up oxygen tanks, and a gaggle of tourists in wetsuits chattering excitedly.

The people staying at the resort were a mixture of Americans, Germans and French, with the occasional Dutch and British. Neil could not afford to stay here himself: until he found a way to sell *The Red Courtesan*, he was broke. He was staying at a two-star place a short walk away, a brick building with no pool and no air conditioning. He came here daily to have coffee at the waterfront bar and keep his eyes peeled for anyone who looked like a collector of fine arts. So far, there had been no likely targets. The fact was that the people with that sort of money holidayed in St Bart's or the British Virgin Islands. The Bay of Islands in Honduras was the Caribbean for people who couldn't afford the Caribbean.

Under his coconut fibre umbrella, Neil sipped his espresso and looked around him. The cheap burner phone that he had now was kept for emergency use only. It didn't have enough data for him to scroll through news sites anyway. So when he saw a copy of *The New York Times* that someone had left, he seized it at once and started to read. He reached page 5, and stopped in his tracks, staring at the page.

## MEXICAN BILLIONAIRE REUNITED WITH HOKUSAI MASTERPIECE

*Ricardo Velasco, 52, was today presented with Hokusai's* The Red Courtesan, *the painting he bought at auction for $14.2 million. Velasco was the successful bidder in the auction held by Van Asbeck's, London, on April 1, but the painting was stolen by Neil Waller, 31, an auction house employee, before it could be shipped to Mexico City. In an unprecedented sting operation by London's Metropolitan Police, the original painting was intercepted and switched for a copy. A known associate of the art thief has been arrested in Mexico City, but Waller remains at large. A spokesman for the Metropolitan Police Art and Antiques unit stated: 'The investigation remains ongoing.'*

His heart thudding in his chest, Neil threw down the paper and ran the few hundred yards inland along a palm-fringed track to the brick bungalow where he was staying. He wrenched open the wardrobe door, pulled out the black archive box and threw it on the bed, his fingers trembling as he fumbled with the false bottom of the box.

Snatching the painting from its wrapping, Neil carried it towards the window and held it under the light, taking in first the brushstrokes on the front, and then the back of the canvas. It was very good, he had to admit that. Whoever created this knew exactly what they were doing. Unlike the insultingly cheap copy he had arranged to ship to Ricardo Velasco after the auction, with a cursory glance you would never know that this was not the real deal.

Putting the painting down again, he took down his backpack from the top shelf compartment of the wardrobe and reached into one of the pockets for the jeweller's loupe he always carried. He fitted it to his eye and used it to examine the surface of the paint. The surface was cracked, not from genuine age but from some chemical process that had been intended to cause cracks. Taking cotton wool from the bathroom, he dabbed it with some vodka from the quart bottle next to his bed and rubbed it tentatively over the paint. Brownish streaks came away, not old, ingrained dirt but watered-down brown paint.

And now he looked at it objectively, it was obvious. The red of the kimono was not subtle enough, the gold of the fan too bright, the white geisha's face a touch too garish. He let the painting fall onto the tiled floor with a clatter and sank down on the edge of the bed with a groan of despair. Was this Hattie's doing? She was the only one who knew the location of the genuine painting. Had she been the one who arranged the switch? It hardly seemed credible, nor did Neil want to believe it. Not sweet, flaky Hattie. Hattie, who had encouraged him to flee just before he could be arrested.

He sat with his head in his hands for a couple of minutes, then stood up with a sigh. Even if *The Red Courtesan* had been real, it would have proved very difficult to sell at this point anyway. Time to write it off, and start again. There was no other choice.

Leaving his bungalow, he walked round to the back of the main hotel building and threw the painting into a dumpster. Then, because he couldn't think of an alternative course of action, he walked back to the Turquoise Bay Beach Club.

. . .

The first thing that caught his attention was the accent. A native English speaker, almost certainly from London or the South East, speaking to one of the waitstaff.

He swivelled in his seat so that he could see her from behind his sunglasses. She was sitting at one of the tables at the edge of the beach. Young – possibly mid-twenties – with long straight straw-blonde hair and a wiry, gym-toned body. She must have recently arrived, because her fair skin had not yet acquired a tan. In fact, if she didn't apply some sunscreen soon, she was going to get a nasty sunburn. The beach tote was Prada, he noted, and the silk kaftan Tory Burch. So she had money. He took in more details. There was a vintage Dunhill cigarette lighter on the table in front of her and she wore a string of natural pearls round her neck, casually entwined with the sort of solid gold necklaces you couldn't buy but had to inherit. There was a signet ring with a family crest on her little finger. Old money, then. Even better.

She scrolled mindlessly through her phone, then held it up and took a selfie. An open paperback and an empty cocktail glass stood on the table in front of her, and she had placed her credit card on top of the saucer containing the bill.

Moving slowly and casually, Neil strolled in her direction, tilting his hip just enough to knock off the book. It was a best-selling summer blockbuster on sale in all the airports, and she had helpfully written her name on the flyleaf. Cleo.

He bent to pick it up, glancing at the credit card as he did so. *Ms C Lawrenson*, it said.

'Here.' He made sure the book was closed before handing it to her.

'Thanks,' she said, still looking at her phone.

Neil pretended to do a double take. 'Hold on, aren't you Cleo Lawrenson?'

He had her attention now. His mark took off her sunglasses and looked at him. She had large protruding eyes and a slight overbite. Not exactly a beauty, but no matter. 'Sorry, do I know you?'

'We met at a party in London. The one at... you know, at that place by the Embankment. Sam's promotional thingy.' He hoped that this was vague enough.

She was looking at him more closely. Taking in a very handsome man with golden blond hair, an impressive tan and a charming smile. 'And you are?'

And then Neil had a sudden, lightning-sharp flash of memory. He was seven years old, and his parents were still together. He was sitting on his bed with his father, who was reading *Dastardly Tales for Daring Boys* to him. His mother was downstairs in the kitchen baking something, and a warm, comforting smell was floating up the stairs. 'Casper Merriweather is really lucky,' he was telling his father, 'because he has a best friend in all the world, no matter what.'

*What had the name of that fictional sidekick been? Ah yes, that was it. Johnny Royle.*

He smiled and extended his hand. 'I'm Johnny. Johnny Royle. Lovely to meet you.'

# A LETTER FROM ALISON

Thank you so much for choosing to read *The Woman in Carriage 3*. If you enjoyed it and want to keep up to date with all my latest releases, just sign up at the following link. Your email address will never be shared and you can unsubscribe at any time.

*www.bookouture.com/alison-james*

Most urban dwellers commute to work on public transport, travelling in close proximity to people they never speak to or connect with. When I was taking a train from Waterloo to the south London suburbs where I live, I wondered what would happen if circumstances forced the people in the carriage to talk to each other. The plot of *The Woman in Carriage 3* was all built around that one question.

I really hope you enjoyed reading this novel, and if you did, I would be so grateful if you could write a review. I'd love to hear what you think, and it makes such a difference helping new readers to discover one of my books for the first time.

I love hearing from my readers – you can get in touch on my Facebook page, Twitter or Goodreads.

Thanks,

Alison James

# KEEP IN TOUCH WITH ALISON

goodreads.com/author/show/17361567.Alison_James

facebook.com/Alison-James-books
twitter.com/AlisonJbooks

Made in the USA
Las Vegas, NV
04 June 2023

72971964R00173